# Vengeance Is Mine...

# Vengeance

## IS MINE...

Cliff Chandler

# Vengeance Is Mine...

## Cliff Chandler

Writers Club Press
San Jose   New York   Lincoln   Shanghai

Vengeance Is Mine...

Writers Club Press
an imprint of iUniverse, Inc.

For information address:
iUniverse, Inc.
5220 S. 16th St., Suite 200
Lincoln, NE 68512
www.iuniverse.com

ISBN: 0-595-21032-5

Printed in the United States of America

# Dedication

*Thanks again to my wife Velma, who sacrificed so much to make my quest successful.*

—V—

It is important to know who your friends are; but it is better to know who are not your friends. I am blessed with good friends. Friends like Dr. Richard Cummings and Alix Kenagy who worked so hard promoting my last book "The Paragons." Thank you Richard, Alix: and thank you Barbara Bird, Barbara Keene, Chan'te Whitley-Head, Jeanine, Jill, Brittney, Birtie and Bob Jones. Vanessa and Ed Gordon, Renee and Guy Banks, Ken Barbosa, and Cousin Inez Hancock. What would I be without Leora Newton and classmates Leontine Espy and Barbara Clowers? Vincent D. Smith, Ben Tucker, Reggie Workman music masters and good friends. St. John Flynn, Rachel English, Jackie Cooper, Ken Mann, Joy Satterfield, Jeanette Le Pratt, David, Debra, and Don Woods, and Keith English Media friends. To my writer friends, Evelyn Coleman, P.T.Deuterman, Faye McDonald Smith, Glenda Ivey, Geri Taran, Anthony Grooms, and Paul Carr.

To Mrs. Hall, Sadie Hutchings. Madeline Squire and Barbara Squire, sisters extraordinaire, two great ladies. Pat and Mark Keller for those wonderful evenings in Cochran, and for their support: the lectures, my readings, and for inviting me to host events at Middle Georgia College most of all, for being my friends. Jodie& John Setran, wherever you are...Rob, you're the greatest keep up the good work, and Margo for styling my hair, and you the readers who make it all possible; thank you.

Last to those who are no longer with us who made this literary journey possible: Duke Ellington, from whom I learned to believe in myself. John Oliver Kilens, a neighbor and from whom I learned that it was possible to become and author. Langston Hughes, whose work floated off a page at the Schomburg and inspired me to return to writing; and to Zora Neal Hurston, Richard Wright, James Baldwin, and Owen Dodson. To Jerry Pratt for the opportunity of acquiring a great education, and Betty Guidry who gave me the courage and guidance to return to the morality my Grandmother taught me, also for teaching me who I really am; and to my son Keith, his sudden death is still a bad dream.

# CHAPTER *1*

*I*t appeared on the horizon, first as a ghostly cloud emerging from the depths as if it was riding on the shoulders of Aphrodite and Poseidon. But this was no ghost. The Beth, one hundred sixty-one feet of fiberglass luxury, her bow honed to a knife-edge, is an Evviva class yacht. She has five staterooms, accommodates ten, and a crew of seven. The early risers and the all-nighters were the first to spot her cruising into the harbor, and word spread like wildfire that the boat had arrived. They hadn't seen anything like the Beth since Malcolm Forbes Highlander's last visit. The Beth sailed straight in, so they couldn't see the helicopter pad on her rear deck, nor could they see the garage below deck, stuffed with all kinds of toys. The Captain chose a deep-water anchorage at Trumbo Point, just off Mustin Street; the deep anchorage would provide a certain amount of security. He toggled the twin 900hp Alaskan diesels until the boat was just inside the harbor and dropped anchor. By this time a small crowd had gathered to gawk at the huge yacht.

A crewmember lowered the motor launch and tied it to the gangplank. An audible murmur of surprise rose from the crowd when Honey and Vic appeared and made their way towards the launch. The Crewman helped Honey aboard and waited for Vic to join them. Someone in the crowd remarked that Vic was "probably a football Jock," and another person in the crowd agreed. Vic looked every inch a football player, and nothing like his real occupation, a New York City detective. Honey, on the other hand looked like Jane Kennedy in her prime.

The big yacht and the beautiful black couple wasn't your everyday "fit," but there they were, and there it was, "The Beth," a gleaming white symbol of luxury—everything on it white—but its owners. Vic waved to the crowd, and Honey smiled. The response was immediate and unanimous, a loud, approving cheer. The only exception, a stone-faced man within the crowd who slithered off to a pay phone and called San Juan; he had recognized Vic as the cop who had cost him ten long years in prison.

*              *              *

Juan replaced the receiver and said, "Damn!"

"Que pasa?"

"Medicon! Putano, mardre…"

"Juan, what is it!"

"That fuckin' cop, that nigger is coming here!"

"So what? You got a new face. He won't even recognize you. Besides you got the cops in your pocket," Lisa said.

"Not when it comes to cops, they look out for each other."

"Maybe in New York, but this is San Juan, think about it," she said.

"Get this, he's coming here in a big fuckin' yacht. He's the one who stole the Cartel's money…"

"Yeah," she said

"Imagine coming here with that yacht…he's got big balls. That's his ass! You don't fuck with our money and get away with it. All I got to do is tell Manero and our problems are over."

"Come here, baby. You're so smart." Lisa pulled Juan closer to her and slipped her hand under his shirt.

*              *              *

They say "money knows no color," and it must ring true, because Vic and Honey found themselves surrounded by the curious and the weirdoes of the fabled Key West. And, Vic's personality suited their circumstances perfectly; but buying drinks for the freeloaders certainly didn't hurt. They did the usual tours, visiting Hemingway's home, dodging the fabled three-toed cats, and listening to endless time-worn stories at "Sloppy Joes," while consuming booze in the Hemingway tradition until dawn. Then, it was a short and happy struggle back to the yacht where they regrettably said farewell to their new-found friends with promises to stop on their way back from Puerto Rico. But the first thing they had to do was sober up; the citizens of Key West knew how to drink from sunrise on…

The Captain gave one blast on the horn, eased the left engine back, and the right engine forward. The Beth rotated slowly until she was headed in the direction of the open sea. He returned the engines to neutral for a moment, and then eased them forward. The maneuvers were so smooth Honey and Vic didn't realize they were moving. Honey was in the bathroom dashing cold water on her face. Vic ordered two "Bloody Mary's," his cure for a hangover. Honey entered the room and shook her head; she couldn't believe Vic was offering her a drink.

"No way!" she said.

"Believe me, it will work, come on, try it." Honey approached Vic slowly. She sat on the couch next to him, and he handed her the drink. She tilted the glass back and took a small sip.

"Not bad. You know, you're right?"

"Of course I'm right, had a lot of practice."

Honey laughed.

"I could get used to this," Honey said.

"So could I," Vic said.

The master stateroom was something to see, designed by Jack Sarin; nothing was left to the imagination. Unlike most master suites, the room had the feeling of a luxurious hotel, walk in closets, twin bathrooms, recessed lighting, and noise suppressers that dissipated the sound of the engines. A room in which Honey swore she was going to spend the rest of her life.

"I don't believe it, I feel better. Let's go out on deck."

Vic pulled Honey closer and kissed her.

"Anything you say, Love."

"Never mind that, let's go out on deck." Honey jumped up and ran for the door.

*The ocean was a mirror of reflections, blurred starlight bouncing off soft waves. Honey turned her back to the rail and pulled Vic closer. He resisted a little, and she urged him forward.*

"You seem to have something on your mind, is there something wrong?"

"No. I was just thinking about Ellis' offer. Jess likes the idea of us opening our own private detective agency. With Ellis behind us maybe we can get used to this."

"What matters is what you think."

"I like the idea," he said.

Vic wrapped his arms around Honey as a tropical breeze blew softly across the deck. In response, she brushed and tickled the soft hair of his forearm and leaned into his chest. The waves softly lapped against "The Beth" and released an enticing scent of the sea into the air—not the sea one smells on land, but a different, enchanting fragrance. They felt the Yacht shift course and rock a little, but the only sound was the soft purring of the engines propelling *The Beth* through the water. Vic eased Honey back against the rail and tightened his arms around her; there was nothing subtle about his intentions. Vic lifted the edge of her skirt with the tips of his fingers as he moved forward. His silk pajamas brushed against her naked thighs enhancing the magic of the moment. *The Beth* rocked in the rolling swells, while Vic and honey created their own motions of the sensual moments engulfing them in a timeless encounter that left them exhausted.

*       *       *

The door of the Gulf Stream V closed. Manero fasten his seat belt and reached for a drink. The attendant checked his seat belt, handed him a napkin and returned to her seat. Chimes sounded in the background and the plane surged forward. Moments later they were climbing above the mountain range that circled Manero's private airfield. A herdsman used his cellular phone and called headquarters.

"Manero just left, this time the direction is north east."

"Thank you," from the recipient.

Off the coast of Columbia, on board a Coast Guard cutter, an officer moved to the radar screen and entered the code for Manero's plane. At the same instance, on the coast near Manero's private field, the supervisor at Colombian flight control glanced at the screens around the room, he spotted Manero's plane and assigned a counterfeit number to Manero's flight.

"Sir, we lost him! "

The Captain of the cutter spun around in his chair and headed for the radar screen.

"How the hell do they do that? We know the damn plane didn't go down. Call Big Bird and let them know he's on the move."

"Yes, sir," the young technician said.

In the distance the special number assigned to Manero's plane would be recognized by a flight controller in Cuban air space and designated the flight's origin as Jacksonville Florida. Manero's pilot turned the autopilot two clicks, the plane banked and headed south to their destination, San Juan, Puerto Rico.

\*                    \*                    \*

They ran into a storm off the coast of Cuba that tossed the boat about the ocean like a rubber duck in a bathtub, and Honey thanked God for the double bathrooms in the main cabin. Vic in one bathroom, and Honey in the other, losing their body fluids in a gray slime that appeared to be endless. Vic cursed the sea after a stream of slime left his body following the motion of the ship. Everything happened at once...He kneeled down and grasp the toilet and continued his donations to the sea. Honey had a better solution, she sat on the toilet, and used as small waste basked to trap her slime.

The storm lasted until dawn. At dawn a crewmember knocked on the door. Honey got out of bed and rushed into the bathroom, while Vic struggled with the bed covers.

"Come in!" Vic said.

"Sir, we have some fresh clothes for you."

The crewman held out some fresh towels and two huge terry cloth robes.

"If you will put these on and come to berth five, we have everything ready for you."

"Thank you."

The Crewman turned and left the cabin.

"Honey!"

"What is it!"

"They have another room for us to clean up in, come on out."

"In a minute..."

Vic hung the fresh clothes on the door just outside Honey's bathroom.

"I left a clean robe on your door," Vic said.

"Thank you!"

Vic pushed the soiled floor mat to the side and entered his bathroom. That was it; he grabbed his stomach and rushed out of the room. Out on deck he took a deep breath. The waters were calm and in the distance a faint glow of light shone on the horizon. Honey called from the hallway and Vic went inside. Honey took Vic's arm and led him to the new room.

"The Cabin Boy said that we can rent a house in San Juan, by the day, or by the week. Why don't we try it?"

"Okay by me, I've had it with this boat. How do we do it?"

Honey picked up the phone and asked for Ralph. Ralph said that he would take care of everything. Honey coaxed Vic into the shower with her. Things were looking up. The crewmen had thought of everything: fresh cut flowers, fruit, juices, and soft music that muted the sounds on the boat. In a short while Honey had forgotten that they were at sea. The bit in the shower exhausted them, they fell into bed, and Vic was the first to fall asleep. Honey sat up in bed and looked at Vic, at that moment he looked like what she had imagined he looked like as a small child. She got up and walked over to the porthole pushed the curtain aside and looked out. Suddenly she saw it, the faint lights of San Juan on the horizon. Honey moved closer to the porthole and look skyward. In the distance a jetliner climbed towards the heavens.

"Vic! Vic, its out there, I can see it!"

Vic stirred for a moment, then sat up in the bed, startled.

"What is it, what's wrong?"

"Nothing, I can see San Juan, I can see it!"

Vic yawned, got up and looked for his slippers.

"Come on, Vic! Hurry."

"I don't think it's going anywhere," Vic said.

"I'm calling upstairs to see if that's it."

"Tell you what I'm going to do, I'm going to sleep, I've had it."

"Captain, is that San Juan I see? Thank you! When will we get there? Fine, thank you," Honey said.

They arrived at 10 a.m. The yacht slowed and maneuvered its way into the harbor and docked. Honey was dressed and waiting at the rail when the gangplank was lowered. She trotted down the gangplank, kneeled on the dock and kissed the ground. Vic held onto the rail, looked down at Honey and managed a smile. Honey threw her head back and let her hair blow freely in the tropical morning breeze. She took a deep breath of the tropical air, looked up at Vic and motioned for him to join her. Vic was surprised when he stepped onto the dock. It was as if something magical had happened, his system returned to normal. Behind them, the crew was busy hoisting a Corvette from the lower deck of the boat. The aft crane lifted the car from the lower deck and sat it gently down onto the dock. Vic took Honey's arm and walked towards the car.

"That's class," she said.

"Nothing but the best for Ellis. Are you sure you want to rent the house?"

"Don't you? We need a little time to get over that storm. By the way, when we go home I want to fly I've had it with that yacht."

"Not, you...I thought you wanted to live on it."

"No, nooo, that was before the storm. I didn't think we were going to make it...and the sickness."

"They say once you've been sick, it doesn't happen again."

"You know what they say about, they say."

Captain Murray leaned into the car and handed Vic the directions to the house. Vic studied the map and thanked the Captain. It was a simple trip. Drive straight ahead until they came to Avenida Ashford, turn right and remain on Ashford until they reached the house. The house was small with a terrific view of the water. Captain Murray didn't overlook anything, including a housekeeper to look after them during their visit. Vic found the address without any trouble. Lena was waiting for them when they arrived. She opened the gate that led to the carport, and stood aside.

"Welcome to Puerto Rico, Senior, Senora. My name is Lena"

"Thank you," Honey and Vic spoke as one.

"I'm Vic, and this is my wife Honey."

"Senior, Senora."

Lena took the two bags from the rear of the car and motioned for Honey and Vic to follow her.

"The house hasn't been used for a while, I was busy preparing it when you arrived. Why don't you go down to Old San Juan, you know, see El Moro, it is beautiful."

"Can we walk?" Honey asked.

"Si, I mean yes, but it is a long way."

"Come on, Vic. I need to stretch my legs. You might as well get used to it, I'm a walker."

"Just what I need. A Corvette sitting in the carport, and we walk, go figure."

Lena laughed.

"Well, first things first. I bought these for you." Honey opened one of the bags and removed a pair of Nike Joggers.

"How did you know my size?" Vic asked.

Honey handed Vic a pair of socks and winked.

"You might as well put these on too."

Vic looked at the outfit and nodded his approval. He opened his bag and fished around until he found a small package. He took the package out and handed it to Honey.

"Two can play this game," he said.

Honey fumbled with the wrapping like a little child, being careful not to destroy the paper. She opened the case and gasped.

"The Rolex! The one I showed you!! When?"

Honey threw her arms around Vic, the wrapping in one hand, and the watch in the other.

"Let's change before we get into trouble, she'll be through when we get back," Honey said.

"Last one to get dressed, is a you know what," Vic said.

*　　　　　*　　　　　*

Manero's plane landed at a private field near Dorado. The sleek aircraft parked between two smaller private jets. An ordinary car moved forward and parked next to the plane just as the door of the plane opened and the steps were lowered. Manero walked down the steps wearing a plain white shirt and slacks. Two men got out of the car, and each of them, in turn, embraced Manero before escorting him to the car.

"Donde esta un, pig?" Manero said.

"Isla Verde. They are staying at a small house."

"Good," Manero said.

The younger of the two men handed Manero a Walther PPK and a silencer. Manero pulled the action of the gun and loaded one round into the chamber. He checked the gun carefully and attached a silencer to the barrel.

"Let's get this thing done, I have guest coming to the house for dinner tonight," Manero said.

The two men laughed.

*       *       *

They walked down Avenida Ashford until they reached Old San Juan, and did a little shopping. Honey bought a few souvenirs and a silk scarf, which she draped around her neck. They walked a little further until they reached the town square. The square had the feeling of old San Juan. The glitter of the large hotels had not reached it. Vic let curiosity get the best of him while walking down one of the narrow streets. He opened the door to what he assumed was the entrance to an apartment building and found himself in the living room of someone's house. He closed the door quietly and backed out. Honey laughed until she almost cried, Vic dragging her along in his haste to get away from the house. That was it, as far as Vic was concerned, they did an about face and started back to their love nest.

*       *       *

Ernesto parked across the street in front of the house. Philippe and Manero crossed the street, walked over to the entrance and knocked on the door. Lena was busy vacuuming and didn't hear them. Manero used picks to unlock the door and entered. Phillippe took one room and Manero the other. Lena looked up just as Phillippe fired. She slumped over the vacuum cleaner, dead before she hit the floor. A small red dot between her eyes oozed the essence of her life onto the roaring machine.

"Stupido! Let's get the hell out of here," Manero said. Phillippe attempted to run, but Manero grabbed his arm and held him back.

"Tranquilo, tranquilo…" he said. The two men walked casually across the street and got into their car. Manero tapped Ernesto on the shoulder and the car moved.

"The airport?"

"No, there's a problem," Manero said.

"Que?"

"Drive," Manero said. Ernesto looked into the rear view mirror; he didn't like what he saw in Manero's eyes. Phillippe behaved as if nothing had happened.

*                          *                           *

Honey and Vic ducked under a tree and watched the phenomenon of a tropical shower forming a wall of rain in front of their rented house. Not a drop of rain fell where Honey and Vic stood in the shade of a huge palm tree, across the street from the house, in the mid-day sun. Vic noticed it first, the front door was open and the rain was pouring into the house. He looked at Honey and shrugged his shoulders. A gust of wind blew against the front door and it slammed closed. The shower diminished, but they didn't wait for the rain to stop; Vic and Honey ran across the street and into the house.

The sound of the vacuum cleaner led them to the body. The woman's body was twisted, one arm extended as if to break a fall, her head against the handle of the vacuum cleaner, a surprised look on her face. Honey turned away. Vic kneeled and took a closer look. He got up, walked across the room, turned off the vacuum machine, picked up the phone, and called the police....

Vic checked the house. Nothing had been disturbed. He checked the body, one shot between the eyes.

*A professional hit, why?*

*       *       *

"Don't touch anything! Who are you?" Lieutenant Santiago shouted from the doorway.

"We leased this house for a few days. My name is Vic Morgan, and this is my wife, Honey. And I didn't touch anything, I'm a New York City Detective..."

"You're the couple from the boat...they must pay you guys pretty good up there in New York." Lieutenant, Santiago said.

Vic gave Santiago a dirty look.

"Hey, no offense, but you must admit that you didn't get a boat like that on a cops salary," Santiago said.

Vic motioned in the direction of the bedroom; Honey nodded her head and left the room.

"All right, Lieutenant, what the hell's going on here?"

"Take it easy, you know the drill. She probably owed a debt and couldn't pay it, you know, dope. The island is infested with it."

"What are you tying to tell me?" Vic said.

"What do you think?"

"I don't know, but it wasn't robbery, she still has her wedding ring on her finger," Vic said.

"You're good. I guess you are a cop. You understand, things look bad for you," Santiago said.

"What the hell do you mean? I don't know a soul on this island," Vic said.

"Well look at it this way. You come here in an ocean going yacht and a woman is killed in your house. What the hell is I suppose to think?"

"You think what the hell you want to think, but I'd better warn you that if you try to tie me in with this hit your ass is going to be in a sling. As for the boat, that's none of your damn business.

"Are you threatening me!"?

"No, I'm promising you. I tell you I'm a cop, and do you show me any respect? Hell no! You jump the gun and assume I'm on the take, more than that, you imply that I'm a dope-peddling killer. Fuck you!"

"All right, all right…I'll check you out. But if you're right the contract was on you," Santiago said.

"On me, why?"

"You're the wise ass New York detective, you tell me. I'm going to suggest that you and your wife go back to your boat; you'll be safe there. Maybe you're right, but somebody out there doesn't like you. By the way are you carrying? "

"No. I'm on my honeymoon!"

"Okay, okay, I'll have someone cover you 'till we get this crap straightened out."

"Thanks," Vic said.

"Hey, we cops got to stick together. Get your wife, I'll have someone escort you back to the boat."

"Good."

Vic knew the signs, fancy shoes, expensive suit, and the white Mercedes Benz. Lieutenant Santiago probably had a good explanation, got the car from a forfeiture. Vic held the door open for Honey, closed the door and took a seat behind the wheel. Santiago's driver followed them to the dock and escorted them on board.

"Man! This is what I call living. You New York cops sure know how to live," the driver said.

He brushed the polished rail along the deck with his fingers and looked at Vic.

"Hey, this is where I came in, you know, I've seen that movie."

"No disrespect, but this is one hell of a boat."

"Thank you. How about a drink?" The driver nodded his approval.

The Cabin Boy poured the driver a glass of champagne. The driver raised his glass and offered a toast.

"To those who watch their backs."

"And to those who don't," Vic said.

"I'm, Rico. "

"Vic."

"I know."

"Let's take a walk," Rico said. Rico put his glass down and motioned in the direction of the dock. Vic followed him down the gangplank and out to the end of the dock. A large cruiser cast small slapping waves against the Beth creating slushy slapping sounds against her hull.

"I'm working on special assignment with your government, and my advice to you is get the hell out of here as fast as you can. I know who you are...Santiago was right; you were the target this morning. He's part of it. Santiago is dirty. What we didn't know is how dirty, until the hit this afternoon.

"Why?" Vic said.

"You mean you don't know?"

"No."

"Your last case."

"Yes?"

"Word is the cartel lost a lot of money."

"The case is over, we took the bad guys out."

"Not all of them. The problem is Wayne Woolford didn't deliver the last batch of money. Feeling is that you took the money and bought this boat."

"That's stupid," Vic said.

"You're right, but we are not dealing with ordinary people. Somebody with juice is behind this, and they want the money and you out of the way. I'll talk to Santiago, tell him you're leaving and let's see what happens." Rico said.

Rico offered Vic a gun.

"Thank you, but I'm okay."

"You told Santiago you weren't carrying."

"I'm not, but I have what I need on the boat."

A police car rolled slowly to the end of the dock and two uniformed officers got out. They spoke to Rico in Spanish for a few minutes and returned to the car, backed it up to the entrance and parked.

"Those are your baby sitters, they're clean, and I picked them. You be careful, hear?"

"Thanks, Rico."

"Yeah. Keep your head down, this isn't over."

"We'll be fine," Vic said.

"Yeah." Vic and Rico walked back to the yacht.

*        *        *

Santiago told Rico to wait for him in the car. Rico stopped in front of the Caribe Hilton and waited for the Doorman to open the door. Santiago got out, and Rico parked on the side near the entrance. Fifteen minutes later Santiago returned.

"Take me home, I've had it for tonight. Tell them at the station I will be in late tomorrow. You won't have to pick me up, I'll take a taxi in "

"Yes, sir," Rico said.

Manero stood at the living room window and watched Santiago's car drive away, picked up the phone and called Columbia. He needed a specialist for what he had in mind.

*        *        *

A Scuba Diver moved close to the Beth and tied his rubber boat to a buoy near the yacht. He opened a plastic case and assembled a small caliber rifle, attached the silencer, loaded the gun, and slipped back into the shadows. The water was calm, but the tropical heat made his suit uncomfortable. He unzipped the front of the suit almost to his waist, picked up the gun, and focused on a deckhand on board the "Beth," after which he laid the gun across his lap and waited. A smaller boat slowed and dropped anchor opposite the Beth .The party onboard the smaller craft was going strong. Couples dancing to the bossa beat of a man on the aft deck playing a guitar. The Diver, comfortable now, smiled, opened his canteen and took a sip of water.

Vic stood and looked down at the party boat. He called Honey to watch the party with him. Vic poured a glass of champagne for honey and extended the drink in her direction. The scuba diver sat patiently in the shadows, gun focused on Vic. The two officers in the car turned on the radio to listened to the ball game. Manero's Driver drove up next to the police car and stopped. His Driver rolled down the window on the passenger side of the vehicle and asked for directions to a hotel. Phillippe took careful aim at the police car, from the back seat of Manero's car and fired two shots. The two cops slumped forward.

"Go!" The Driver of the van waiting in the shadows gunned the engine and sped up to the boat. A crewman on board the Beth saw the van coming, kneeled in the combat position and fired at the van.

"Honey! Get down!"

Vic ducked behind a table and fired once at the car, following the van. The bullet hit the windshield above the driver's head. The car swerved and smashed against the yacht.

"Damn! " He said.

The Scuba Diver took advantage of the activity and made his way onto the deck of the Beth. He clubbed Vic from behind, pointed the gun at Honey, and motioned for her to keep still. He gave a hand signal to Manero and kneeled behind a chair. The Captain was on the phone. He completed his call and crawled out of the wheelhouse onto the deck. Manero and Phillippe walked slowly up the gangplank, guns drawn. The Captain stood and fired, hitting Phillippe in the shoulder. The Diver stood and fired, and the Captain dropped where he stood. The only indication that he had been shot was a red spot in the middle of his spotless white uniform. Vic stirred…

"Take them to the van, hurry!" Manero said. Vic tried to resist, until he noticed the gun pressed against Honey's skull.

"All right, all right."

The van backed up to the gangplank. Honey and Vic were shoved inside. In the distance the sound of sirens filled the quiet evening.

"Hurry, and get rid of that car." Manero said. The Driver of the van used the van to push the car off the dock and into the water. He turned the van around, sped off the dock, and vanished into the night.

Rico watched the action from the roof of a building across the street from the docks. He was too far away to help, but he got the plate number of the van. He ran to the edge of the building and slid down a ladder to the ground. The dock lit up like a Christmas tree, at least ten cars arrived with blue lights flashing. Rico went to the back of the building and got into his car. A few seconds later he heard his beeper, he didn't have to guess who it was. He acknowledged the beep and headed for Santiago's house. Rico made a phone call to his command and reported the action down at the docks. He requested a search for the Van, gave dispatch the plate number, and headed for Santiago's house. Santiago was waiting in front of his house.

"Did you hear what's happened?" Santiago said.

"Yeah."

"Good, let's go!" Santiago said.

Santiago had selected Rico because he was quiet and didn't ask any questions. Internal Affairs had arranged for Santiago's regular driver to be given another assignment because of his health. Santiago's regular driver accepted the suggestion rather than go to jail. Lt. Santiago had interviewed three men before selecting Rico and he had given each man the same test; a share of the money he took from a small time gambler. Everyone had refused the bribe except Rico. Rico accepted the money and didn't ask any questions….

Rico waited for one of the officers on the scene to move a car so they could get closer to the crime scene. He parked near the gangplank and joined Lt.Santiago.

"Damn! This is a mess…" Santiago was visibly shaken. Two people dead and three missing. He checked the scene carefully for anything that might have been left behind by the perps. Satisfied that they hadn't left any clues Santiago motioned for Rico to follow him. Santiago made a few notes, gave a few instructions to the forensic team, and left the boat.

"What do you think, Rico?"

"Kidnapping?"

"Could be, but who?"

"You got me Lieutenant. I'll question the crew members who were off ship when it happened, maybe they can tell us something."

"Good thinking. You've got everything covered here. I'm going home. We're going to have a busy day tomorrow."

"Yes, sir."

*     *     *

Eddie Sullivan, the engineer on the Beth, waited quietly in the shadows of the giant engines during the gunfire. The killers didn't bother to check the boat. Sullivan watched the van leave and hurried to the aft deck and started the helicopter. The small custom-designed copter lifted off, and Sullivan followed the van's lights. Sullivan took advantage of his perspective and determined that they were headed for the private airfield near Dorado, he flew ahead of them and landed near a Biz-Jet parked at a hangar. A security vehicle headed for his craft and he ducked behind one of the large planes and took cover. Sullivan moved cautiously around the craft, dodging the beam of the guard's flashlight. In the background he could hear the van rushing towards the planes.

The Guard pocketed his flashlight and returned to his car. He stopped the two vehicles and asked for their identification. Manero handed him his parking permit, then followed the Guard's vehicle to the plane. Manero thanked the young man and waited until he drove away before getting out of the car. Manero motioned for the van to back up to the plane. Phillippe got out of the car and waited until the van had reached the steps of the jet. He gave a hand signal for the driver to stop and opened the van's doors.

Sullivan shifted to a position directly in front of the activity at the plane. Phillippe helped Honey out of the van, the driver and Manero reached for Vic. Sullivan fired and dropped the man holding Vic. Manero released Vic and dove for cover. Honey broke away and ran for cover. Vic watched Manero raise his gun and aim it at Honey. He struggled to get to his feet, but his hands were tied behind his back. The pilot started the engines and the noise drowned out Vic's voice as he shouted for Honey to get down. Manero fired once, and Honey fell backwards in a rolling motion to the ground. Vic yelled "Nooooo!" Just before Manero fired at him.

Sullivan took out the driver and focused on Manero who had turned his attention to Vic. Sullivan fired and Manero screamed, dropped his gun and grabbed his groin with both hands. Someone inside the plane grabbed Manero by the hand and pulled him into the plane. A barrage of gunfire from the van pinned Sullivan down long enough for the plane to taxi out to the runway and take off. Sullivan used a grenade launcher to take out the van, and then rushed to Honey's side. The Jet roared forward and lifted off the runway half way down the field. Sullivan didn't bother to fire at the plane. It was gone. He rushed over to Vic and searched for a pulse, he didn't have time to look at Honey. Vic was breathing. He would survive. Sullivan glanced at the Guard hiding under his car, returned to the copter, and took off before the blinking lights in the distance arrived on the scene.

\*  \*  \*

Margaret and Ellis boarded their private plane at Republic Aviation. The pilot had been given a clearance for an unlimited take off. He waited until the Flight Attendant indicated that the passengers were belted in, and then he turned the plane and prepared for takeoff. The huge Hawker screamed up the runway and tilted upward. The angle was steep, and the ascent was swift. The pilot looked over his left shoulder and smiled, the last time he had experienced a take off like that, was his last flight in a F-15. He banked the plane to the right, continuing his climb. The compass locked on SSE, they continued their climb until they reached 30,000 feet and leveled off.

"Well that's, that. I guess we can have a drink now."

Ellis nodded and the Attendant prepared a Martini for Margaret and a bourbon and branch water for Ellis. It was a ritual that took place when their plane reached altitude.

"Have you heard anything from Vic?"

"Not a word, and that bothers me."

"Well, you can't expect too much from him right now, after all..."

"I guess you're right. What a terrible thing to happen...it doesn't make sense."

"Murder never does," Margaret said.

\*  \*  \*

Rico asked Vic did he want a drink. Vic didn't respond, but Rico prepared one for him anyway. Rico nodded his head, and the uniformed officer assigned to Vic left the cabin.

"Vic, you've got to get a hold on yourself. I know it's hard, but we have a job to do."

Vic didn't respond. Rico pushed a glass of Harvey's Bristol Cream towards Vic. Vic reached out and picked up the drink and took a large swig.

"We picked up Santiago and he gave us some information."

Vic blinked and looked at Rico.

"He gave us something that might help us.

"What?" Vic said.

Rico smiled.

"The hit was set up by a guy here on the island. Seems you had some dealings with him back in the States. The guy who set it up was Juan Acevedo."

"Impossible, your people killed him in a shoot out," Vic said.

"No, it was a setup. That's what Santiago gave us to keep them from putting him in with the regular population," Rico said.

"But why?"

"Juan thought you bought the yacht with the Cartel's money. It looks like their guy in New York had about twenty million of the Cartel's money. They couldn't find it so they assumed you took it."

"Damn! Honey died for nothing, no. She died because of me…"

A tear rolled down Vic's cheek.

"I want that bastard, and I want his boss," Vic said.

"That's not going to be easy." Santiago said Juan had a face job, and he's clean. Besides, when he heard that you survived, he left the country."

"Where did he go?"

"You're going to like this, New York. He's using the name Guzman."

"I'll find him, him and his boss," Vic said.

"We know where to find Juan. Manero went back to Columbia."

"First, Juan, then Senior Manero," Vic said.

"We'll take care of Manero, Juan is yours."

Vic stood, stopped for a moment, and rubbed his forehead.

"The bullet grazed your head. It didn't penetrate, but the force of the impact gave you a concussion."

"She was so beautiful, Rico…"

"I know…I'm sorry, Vic."

"I have to call her sister," Vic said.

"She's on the way. The Crainsworths are coming too." Rico said.

*Vic put his drink on the table and lay back in his chair. Rico left the cabin closed the door, walked out on deck, and looked out to sea. Sullivan came up from below with a pail; he apologized for disturbing Rico and made his way to the bloodstained wall outside the wheelhouse. Rico watched Sullivan work and thought how lucky he had been not to be discovered below deck. Sullivan finished his task and moved to the rear of the vessel, he checked the locks on the helicopter; he had been interrupted when he returned to the yacht. He pretended to clean the locks until he was satisfied that Rico wasn't watching him, then proceeded to lock the craft to the deck.*

The new captain and replacement crew would arrive later in the day and it would be Sullivan's task to prepare their quarters. He went below and packed his friends clothes. He removed a picture from over the Captain's bunk and held it in his hands. It was a picture of the three of them taken after a run on the Cong. Sullivan bit his lip. *What a hell of a way for them to go, after all we've been through.* He packed the picture with the Captain's things and moved to the next bunk. "Billy and Carl," he whispered. "I got two of them." A tap on the door interrupted his thoughts. Sullivan put the clothing bags back on the bunk and opened the door.

"We are the new crew. I'm Mack, Captain, and this is Waldo. That's his real name and he's real touchy about it." Waldo stared at Sullivan, looking for any signs of disrespect.

"I was just removing a few things."

"Hey, we're sorry about your friends. How did it happen?"

Sullivan didn't answer.

"Mr. Crainsworth said to tell you he hired us from the same company."

Sullivan relaxed a little.

"They rushed the boat, and used a sniper."

"How do you know that?"

"That's the only way they could have gotten to them. Besides, I didn't hear a thing. I was checking the engines. When I went upstairs I caught a glimpse of them leaving. The sniper went over the side and disappeared."

"Too bad they got away."

"Two of them didn't, and I'm sure I wounded the third."

"Good work. What else do you have?"

"They killed one of our clients, and injured the other one. "

"Damn," Mack said.

"Our killer got away in a Biz Jet. I checked the registration, it was phony."

"Okay. We'll wait for Mr.Crainsworth and see how he wants to handle the situation," Mack said.

"Yes, Sir," Sullivan said. Sullivan took the two large bags and carried them topside. He left the boat and took the bags into town.

*　　　　　*　　　　　*

Vic finished his drink. He stood and wavered a little.

"You'd better take it easy." Rico said.

"I'll be all right. I want to see Santiago."

"Vic, you're in no shape to see him. He's half way across the island."

"I want to talk to him," Vic said.

Rico thought about it for a moment.

"Tell you what I'll do, I'll have him brought here."

"That's no good, we have to do it my way…"

"I know, but…"

A limousine pulled up along side the dock and Mr. and Mrs. Crainsworth got out. Vic saw them and tried to stand again, but his legs failed him.

"You're right about me not being ready. I'll wait, Santiago isn't going anywhere."

"Right," Rico said.

"Vic, Vic. We're so sorry," Margaret said. Ellis nodded in agreement.

"Thank you." Vic looked up at the Crainsworths, tears flooding his cheeks.

"We're here for you," Ellis said, Vic nodded his head.

*      *      *

Monica hugged her nurse, it was over, and she was clean again. Her Mother stood by beaming with pride. This time she would make sure Monica didn't end up in a rehab facility again. It was the news of her father's death that did the trick.

"Her recovery was astonishing," Helen would say to her friends.

Helen chartered a helicopter; she didn't want to take the long ride home in a car. She had taken the car to visit Monica because she didn't want to appear ostentatious. Monica changed into her new clothes and joined her mother in the lounge. The meeting was brief, Monica said goodbye to the staff, hugged her nurse, and they were off.

The copter lifted, cleared the trees, and climbed slowly over the hills surrounding the hospital. Monica had stared at those hills from her private room and wondered what was on the other side. Now the mystery was sprawled below her, a mass of rolling hills that blended into model-size scenery. The copter flew in a straight line from the hills of Vermont to the Massachusetts state line, and across the green hills to its destination Bishop Island. Helen watched Monica taking in everything in. Monica took a deep breath and relaxed when the copter approached their home, she looked at her mother and smiled. Helen returned the gesture.

The servants met them at the helicopter and took Monica's bags. Louise hugged Monica, her husband, Robert, patted Monica on her shoulder. Monica stood there for a moment and absorbed her surroundings. She looked towards the Crainsworth estate and turned away.

"What is it, Monica?" Helen asked.

"Nothing."

"It's all over. Try not to think about it. Get on with your life."

"I'm fine, Mother, really."

"Good. Let's go into the house I want to show you something."

The servants had left them standing in the yard. Helen motioned towards the entrance and Monica took her mother's arm. They entered the grand room and took the stairs up to the second floor. Helen reached for the door to the study. Monica froze; she had always hated that room, the room in which Wayne had molested her.

"It's all right, come on. I know how much you hated this room so I changed it." Helen pushed the double doors open with a powerful thrust and daylight flooded the hallway. The Study had been changed into an exercise room. The bookshelves were gone, replaced by exercise rails and mirrored walls; stationary bikes, treadmills, weight machines, and mats completed the space.

This is where I keep in shape; the servants use it as well. What do you think?" Helen asked.

"I love it!" Monica took a deep breath, her eyes roamed the room, and then she turned to her mother and kissed her. Helen turned on the music system and the "Stones" rocked the room with "Satisfaction." Monica couldn't believe it. Wayne Woolford hated rock music. Helen took Monica's hand, led her to a bench, and sat down.

"I know what he did to you...but I didn't know then. You know how clever your father was." Monica nodded her head. "Can you handle this?

I asked them at the hospital about pressure, and they assured me that you were okay."

"I can handle it. How did he die?"

"He was shot..." Helen said.

Monica shrugged her shoulders, casually.

"Good. Let's get on with our lives. I had your place in town painted. Its there whenever you want to go back. I took Wayne's apartment, got rid of everything, and had it decorated."

"Thank you, but I want to stay here for a while. It's funny what you miss when you're in a place like that. One would think that you would miss our lifestyle. You know what I missed, after you of course?"

Helen shook her head.

"I missed the water, the horses, riding, and the ability to enter and leave a room without asking permission. Things we take for granite. To sum it all up, it was freedom."

"Let that be your motto and you'll never have to go back there. It's time for lunch. Let's go down stairs and have some real food for a change."

"Cool," Monica said.

"Cool?"

"Yes, Mother, cool."

*       *       *

Bee didn't tell anyone that Jess was coming with her. She knew that Ellis had provided protection for her, but she wanted her own. Jess called the Commissioner and he cleared Jess with the authorities in Puerto Rico, to pack two semi-automatics pistols. Ellis had a car meet them at the airport and bring them directly to the boat. Vic tried to stand when Bee arrived, but she looked so much like Honey that he was overwhelmed and sank back into the chair.

"Vic! Vic! Are you all right?" Bee asked.

Vic waved his hand in response. Jess stood behind Bee nodding his head. Vic looked at him and repeated the motion. It was cop talk. They didn't have to say anything to each other. It was time for business. Bee leaned down and hugged Vic.

"They are going to pay for this," Vic said in a whisper just loud enough to send a chill through everyone there.

"I know how you feel, but you're too close to the problem. Let Ellis and Jess handle it. You know I'm right," Bee said.

"She was my wife!"

"And my sister…I don't want to lose you too, Vic."

"I'm going to be fine. They are preparing Honey. She wanted to be cremated. We'll take her back when we finish here. Right now Jess, I want you to meet someone."

"Anything you need, Vic, anything," Ellis said.

"We have to see a man in Ponce, on the other side of the island, when I'm feeling better," Vic said.

"Can I come along," Ellis said.

"You don't want to be a part of this. I'll call Rico," Vic said.

*          *          *

Bee suggested the simple ceremony, after which they would keep Honey's ashes with them until they finished the business in Puerto Rico. The doctor had given Vic a green light; his x-rays were negative. The first picture taken, had an imperfection that had appeared to be a fracture. Ellis' private physician had flown down to examine Vic, and ordered new pictures. The diagnosis was a mild concussion, and the prognosis was for a speedy recovery. That was enough for Vic; he called Rico and asked to be taken to see Santiago.

Santiago was locked in a special facility, a place hidden away from normal traffic. Internal Affairs wanted everything Santiago knew, and didn't want to take a chance on the Colombians blowing him away.

Santiago had already given them twenty bad cops. Who knew what else he had to offer. The secret base was just outside of Ponce. Wayne's copter left Rico, Vic and Jess off at a ball field in the heart of town where they transferred to an army craft. The olive drab helicopter lifted off, its engine loud enough to wake the dead, and ten minutes later the craft landed at the secret base.

The place appeared to be empty but Vic and Jess could feel the eyes watching them. They were taken to an ordinary hut in the middle of the base. Vic, Jess, and Detective Rico followed their heavily armed escort through the door and watched him place his palm on a sensor. A few seconds later they heard a buzzing sound and the wall opened, each side rolling back into the side of the hut revealing a large door that opened to a long corridor that ended at an elevator.

Vic looked at Jess, his mouth twisted into "get a load of this crap." Jess nodded his head. Rico laughed, their escort was stoned faced. They entered the elevator; listen to the doors hiss closed, and braced themselves when the elevator appeared to fall. They had no reference, but they knew they were traveling at a high rate of speed, too fast to be comfortable. The elevator decelerated and slowed to a stop. Vic took a deep breath and waited for his body to adjust to the change. Their escort looked and smiled for the first time. Vic looked at him and gave him one of his smart-ass looks. The soldier laughed out loud.

"Wise guy," Vic said.

"Follow me, gentlemen," the Soldier said.

This was no ordinary prison, but a prison it was. They removed their weapons and left them with a guard who sat at a desk in the middle of a kiosk of television monitors. Vic scanned the monitors; television cameras covered every section of the outer area of the site. To anyone that too got close to the facility it would appear to be a motor pool. There were three buses, a few trucks, a couple of vans; one of which was up on a lift, and a gas pump. In the shadows concealed by the mock equipment, stood a heavily armed specialist.

Vic, Jess, and Rico were taken to an interrogation room on the second level of the prison. There was one more identification check, after which they were permitted to enter the room. A spit-and-polish lieutenant greeted them.

"Gentlemen, I'm Lieutenant Price. I hope you don't think we are paranoid. We are dealing with the most dangerous criminals in the world. The situation is complicated by the fact that they have so many resources. Their tentacles reach to the highest levels of government. You are the first people to ever visit this place. I don't know how you managed it, so I hope that you can be trusted. That aside, I must ask you to sign these forms we have prepared for you. It is a form that swears you to secrecy, and should you reveal anything you've seen here, you are subject to imprisonment, or worse. Any objections?"

Lieutenant Price scanned their faces. He was Satisfied that they understood. He placed the documents on the table and watched the three men sign. Lieutenant Price gathered the forms, put them in his attaché case, and motioned for the two soldiers standing at the door to bring in Santiago. Santiago shuffled in, handcuffed, a chain around his waist. Another chain passed through a ring on the waist-chain and dropped to a second ring that was attached to his leg irons. He looked pale; a sign that he was getting off drugs the hard way, cold turkey. He wouldn't look at Vic. The soldiers put him in a chair across the table from his three interrogators. Rico was first.

"We want to know where Juan Acevedo is in New York?"

Silence. The two soldiers who escorted Santiago into the room winked and left the room.

"You can't do that! You can't leave me alone with them!"

The door slammed and the soldiers were gone. Vic got up and walked around the table and reached for Santiago's leg irons.

"You can't touch me, they promised! Help! Get me out of here!!" Santiago looked towards the door. Panic seized him; he was alone in the room with two strangers, one of whom had lost his wife because of him.

Vic walked slowly towards Santiago and Santiago whimpered. Santiago didn't wait for Vic to ask him anything. He pulled against the chains that held his cuffs and tried to raise his hands to protect his face, but the chains didn't bulge.

"All right, all right! He went to his friend in the Bronx, the black dude. I swear!" Santiago said.

"A name," Vic said

Santiago leaned forward and tried to cover his face.

"I told them not to do it, I told them…but they wouldn't listen," Santiago said.

"Okay," Vic said.

Vic looked at him for a long time. He wanted to kill him, but instead he turned around and signaled for the guards to take Santiago back to his cell.

"What will happen to him?" Vic asked

"He'll never see the outside again," the Guard said.

Vic handed the Guard his card, but the soldier ignored it.

"We are here for one week. We never see the same prisoners more than once, after the week is over we move on."

"Move on?"

"Yes, to the next assignment," the guard said.

Vic tucked his card into his shirt pocket.

*       *       *

Ellis watched Vic and Jess return. The sun was setting in the background. Ellis looked at the tranquil scene and shook his head. "This is paradise," he whispered.

*How could such horrible things happen here?*

He turned and greeted Vic.

"How did it go?"

"I got what we needed," Vic said.

"You're not the only one who has been busy. Vic I want you to go downstairs and try to get a couple of hours sleep, we have a mission."

"A mission?"

"Yes. You're going to like this one, we're going on a trip south," Ellis said.

Vic shrugged his shoulders.

"Yes!" Jess said as if he understood Ellis' meaning.

⋆ ⋆ ⋆

Vic turned, opened his eyes, and tried to determine where he was; someone was knocking on the cabin door. Vic turned on the light and checked his watch. It was eleven o'clock on the head. He had been asleep for almost eight hours. Vic got up and opened the door. Ellis was there with another man dressed in black fatigues.

"Vic this is Duke. Duke and his team are going to take us into Columbia, and lead us to Senior Manero," Ellis said.

"I brought these for you," Duke said. We leave as soon as you can get dressed."

"How do you know he's going to be there?" Vic asked.

"We know his every move, but we had no idea that he was in Puerto Rico to do a hit. You must have hurt him pretty bad for him to come after you personally."

"I don't even know the man."

"He knows you."

Vic changed into the battle gear. He checked his gun and locked it in its holster. Jess walked past the cabin, fully dressed.

"Well, that's it. Let's get the show on the road," Vic said.

"I wish I could go with you," Ellis said.

"This isn't your kind of work," Duke said.

"You'd better get going before Bee gets wind of what going on," Ellis said.

Vic and Jess followed Duke to the rear of the yacht and boarded a small rubber boat. Duke released the rope at the stern and gunned the motor. The light craft lifted and stood higher above the water with each knot of speed. They traveled out to sea in a southerly direction. In the distance, Vic could see blinking lights. Soon they pulled up and docked with the damnedest looking seaplane Vic had ever seen. Duke held the boat while Jess and Vic climbed through a huge door into the plane. His assistant revved the outboard just enough to keep the boat near the plane. Duke jumped onto one of the pontoons and held the boat until his man climbed aboard. They lifted the boat on board, and Duke closed the door. He led the team forward to a compartment behind the pilot. The Pilot, like the man in the boat, said nothing. He turned the plane into the wind and accelerated. The plane's two jet engines roared as it raced along the water, lifted off, banked, and headed south.

"What in the hell is this thing?" Vic asked.

"Its an old navy job. They didn't have any use for it so we borrowed it," Duke said. "Try and get some rest, this is going to take a little while. We should make landfall about 0400. That will give us enough time to make it to our target before daylight. If things go well we will be picked up by a copter and taken to safety."

The plane was noisy, but not noisy enough to erase the reoccurring picture of Honey falling and rolling into the arms of Death. Vic broke out in a cold sweat.

Jess watched Vic struggling and reached under his bulletproof vest and removed a flask. He leaned forward and reached over the back of Vic's seat and passed the flask to him.

"What the? Thanks, Jess I can use this," Vic said.

Jess tapped Vic on the shoulder. Vic took a big swig and passed the flask back to Jess.

"Is this a private party, or can anyone join in?" Duke asked.

Jess gave Duke the flask.

The drink did the trick. Vic adjusted his seat and fell asleep. The dream this time was of the good times…

         \*        \*        \*

"The coast is dead ahead, sir."

"Make the call."

"May day! May day! Alpha Bravo Nelly, engine failure! May day!"

The pilot pressed a button, released a drone, and followed it in a steep dive. At two hundred feet he leveled off and watched the drone crash into the forest and explode. He leveled off at one hundred and fifty feet and turned on his terrain guidance system.

Jess sat up and gripped the back of Vic's seat.

"Shit!" He said.

"Relax," Duke said. "This plane can fly on the back of a mosquito."

The plane banked and climbed, following the contours of the forest. The last obstacle was a small peak that appeared out of nowhere. The plane's engines roared and the plane climbed and skimmed the ridge above the peak at tree top level. Jess reached for the small bag attached to the rear of Vic's seat and threw up. Vic was sound asleep, lost somewhere between dreams and reality.

"Target dead ahead, Sir"

"Good," Duke said.

In the distance a small light interrupted the darkness. Vic stirred and sat up. He rubbed his eyes yawned, and turned in the direction of the pungent odor behind his seat. Jess, head lowered, raised one hand and waved him off. The plane bumped once and landed on a small lake. Vic couldn't see anything. Suddenly, Vic caught a glimpse of the blinking light. In the distance the light looked like a firefly. The pilot cut the engines and let the plane drift up to three small boats. Duke opened the door and threw a rope to one of the boats and tied it to the plane.

"All right you guys, hit the deck!"

Vic stepped carefully onto the edge of the boat, balancing the weight of his pack, while holding onto the plane. Jess fumbled his way out of the plane and followed Vic. The three small boats were loaded in tandem, with supplies, after which they eased away from the plane and made their way to shore. Behind them the black behemoth surged forward in a thunderous roar. The flames from the engines gave the darkened craft the appearance of a demon from hell.

Vic and Jess followed duke up a slight embankment to a small clearing. The green glow of the night glasses, new to Vic and Jess, caused them to stumble and make false steps. Later they adjusted to the phenomenon and kept pace with the rest of the team.

"I hope you guys can ride. We go the rest of the way on horses." Duke said.

"Hey, we had horses in New York," Jess said.

"Yeah, but these aren't rent-a—mounts," Duke said.

The one thing about Duke's crew that was consistent was their silence. They went about their duties without saying a word. The team consisted of three men, boys rather, they appeared to be no older than sixteen. One of the crew was smaller than the weapon he carried. Duke checked the loads and used a hand signal to move out. He approached Vic and Jess and said, "We can't talk from here on."

The sound of the horses' hooves crushing leaves sounded like any other group of animals in the jungle. If there were anyone out there watching for them they wouldn't be disturbed by the sounds. Above the peaks, dawn glowed like a weak flashlight. Then, as if someone had turned up the wattage, the trees filled with light. Duke raised his arm and gave the signal to dismount. He led his horse off the trail into the bush. One of his young assistants passed his reigns to another silent companion and worked on obliterating their trail. Duke led them to a cave and took the horses inside. The cave was large, damp, and smelled of tragedy.

"Luis, take care of the horses,"

"Si!"

"So, they can talk," Vic, said.

"When it's necessary," Duke said. "We had a strong head wind coming down and we arrived late, but no problem, we'll stay here until it's dark. Might as well make yourselves comfortable."

"Is this place safe?" Jess asked.

"No place is safe, but this will do," Duke said.

Vic needed the break. Too many things were happening too fast. He opened his bedroll and chose a spot with a slight incline. Duke had rigged a blanket near the front of the cave to prevent the light from their lamps escaping. The two young warriors were busy preparing food. Jess opened his bedroll and placed it close to Vic.

"That food smells good. Do you think it will arouse suspicion?" Jess asked.

"Out here, I don't think so. The things out there eat raw meat," Duke said.

"Did I ever tell you that you're a nut?" Vic laughed.

"Damn! That's better, that's like my old partner," Jess said.

"Alimento, Senior?"

"You bet," Jess said.

"Damn! This beats the hell out of k-rations," Jess said.

"We don't live that way anymore," Duke said.

"You're damn right," Jess said.

Fernando pushed the blanket aside and left the cave.

"Fernando is taking the first watch. Each of us will take turns until nightfall. After you eat, try and get some sleep, we're going to be busy when it gets dark," Duke said.

*          *          *

The food or the wine worked like a charm, or Duke put something in Vic's food to make him sleep. Vic slept the whole nine yards. Duke waved Jess off when it was Vic's turn to relieve Fernando. At 21:00 hundred, Duke gave the signal to pack. He nodded his head towards Vic, and Jess shook Vic. Vic jumped up and reached for his gun.

Easy…easy. We're getting ready to leave," Jess said.

Vic rubbed his eyes and waited for them to adjust to the dim light in the cave.

"What time is it?"

"Nine o'clock," Jess said.

"Why didn't you wake me?"

"Duke thought it was best for you to sleep."

"Thanks, Duke, I'm ready now."

Duke gave Vic a thumbs up.

They loaded the heavy weapons onto the backs of the packhorses and saddled their riding horses. Duke led the group out of the cave.

"We ride to the top of the next hill, leave the horses there, and go the rest of the way on foot. We're back to hand signals again," Duke said.

The caravan moved out into the wet wilderness, head to tail, moving slowly towards the next mountain. In the background beyond the peak, the light from Manero's estate set the vapors of the evaporating mist aglow. The leaves were still wet from the rainfall and all was quiet. Vic looked through the sweaty infrared screen clamped to his head at the huge animals moving ahead of him in ghost-like movements, their hooves silent.

At the crest, just before the top of the peak, Duke stopped and led the horses off the path. He pointed to the trees and tied his horse. Duke unpacked the heavy weapons and laid them on a canvass Fernando had unrolled near the packhorses. Luis assisted Duke; Fernando vanished into the night. Each man checked their weapons and waited for Duke to give the go-ahead signal. A bird song echoed across the area, answered by other birds, then silence. Duke raised his hand and the group moved out. Near the top of the hill Duke got down on all fours and directed the group to follow him. Soon they were on their stomachs crawling toward the top of the hill.

Manero's ritzy estate looked like a set from Disney Land. The place mirrored the model they had used to practice on. Duke hesitated, something was wrong…he didn't see any guards. Duke rolled on his side and gave the sign to "stay put." He motioned with his head to Fernando and Luis to follow him. The two men crawled a few feet and froze. Duke moved first, sliding slowly backwards, Fernando moving and stopping whenever Duke used his foot to tap him on the shoulder. They turned around, a few moments later, and crawled back to the group. Duke used a small pen light to light a slate board and wrote LASER TRAP on it in large letters. He passed the slate and light to each man, and then signaled for them to follow him. Duke pursed his fingers to his lips and used hand signals to indicate that he wanted Jess and Vic to stay with the horses while he and his crew looked for another way into Manero's villa.

# CHAPTER *11*

---

"*T*hey fucked up, Lisa. We have to get the hell out of here," Juan said.

"What happened?"

"Those crazy Colombians, they killed the cop's wife, but he's still alive. Something else, they got Santiago and he's talking his head off."

"Damn," Lisa said.

"We're going back to New York. I want you to get a face job, and while you're healing we'll cool it for a while. We have enough money," Juan said.

"When do we leave?"

"Now. I got a charter job to take us to Tetaboro."

"What about your mother?"

"She's cool. They won't bother her; its me they want," Juan said.

Lisa threw a few things into a bag, looked around the house, as if it would be the last time she would ever see it again and hurried through the door behind Juan.

"Don't worry, Lali will take care of the place. I told her what to do and made arrangements for her to pick up her check every week at the bank."

"You think of everything, baby," Lisa said.

*　　　*　　　*

"We've found it, a drainage ditch at the rear of the house. It's all clear here, not even wired. Follow us and once inside, find your objectives. The only difference is that we will be approaching our targets from the rear of the house," Duke whispered.

"What about the guards?" Vic said.

"They're probably inside watching television monitors, and you know how that goes," Duke said.

"Right, they're asleep."

"Let's hope so. Okay, back to the top of the hill and around to the drainage ditch. Move out!"

"Damn, this guy takes this shit seriously," Jess, said.

"You'd better be just as serious. These guys don't play. And if we don't get them in the first round you can kiss your butt goodbye," Vic said.

Jess was silent.

Fernando had remained at the drainage ditch; he had an opening ready when they got there.

"I'll go first and take out the powerhouse. As soon as the lights go out get to your targets," Duke said.

They crawled through the opening and followed Duke up the path, running through the drainage ditch. Ahead of them at the other end Fernando clipped the wire mesh covering the opening that led to the backyard. He eased the circle of mesh from the large hole and placed it gently into the ditch and stood aside. Duke climbed through the hole and ran across the yard towards the powerhouse. He used his knife to take out the guard sitting at the entrance and entered the building. Moments later the estate plunged into total darkness. Each man ran toward his assigned target. Vic grabbed his man from behind and snapped his neck. Jess garroted of one of the guards at the entrance to the house while Luis took out the other one with the hiss of his gun. A thunderous sound broke the quiet; suddenly the place was flooded with light. A volley of fire raked the yard and everyone ducked for cover. The light moved skyward until the only thing recognizable was the pink darts spitting from a machine gun mounted under the helicopter; its blinking strobe light vanishing into the distance.

"Damn! We missed him. Move out! We have to get the hell out of here…let's go, let's go!" Duke said.

Manero covered on ear with his hand and used the other hand to dial a number on his cellular phone. The conversation was short. He used the intercom to instruct the pilot to take him to his airfield.

"Abort! Abort…we have to make it across the river, or else we've had it,"

"He was tipped off," Vic said.

"No way, he's just lucky this time. Our problem right now is to cross the river and lay low until the heat is off. Borders don't mean a thing to these guys, but if we can hide until they leave we'll be picked up and taken home. The land on the other side of the river is friendly territory. Each man took as much ammo as they could carry and mounted their horses. Carlos led the way. There were no subtleties this time; the group hit the trail at full gallop. Thank God horses followed commands, a mule wouldn't even gallop in the dark. Night goggles turned the dense, dark jungle into a maze of tricky paths, all of which Carlos knew like the back of his hand. They made their way back to the cave and took cover.

"Walk the horses before we rest or else they will be winded," Duke said. He pointed to Carlos, Carlos nodded his head and handed the reigns of his horse to Fernando, after which, he left the cave.

"When you finish with the horses get some rest, we're going to be busy as soon as day breaks," Duke said.

"Think we're going to make it?" Jess asked.

"We might have to fight, but we'll make it," Duke said. Vic sat silently cleaning his knife. He held it up to the Coleman lamp, twisted it, and put it in its scabbard. The sound of helicopters overhead broke the silence. They were flying high and appeared to be heading south.

"We made it just in time. They would have picked us up with their heat devices if we had stayed on the trail," Duke said.

"Damn technology," Vic said.

"Yeah, its good when we use it, and bad when they use it," Jess said.

"Chill out, Jug head," Vic said.

"Yeah," Jess said.

*        *        *

"Who the hell were they?" Manero said.

"We don't know. It looks like they got away."

"How is that possible, what do I pay you for?" Manero said.

"It is not over yet."

"I want them and I want them now!" Manero said and closed his phone.

The clouds below were filled with night and day, darkness on one side of the plane and dawn on the other. In the distance the white beaches of Portugal came into view. Beyond the shores of Portugal, in the distance, the mountains of Spain rose from the earth like bumps on a log. Manero's pilot called Malaga Control and asked for clearance to land.

*        *        *

"All right, you sleeping beauties rise and shine!"

Duke was in a good mood, the anxiety and fear of the night before, gone. Jess rubbed his eyes and looked for Vic. Vic jumped up, and grabbed his gun.

"Easy, easy. It's daylight, now we will have the upper hand," Duke said.

"What was all the caution about yesterday?" Vic asked.

"Surprise, we needed the element of surprise. Now that they know we're here it is just a matter of making our way out."

"I like that, making our way out," Vic said.

"Let them look for us until we find them," Duke said.

"Right, we set a trap for them," Vic said.

"Give the man a cigar. Okay, move out," Duke said.

The jungle outside seemed thicker after the rain. It had lasted all night and the vegetation was rising in a ritual of worship. Fernando took the point on foot, leading his horse and whacking away at the bush with a machete. At seven in the morning the trail had turned into a green sauna. Vic wiped the sweat from his face and cursed the wine he drank the night before. A thumping sound somewhere in the distance brought everyone to a halt. Duke looked skyward and pointed to the three small specks moving towards them.

"Everybody, under the trees and keep still," Duke said.

Fernando was caught out in the open. The copters began their descent, moving towards Fernando. Fernando didn't panic; he removed his hat and waved to the three craft. One of the copters broke away from the formation while the other two hovered over the trail. Fernando waited until the copter was in range and opened fire. The shots penetrated the copters windscreen, and the craft tilted on its side and crashed; in the same instance Duke and Carlos fired their rocket launchers at the two remaining copters. Vic watched the rocket's trail of death tracking the two remaining helicopters. Two large balls of fire singed the treetops and a large cloud of black smoke plumed toward the heavens.

"Move out! On the double!!" Duke said.

Vic and Jess mounted their horses and joined Carlos and Duke at the gallop. The border was less than a mile away; they had to make it before reinforcements arrived. This time they would come in jets. Suddenly they were in the open, and a vast area cleared between the two countries. It was a border without fences, protected by a huge gorge. Fernando stopped, got off his horse and walked it down a narrow pass that led to the river. The rest of the team followed him. At the river Fernando waded into the water up to his waist. He slapped his horse on its rear end and watched it swim towards the opposite bank. A salvo of shots rang out from somewhere to his left and the horse fell. Fernando dived into the river and swam under water towards the riverbank on the other side. Duke and his group hit the deck and remained still. The ambush was a total surprise.

Fernando held his breath. He felt his fingertips touching the riverbank and pushed himself slowly to the surface. Two shots rang out, and bullets whistled over his head. Moments later a volley of shots burst over his head, firing in the direction of the bushwhackers. The exchange of gunfire lasted thirty seconds, but it seem like a lifetime to Fernando. Then it was quiet again. Duke and Carlos had climbed trees and blended into the leaves. They attached scopes and silencers to their weapons and scanned the bush around them. Vic and Jess lay flat on the ground, bellying to cover. Fernando climbed out of the water and joined the backup team waiting on the embankment. He dried his weapon and took a position that gave him full view of the area from which the gunfire originated.

He used his automatic weapon to raked the riverbank to the right of where he had left Duke and the rest of his team. A man fell out of the bush, clinched his shoulder and screamed. Duke raised his rifle and fired. Fernando spotted movement in the leaves and fired in the direction of the movement. A soldier rolled down the bank and fell into the river. Duke pointed to their left, up the hill about fifteen feet. Fernando nodded his head and took a grenade from his belt and pulled the pin, he counted to five and tossed the grenade to the spot Duke pointed out. Two large explosions and a ball of fire cleared a massive area around them. Three attackers were left; they dropped their weapons and fled.

Duke climbed down out of the tree and joined Vic and Jess. "It's over for now. We cross the river and go home," Duke said.

∗    ∗    ∗

Manero had a passion for flamenco, and Toremollinos offered a unique experience for aficionados. Castro warned him that it was dangerous to be seen so soon after the attempt on his life, but Manero shrugged off his advice.

"What am I some kind of jerk! I will not hide like an animal. It is your job to find these people and solve this problem...is that clear?" Castro nodded his head. This was a bad time to reason with Manero. Someone had had the nerve to attack his home and they could not have done it without the help of the DEA. There was a leak in his organization and he was going to find it. But for now, it was time to enjoy Spain. Bar Tanos sat at the top of a hill away from the tourist crowd. It was a place where flamenco dancers gathered after performing in theaters and local clubs. The dancing started at midnight and lasted until dawn; it was a flamenco jam session.

Manero entered the club and everything stopped, a pregnant moment in which everything fell quiet, then, cries of "Hombre!" Tonight the drinks would be free, provided by the rich hombre who loves flamenco. He gave no name so they called him "Hombre." The audience composed of locals and old performers, who sat at their favorite tables, broke tradition for their guest of honor, who was allowed to sit at the center table in the middle of the room. Manero's bodyguard sat next to him. One of his men covered the rear entrance, two were at the front entrance, and one man waited in the car. There was no ceremony at Bar Tanos, the music began at midnight and the dancers entered the room in mass. Manero loved flamenco for many reasons; one was the dancers, dancers with a certain predilection for his craving...

At four in the morning Manero's bodyguard paid the check and tipped the waitress. It had been an exciting evening. As was the custom during the performance, members of the audience were selected by the dancers to join them in their performance. A striking young woman with pure black hair and olive skin, the dark color of many women who come from Seville, danced over to Manero's table and pulled him onto the dance floor. A dancer he was not, but his movements attracted one of the younger male dancers who pushed the woman off the floor. The crowd went wild. It was as if they had anticipated the encounter. Later the young dancer left with Manero and his entourage...

An older man in the audience was the first to leave. He walked down the hill to his car and waited for Manero to leave. Manero's driver laughed when the old man stumbled against his car. The old man staggered, apologized and went on his way, but not before stumbling again and in the process attaching a small transmitter to the car's license plate. He made it to his car, fumbled with the lock, opened the door and stumbled inside. He turned on the homing device; a red light on his dashboard blinked intermittently. Ten minutes later, three cars left Bar Tanos. The first car was occupied by Manero's security, followed by Manero's car; the backup car completed the caravan. They drove back to a condo a large white palace of a place at the end of a dead end street. The old man followed them, and parked innocently in the hotel parking lot next door. Manero had chosen the place because his apartment faced the sea. On a clear day he could she the shadowy coast of Algeria, and from his window he had a clear view of the beach below.

The old man made a phone call, after which he went into the hotel and registered. He waited for his backup team to arrive and chose a room that gave him a perfect view of the entrance to the condo next door.

&midast;    &midast;    &midast;

Fangio met Lisa and Juan at Tetaboro Airport. Fangio had moved up in the world, as the famous owner of Fangio's Limousine Service. The car rolled up to the plane and the ritual of doors opening and closing was repeated, Fangio waited in the car.

"Hey, Dude!" Juan said. Lisa stooped, entered the car, and sat beside Fangio. Fangio moved over to make room for Juan.

"Hey amigo! Welcome home. If it weren't for Lisa I would think you were somebody else. I couldn't believe it when you called. I thought you were dead."

"That was my plan."

"Cool. Juan, anything you want, anything you need, you got it," Fangio said.

"Take me to the Palace Hotel, then, I want you to take Lisa to this address on Park Avenue. When you drop her off, come back to the hotel and call my room. We have to make some plans. I'll be registered as a Mr. Guzman, " Juan said.

*      *      *

It was good to be back in New York again, away from the tragedy of San Juan. The familiar surroundings comforted Vic, and for a while his anger subsided. Commissioner Chapman asked him to lunch at Peter Luger's, the Commissioner's favorite restaurant, and another touch of the familiar, it was good to be home again. The restaurant was full of the usual crowd, businessmen making deals and politicians doing whatever politicians do.

"Commissioner Chapman," Vic said. The headwaiter nodded and motioned for Vic to follow him. Vic followed him, but he knew exactly where to find the Commissioner in the back room at the corner table.

"Vic! Good to see you, sit down..."

"Commissioner."

"You know how I feel about your wife...I...er...I just..."

Vic interrupted.

"Thank you, sir."

"What do you want to do, you name it and it's yours."

"I haven't had time to think about it. You know what I have to do?"

"Yes, and the whole department are at your disposal. A special team, equipment, its yours."

"I'm thinking about going private," Vic said.

The Commissioner nodded his head. If he knew Vic, it would be better for him to operate as a civilian.

"Your paper work is still on my desk, but like I said, it's up to you. Stay with the department and we'll make this a major case."

"I appreciate it, but somewhere along the line I would step on someone's toes and the shit would hit the fan. You don't need that, Commissioner."

Commissioner Chapman looked at Vic and smiled.

"It's not going to be that easy. You're going to need all the help you can get. Just cool down for a while…take your time."

Vic nodded his head, but he didn't look at the Commissioner.

"Yes, sir."

"Good. Let's have lunch," the Commissioner said.

∗       ∗       ∗

Fangio arrived at the hotel and called Juan from the limousine. The doorman asked Fangio's driver to please move away from the entrance and park in front of the restaurant next door. Fangio chose the spot in front of the Lobster House and parked. A meter maid approached the car and motioned for the driver to move on. Fangio rolled his window down and told the woman they were waiting for a friend who should be out in a moment. The meter maid thought about it for a moment, shrugged her shoulders and said, "Five minutes." Fangio thanked her.

The doorman motioned for a taxi and hesitated, Juan waved the taxi off.

"The gentleman in a limo is waiting for me," Juan said and tilted his head towards the limo.

The doorman walked hurriedly over to Fangio's limousine and opened the door.

"Thank you."

Juan said and slipped the doorman a five."

"Than you, Mr. Guzman."

"You're welcome. You'll let me know if there is anyone inquiring about me, right?"

The doorman winked, said "Yes, sir," and closed the door.

Fangio nodded his head and the car moved forward.

"Where do you want to go?" Fangio said.

"How about The Cantina, you know that restaurant on the parkway, its a good place to talk."

"Right, Gill, do you know the restaurant on the Hutchinson River Parkway?"

"Yeah, its in Westchester."

"Good, take us there."

"Right, boss."

"You look good. Sure had me fooled back there in San Juan. Man, they scared the shit out of me...all of that shooting. And, there was blood all over you. How did you do that shit?"

"Chicken blood. We knew that they had you on the hook, so we set you up. Worked out, didn't it? They gave you a suspended sentence, didn't they?"

"Yeah, that was then and this is now. I would like for them to try that shit again," Fangio said.

"What's so different now?" Juan said.

"I've worked hard, paid off a lot of people to get this far, and nobody is going to take it away from me."

Juan slapped a high five on Fangio.

"Hey, that's what its about. When I think about where I came from it makes me sick. Strung out on drugs, shit, that stuff is for assholes."

Juan banged his hand against the side of the seat.

"One of the things I learned is that business people don't do anything, Manero taught me that. Watch yourself at all times and don't use the merchandise."

The two men exchanged high-fives.

"That's what he taught me, and he made me go back to school. Imagine that, me going back to school. All of that happened after I buried the old Juan. Like you, nothing is going to take what I have from me," Juan said.

"Yeah, we got it pretty good. I never knew why he took me in; it wasn't until now that I realized it was you who put Manero on to me. Thank you." Fangio said.

"Hey what are friends for? Now it's time to work on a problem. I'll tell you more when we are alone." Fangio nodded his head in agreement. He reached for the remote and turned on the CD player. The two men relaxed and listened to a little vintage Tito Puente…

*            *            *

At dawn the Dancer left Manero's place. Fernandez's relief jotted the information down in his notebook, copied the license plate and number of the taxi, and called the information in. It was ten in the morning and the temperature had already reached ninety. Manero was the first one up. The aroma from the kitchen was too much for him. It was his favorite Tarta Español, hamon, and cafe solo. No matter what he tried, including taking a large bag of Café-Christina home, he couldn't make the rich Spanish coffee like the Spaniards. It was as dark as espresso, but not as bitter, it tasted like a good piece of chocolate. He opened his laptop and logged onto the Internet. "You have mail" greeted him. Manero had two messages, one from a friend in Madrid, and one from Juan in New York. Manero logged off the Internet, finished his breakfast and called his pilots. They had to move, Manero's informant had read the report from Detective Fernandez before Fernandez had awaken to take over the watch from his fellow officer. It didn't matter if Fernandez had spotted them; they were going to Madrid where they had protection.

Fernandez stumbled into room half dressed. He got to the window just in time to see the three cars drive off. He didn't bother to put on any socks; he grabbed his pants, put them on and stuffed his feet into his shoes. He put his shirt on, strapped on his shoulder holster, and buttoned his shirt on the fly. His partner carried his jacket and hat. Fernandez called in, gave a description of the three cars, and asked that they be observed, not apprehended. A minute later a motorcycle officer spotted them on the road to the airport in Malaga. Fernandez arrived at the airport just in time to watch Manero and his entourage board Manero's private plane. Fernandez watched until the plane took off, after which he called the tower for Manero's flight plan.

*   *   *

"We have to lay low for a while. Our friends in Madrid won't bother us if we don't conduct any business," Manero said.

"What's the problem?"

"The problem is that we missed the cop and killed his wife…that's the problem. You know we pay these mother-fuckers and they let you do anything you want, as long as you don't touch one of them. Who the hell do they think they are! Look at my condition, where was my protection?"

Gill moved away from Manero, it wasn't safe to be near him when he was in one of his rages. Manero had that strange look in his eyes again. Gill wondered how he had managed to become so rich….

"Get you ass back over here and sit down, Gill! What the hell is this? You think I would hurt you? Sit down," Manero said. The wicked glow was gone as sudden as it had appeared. That was another thing Gill feared, Manero made him feel like he could read his mind.

"Gill, I'm going to give you this job. I want that fucking cop dead. You know he's after me now and I don't need that shit…When we get to Madrid, I want you to go back to the states, find that cop and get rid of him. Do this for me and I will make you a partner."

Gill smiled and nodded his head.

"Let's have a drink," Manero said.

\*        \*        \*

The sun shone brightly; as if God had opened the heavens to say take Honey inside. The service was quiet, a few of Honey's closest friends, her family, the Crainsworths, Jess and Debbie. Vic hadn't discussed his family, or the lack of one. Only honey and Jess knew that he didn't have anyone. Now he was alone again. Reverend Genzel had arranged the jazz group, and Vic asked for and they played Honey's favorite tune, "The More I See You." The moment crushed Vic. Bee rested Vic's head on her shoulders, she patted his hand lightly, unable to do anything else.

After the ceremony Jess helped Vic to the car. The Crainsworth's chauffeur eased the car out of the parking space and headed for the Midtown Tunnel. Bee and the Commissioner rode with him back to the Crainsworth estate. Commissioner Chapman forced Vic to have a drink. By the time they reached Connecticut, Vic was singing Honey's song. He wasn't a singer but that didn't matter because there was a glow in his eyes.

\*        \*        \*

Juan helped Lisa into the car. There were dark blotches around her eyes. The panda affect didn't startle Juan as much as the change in her face. Her nose was bandaged, but it looked smaller, not smaller, and not as wide as before. Her lips were swollen a little and her hair had been dyed a warm brown. She edged back into the seat, opened her purse and removed a pair of sunglasses.

"There, that's better," she said.

"How you feeling?" Juan asked. For a moment he had digressed into the street lingo. He dropped his head and laughed.

"Did you hear what I just said."?

"Yeah. You sounded like the old Juan," Lisa said. Juan waved his hand and the car moved out.

"I want to move out of the hotel Manero has a place for us on Seventy-second Street. It belonged to one of Manero's boys before he had an accident. The place is registered to one of Manero's phony companies so we won't have to worry about anybody finding us."

Lisa nudged Juan with her elbow and nodded towards the limo driver.

"It's okay, he's working for me."

"Good," Lisa said and sat back in the seat.

The driver turned onto 50th Street from Fifth Avenue. He drove across 50th Street and stopped at the hotel A taxi driver cursed at him and turned to his left to avoid hitting the limo. The taxi driver extended his arm out of the taxi and gave the limo driver a single-finger salute.

"Baby, it's good to be back the hotel is fabulous."

"Riiight, and think about it we have new faces, and money. I'm going to help Manero wrap this thing up and we're getting out of this business," Juan said.

"You can do that?"

"Yeah, it's not like the movies."

"I don't know, Baby, Manero did a lot of things for you, he might not like you getting out."

"As long as I don't get into the business, I can get out. I might have to help him once and a while, but it won't be a full time thing, you'll see."

"I hope so. Here, Baby, take these things for me." Lisa handed Juan a small bag and the flowers.

*      *      *

Jess waited until he was sure Vic had a grip on things before giving him the news. Fangio had been found. Jess told Vic how well Fangio was doing and that he had friends. Vic had said "There's nothing like having friends where it counts." The friends were a couple of local police officers. One of them drove a white BMW around the neighborhood in uniform, go figure. It was the shot that Vic needed. By the end of the evening they were making plans on how to handle the situation.

"I thought about it, maybe we shouldn't be in such a hurry to leave the department," Vic said.

"Yeah, we'd need a office, a couple of cars, radios and all kinds of things."

"Right, and we couldn't go to the motor pool any more, either," Vic said.

"Couldn't even go into headquarters unless someone gives us permission," Jess said.

"Don't forget what the Commissioner said, anything we need."

"Right, I forgot about that. Hey, maybe we are going to make it after all," Jess said

"Yeah, as soon as we find Juan and Manero."

"Yeah," Jess said.

Vic grimaced; he had Juan and Manero to hate that was what kept him going.

*　　　　　*　　　　　*

"We have to leave the hotel." Juan said.

"Why, I like it here?"

"They know we are here."

"Damn! I'm tired of these mother-fuckers, Juan. So they know we are here, so what?"

"If they know that, they might know what we look like, that's what! Get your things together!"

"Don't yell at me. You told me everything was going to be different. We could have stayed in Puerto Rico, shit!"

"Look…get your things together," Juan said. Lisa didn't argue this time; she knew she was treading in dangerous waters. Lisa got up off the bed, opened the closet and threw her clothes on a chair. Juan opened a bag and put it on the rack. Lisa was in the shower now, and for a moment the sound of the water running erased the troubles ahead. Lisa entered the room with a towel covering her head, arms extended upward, exposing her lower torso.

"It's all yours," she said.

Juan threw the rest of his things in the bag and put a larger bag on the rack for Lisa.

"Thank you, baby," she said.

"Yeah, you're welcome, and that's more like it," Lisa said.

"You think you're hot shit, right?" Juan said.

"Damn straight."

Lisa popped Juan with the towel and Juan grabbed her and threw her on the bed.

"I thought you said we were in a hurry," she said. Juan eased his hand between her legs and pushed them apart.

"Well," she said.

The Concierge knocked on the door but there was no answer. He knocked once and Juan yelled, "Come back in fifteen minutes." The sounds from the room told the rest of the story. He returned twenty minutes later, this time Juan opened the door and let him in.

"I'm here for your luggage, Sir."

Juan pointed to the luggage rack and called Lisa.

"Lisa, the guy is here for the bags, are they ready?"

"Yes."

Juan tipped the Concierge and stood aside until he had left the room. Lisa entered the room wearing a Bellini suit.

"You look good in black," Juan said.

"Here, put this on, I bought it for you," Lisa said.

"Hey! Its as light as a feather, wow!"

"For the price, it should be. Its silk," Lisa said.

"But it ain't shiny," Juan said.

"That's the idea," Lisa said.

Juan buttoned the shirt, stuffed it into his pants and stood in front of the mirror. He liked the look, but the shirt felt like was going to fly away at any moment. It was a strange feeling, but the shirt looked good. The phone rang and Lisa answered it.

"Thank you, we'll be right down." Lisa took one last look around the room, picked up a smaller bag and joined Juan at the door. The doorman tipped his hat and pushed the luggage cart to the limousine waiting at the curb. Alston, Juan's new driver, assisted the bellhop with the bags, being careful not to scratch the Louis Vitton luggage. The doorman gave Alston a dirty look as if to say "the luggage can take it, how about you?"

Alston ignored him, stood back and waited until he stuffed the last bag in the car and closed the trunk. Juan called the doorman over and gave him a generous tip. Alston was already in the car, he looked back to make sure the door was closed, locked the doors, and moved out into the slow moving traffic, nudging his way in front of a taxi.

"What are we going to do now?"

"We're going to an apartment on Seventy-second Street. It's not too far from here and we will be safe there," Juan said.

"But what about the people looking for us?"

"They won't look for us here in town, not midtown, that is" Juan said.

"Juan I don't want to say nothing, but it don't sound right to me," Lisa said.

"Baby the best place in the world to hide is out in the open, nobody looks for you there."

"What about the limousine, you mean they're not going to notice it?"

"Where we're going everybody travels by limousine," Juan said.
"That's cool," Lisa said.

*      *      *

Having settled the idea of resigning, Bee had suggested that Vic and Jess should open the place on Wards Island again, since they would be concentrating on one case. They would only need two rooms and she agreed to help them after work. Vic and Jess accepted her offer, that done, they were in business.

*      *      *

Vic was functioning at about eighty percent; he still hadn't solved the problem of where he would live. Honey and Vic hadn't even had time to resolve the question of where they were going to live. Vic thought about their dilemma and a painful smile forced its way to the surface. Most people had a problem finding a good place to live; now he had two places to live. Vic couldn't bring himself to even visit Honey's place, Bee had asked him to do so a couple of times, but it was too difficult. He knew he would have to go there one day but for now....

Jess dropped Vic off at his place and offered to stay with him for a while, but Vic would have none of it. Jess tried to argue with Vic, but he knew it was hopeless. He agreed to leave after Vic promised not to leave the house.

"Vic, I got a feeling this thing is just beginning. Don't you go anywhere without me, right?" Jess said.

"Hey, it's gonna be all right. I'll hang here until you come for me," Vic said.

Jess gave Vic a questioning look.

"Naw, naw, I'm not jiving, I'll stay here," Vic said.

"Don't fuck around, these guys don't play."

Vic nodded his head in agreement. He stood back and watched Jess drive off. Vic turned and walked towards the entrance of his place. He opened the gate and entered his yard. He turned to latch the gate and thought about the first time he had done so. His parents were still alive at the time and they kidded him about moving into a house alone. What they said was "Don't you take anybody's wife up there to your place. All we need is for some man go up there and shoot you, especially since you're a cop." Vic hadn't thought about that warning for a long time, but it always made him look over his shoulder whenever he thought about what his mother had said.

Vic climbed the one flight of steps to his porch and felt for his keys. He didn't look in the direction of the black Mercedes parked across the street; he pretended that he hadn't noticed the swanky car parked in the block. Vic entered the house and ran toward the back door. He unlocked the door, ran across the yard, and jumped the fence that led to the street behind the house. A loud "whump!" interrupted the customary sounds of the quiet community followed by a huge fireball mushrooming into a massive cone of destruction.

Vic hugged the ground and covered his head to protect himself from the falling debris. He got up and ran towards the nearest house and took cover in an open garage. He looked back at his place, but there was noting there. It was strange, the explosion did very little damage to the house next door; it was as if a demolition expert had planned the bombing. Vic lay there hugging the ground, listening to the sirens screaming in the distance. He raised himself up slowly. Through the glow of the dancing flames he caught a glimpse of the driver in the Mercedes moving slowly past the burning remains of his house. He would never forget that face. The man sitting next to the driver was obscured, but at the last moment Vic caught a glimpse of an unusual earring the man was wearing.

Emergency vehicles crisscrossed 233rd Street slowing traffic to a trickle. Two police officers were busy detouring drivers who had stopped, or were rubbernecking at the flaming empty space. Vic took advantage of the confusion and walked causally over to a bus waiting for its turn to move. He tapped on the door to get the driver's attention. The driver shrugged his shoulders, hesitated and pointed to the bus stop further up the street. Vic pointed to the cops detouring the traffic ahead and made a pleading gesture. The driver tilted his head in a gesture of agreement and opened the door. Vic thanked the driver, and dropped the fare into the box.

"Thank you."

"Yeah. You know I'm not suppose to pick you up there, right?"

"Yeah, I know, thank you."

"Okay. I just don't want to get in trouble, you know?"

"Sure, I appreciate the favor," Vic said.

"Hey! What happened back there?"

"A house blew up."

"Were you in it? I mean your clothes are...you know," the Bus Driver said.

"No, I was on the next street and when I heard the explosion I dropped to the ground," Vic said.

"Vet huh?"

Vic nodded a yes.

"Me too, Nam," The Bus Driver said.

"Korea," Vic said. The bus reached the intersection and joined the traffic detouring one street over where it moved west for two blocks and returned to 233rd Street. Vic got off at the subway station and took the train downtown. He didn't know why he ran from the house, it was as if someone said, "run for your life," but that couldn't be, no one was there with him....

# CHAPTER *III*

$G$ill paid his driver and entered the private jet chartered to take him home. The ritual of vehicles parting followed their traditional sequence, the limo moving towards the entrance gate and the plane following the Avitat vehicle to the runway paths. The white Avitat van moved to the left and the Lear Jet moved to its right and followed the arrows leading it to the takeoff runway. Traffic cluttered the Jersey Turnpike just over the fence. Gill looked down as they rose above the traffic. Inside the luxurious craft the sound was a faint hum. Outside, the engines thundered over the traffic, forcing drivers with opened windows to look in the direction of the ascending craft. Gill phoned Manero and said simply, "Bueno" and put the phone away. Manero handed his phone to his valet and told him to turn on the television. The screen glowed and Manero used his remote control to find CNN. It was as Gill had said, "Bueno." The top story was the tragic death of one of "New York's Finest.

> *"In the Bronx today a tragic explosion. A building exploded, killing the single occupant. The victim was Detective Vic Morgan. The tragedy is compounded by the fact that Detective Morgan's wife was killed recently on their honeymoon. It appears that the explosion was caused by a gas leak, but the matter is still under investigation. Mari Hill CNN, New York"*

Manero waved his hand and a servant prepared a drink for him. Inside he wanted to jump for joy but he had learned the hard way that you can't trust anybody. He waited for the drink, took it out on the terrace, and waited for an opportune moment to say "Yes!" followed by an arm-jerking motion.

*         *         *

Vic took a bus from the Port Authority Bus Station to Washington D.C. There he would meet a friend. A friend who had convinced him to take advantage of his reported death. Vic took the last seat on the bus. From his seat he could see everyone entering and leaving the bus. Edmond Duke had made the suggestion, or as he put it, "Who would expect you to travel by bus?" Somewhere between the end of the New Jersey Turnpike and Maryland tollbooth, Vic fell asleep and slept undisturbed until the bus stopped. He jumped, reached for his gun, but relaxed when he grasped what was going on around him. The Driver was taking a break. The Driver got on the bus, returned to his seat, and moved the giant vehicle forward. A few minutes later they were crossing the Delaware River. They would reach their destination soon. Later at the bus station, Vic followed his instructions. He bought a copy of "Time Magazine," tucked it in the crook of his arm, and walked to the corner. Taxi number 385 stopped next to him and the driver asked him if he knew any Ellington tunes.

"Are you speaking of Duke Ellington?"

"Who else?"

Vic opened the door and entered the taxi.

"I don't believe we just went through that," Vic said.

"You have a better idea?" The Driver asked.

"I guess not."

"The Major is waiting for you at the National Gallery. He'll be standing near the *Hope Diamond*."

"Thank you," Vic said.

Vic relaxed and enjoyed the ride. The driver followed the slow traffic moving towards various government building and tourist sites. Vic used the opportunity to change clothes in the car. The clothes Duke sent him were a perfect fit. He smiled when he put them on, reaffirming his respect for Duke and his thoroughness. They stopped in front of the gigantic white building and Vic got out. Vic went through the motions of paying the driver, after which he climbed the steps to the entrance to the National Gallery of Art.

Vic walked over to the display window and looked into the box that contained the blue-white diamond. He thought of the alleged curse on the stone and wondered if it were true.

"That could set you up for life," Duke said over Vic's shoulder.

"I thought you were going to be late, I should have known better. What's with the disguise?"

"No one on this side knows what I look like," Duke said.

"I guess that makes me special," Vic said.

"What has happened to you makes you special, you're one of us now," Duke said.

Vic didn't speak, but his expression made what he wanted to say clear.

"We want you to join our special unit. Follow me, I'll explain later," Duke said.

They took the service elevator to the basement of the building and made their way out of the building to a building nearby and entered what appeared to be a workshop. The rest of the visit was straight out of a James Bond movie, sliding doors and all.

"You've got to be kidding?"

"It's no joke." Duke led Vic to a large office on an upper floor where the Bondesque routine continued, complete with an American version of "Money-penny." Duke laughed when he caught a glimpse of Vic's expression.

"Come in, Major." A middle-aged gentleman, who had the appearance of a small town store keeper stood and extended his hand to Duke.

"Ah, Detective Morgan! Sorry about your wife, disgusting, the kind of people out there nowadays. Well, on to the point. Everyone thinks you're dead; hum...works well for us...that is if you choose to join us, lots of advantages in being dead in our work. "

The meek looking little man actually moved forward and used the tips of his fingers to turn Vic's head from one side to another.

"Yes. A tuck here and a tuck there, Perfect! When we finish with you your own mother won't recognize you."

"What the hell is going on? I know you're not talking about plastic surgery!" Vic said.

"They'll never stop trying to kill you, and I know you want to get them. Well, here's your opportunity to get them, and in the process help us. The job pays well, you know," the little man said. Vic thought he was British, later Vic would learn that this was a part of his demeanor. The little man had worked in England during World War II and he liked the British so much that he adopted their accent and mannerisms. Vic looked from one man to the other, puzzled by the events taking place, but he knew that it was decision time. And, if he didn't agree to the offer before he walked out of that office he would have more than Manero to worry about.

"How long will all of this take, the surgery?" Vic asked.

"Good man thought you'd see it our way. Everyone is doing it these days. As a matter of fact the little fellow you're looking for has taken advantage of the process. If we start today, given the normal recovery period, you should be ready in about six weeks. While you're recovering you'll have time to study our routines. One more thing, Vic Morgan is dead, clear? I think for the nonce it will be Vic Wayne."

Vic nodded his head in stunned silence.

*   *   *

The Department gave Vic an Inspectors funeral. The Coroner's office gathered symbolic ashes from Vic's old house and used the ashes to complete the ritual of the deceased. Policemen, Federal Agents, State Troopers, and cops from all over the nation participated in the ceremony. A reward of fifty thousand dollars was offered for information leading to the arrest and conviction of the persons responsible for bombing Vic's house. No stones were left unturned; the media did its part as well. Jess had his own ideas. He asked the Commissioner for permission to take over the investigation of Vic's murder. Everyone knew Manero was responsible for the bombing and somehow Jess vowed to make him pay. Bee, on the other hand, was devastated by Vic's death, and for the first time Commissioner Chapman had the dubious task of taking care of her and the job of running his office.

Detective Tina Martinez was assigned to the Commissioner's office until Bee was able to resume her duties. The woman was good, but she was not Bee. Then there was the other problem. Jess was a good detective, but he was no Vic Morgan. The problem was to find someone to back him up, someone with the kind of skills Vic possessed. Instinctively Commissioner pressed the intercom and asked Bee to get him Captain Weeks at Midtown South. He apologized to Detective Martinez and released the button. He hesitated, then dialed Bee's number. The call was good for both of them, the comfort of knowing she was there, and for Bee, the idea that she was needed. In less than a blink she had reminded him of a detective who had exhibited the kind of qualities he was looking for. The Commissioner thanked Bee and ended the call. The intercom buzzed and Detective Martinez announced Captain Weeks on line three.

"Captain."

"Commissioner."

"Where is Detective Fuchs?"

"He's riding a desk at the 34, sir."

"How did that happen?"

"You know Fuchs, got a little heavy handed with a suspect. I had to move him," Captain Weeks said.

"I see. Thank you, Captain."

"Yes, sir."

Commissioner buzzed Detective Martinez and asked her to come into the office. The young woman, pad in hand, checked her appearance and went into the Commissioner's office.

"Detective Martinez, contact the 34th precinct and instruct Detective Carl Fuchs to report to this office, bag and baggage."

"You don't mean "Loony Fuchs," do you sir?"

"The same. You know him, is there a problem?"

"Well, Sir. I was told that part of my responsibility was to kind of...watch out...er...I mean."

Commissioner Chapman interrupted her.

"Cover my tail, right?"

"Yes, sir."

"Go ahead then."

"Detective Fuchs is from the old school, you know, he's a "Billy-club cop." You know, spare the Billy and spoil the Perp."

Commissioner Chapman laughed.

"Thank you, Detective. Billy-club cop, that's good. But on this case I think he is what we need. I'll tell him to leave his nightstick, er I mean billy-club at home."

"Yes, sir."

"After you get that task done, call Jess Norman and have him come to my office."

"Yes, sir."

"Thank you, Detective.

"Sir, I'd feel better if you called me Tina instead."

"Fine, Detective, I mean Tina. Let me know when they arrive, will you, I'll be at the Mayor's office."

Detective Martinez nodded her head and closed the door.

*       *       *

Manero met Gill's plane; he wanted to congratulate him personally. The idea that the cop that had been a part of a raid on his house had been killed was terrific news. That was when it hit him, the job wasn't complete, someone had led the cops to the house, someone much more dangerous than the late Vic Morgan. Manero pushed a button and a small door opened in a special unit of the limousine. He removed a mixed drink from the small frig and took a sip. He had a leak in his organization; someone on his payroll was double-crossing him. The car rolled to a stop next to the plane and Manero got out and embraced Gill at the foot of the steps leading from the plane.

"Hombre!"

"Gracias, El hefe," Gill said

"No, mas. From now on you're my partner."

"I don't know what to say," Gill said.

"There's nothing to say. I have more money than I will ever spend. What I need now is someone who has as much to lose as I have, some-one who appreciates what we do. You're that man." Gill attempted to speak but Manero waved his hand in a motion to stop him. " We have a big problem. The problem is right here at home," Manero said.

"Que?"

"We have to find out who helped that cop get so close to me."

Gill nodded his head in agreement, embarrassed because he hadn't thought of the idea first…Either Manero was a mind reader or he had great respect for him, because the expression on Manero's face told him he knew what he was thinking at that moment, he said. " I didn't think about it until a few minutes ago, either. Let's go back to my place. I'll have a few people over tonight. Stupid bastards! Did they think I had only one place to live? The people I invite tonight will be the ones I have on the payroll at DEA. I want you to put someone on everyone of them until we find out who betrayed us."

"Consider it done." Gill said.

# Chapter *IV*

"**I**'m getting too old for this crap," Vic said.

Edmund Duke, Junior ran ahead of him with a hundred pounds of equipment strapped to his back, the same load Vic struggled with. Duke looked back, raised his right arm and did a pumping motion, a signal for Vic to pick up the pace. Vic muttered something under his breath that even he couldn't understand. He had given up a long time ago, but his body continued in spite of his exhaustion. That queasy feeling was back again, the feeling you get just before you pass out. Vic shook his head to clear his thoughts and took a deep breath. He stopped and kneeled on one knee. Duke had cleared the top of the hill that was more like a small mountain, as far as Vic was concerned. Pins and needles taunted Vic's body and a vision appeared before him...There in the mist of his failing body stood

"AAAAAH!"

Vic's yell broke the silence in the woods. Small birds in the brush nearby fluttered and scampered for safety. In the next instance Vic was on his feet running to the top of the hill, full hilt. Duke heard the yell, looked back and smiled; he knew that Vic had broken through the threshold. Duke slowed his pace until he heard Vic coming up behind him....

Later the two men forged a creek and rested under a tree on the opposite shore.

"Welcome to hell," Duke said.

"How did you know," Vic said.

"I didn't know, we hoped. That's the way it is with us."

"What do you mean?"

"Our unit is very special. We are chosen because we have paid the ultimate price. All of us have lost someone to crime in a dramatic fashion. For me it was my wife and child in a drive-by."

"Is that why you were selected, just because you lost your family?" Vic asked.

"No, I was military, special forces, the whole bit. But that wasn't why I was selected. Like you I stood for something. They couldn't buy me, so they got rid of me, in the same manner they tried to kill you. That's when I was chosen. As for the rest, we train until we drop, and then we train some more. We either progress to the vision, or we give up. Those who give up are given other tasks. Gathering info, spotting, managing the equipment..."

Vic removed his pack and stretched out on a cool spot under the tree on the creek bank. The thought of Honey, even in a vision was comforting; that was, until Manero's ugly face appeared. Vic would never forget him or his scowl of pleasure when he fired the fatal shots at Honey. There were others involved in the incident: Juan and the two men in the car.

*All of them will pay,* Vic thought.

Duke left Vic to his solitude. The fire in Vic's eyes told the whole story. Now that the fire was back they would really get down to business.

"It's time to move," Duke said.

"Where?" Vic said.

"Back to the base of course." Duke stood and trotted off in the direction they came from.

"Damn!" Vic said.

&#42;   &#42;   &#42;

Juan closed the phone and stuck it in his pocket. "What, what, what...." Lisa said.

"They did it! They got rid of that fucking cop, yeah!"

"When?"

"He didn't say. He just said he owed me a favor and that it had been taken care of."

"We can go back to Puerto Rico?" Lisa said.

"Not right away. I want to meet with him and tell him I want to get out," Juan said.

"I don't think you should do that, Juan."

"Why? We have enough money, why not?"

"You know it don't work like that," Lisa said.

"It doesn't work that way."

"Never mind all that college shit, about this and that, this is business. How the hell are you going to walk away with all you know about him?"

Juan didn't answer right away. He walked over to the window and looked down at a barge cruising down the East River.

"I think you're wrong, Lisa. He doesn't need me."

"It's not about needing you. Shit! He don't fucking need you! Once you're in, you're always in. You know that."

"Its different now, things are different, you'll see."

"Why don't we just leave? We got new faces, nobody knows us but your driver. If I change your hair and if you grow a mustache your own mother won't know you. Then, we can get our money and go somewhere and start over again, maybe out of the country," Lisa said.

'I think that would be a big mistake. It's about respect, that's what all this is about. I'll approach him like a man and you'll see, he'll let us walk."

"We'll see," she said.

"You damn right! He's coming here tomorrow."

"Killing that cop must have made a big difference. Wait a minute, didn't you say he had a partner?"

"Yeah, but he wasn't on the boat," Juan said.

"Those don't mean he's not part of the rip off."

"Hey, you're right! That gives me an idea. I want you to go out tomorrow before Manero gets here. I don't want him to know what your new face looks like, okay?"

"Yeah, yeah, fine. But what is this great plan?"

"Don't worry about it!"

"You'd better worry about getting your ass killed," Lisa said.

"It will work out, you'll see."

"I'm scared, Juan."

Juan took Lisa into his arms and held her close.

"I know what I'm doing," he whispered. Lisa rested her chin on Juan's shoulders, a tear trickled down her cheek. She rubbed her cheek against Juan's shoulder, holding tight to hide her tears. Juan released her, looked at her and faked a blow to her chin.

"Get the hell out of here before he gets here. I told you I don't want him to know what your new face looks like," Juan said.

"Okay, okay, later." Lisa removed her purse from the table and strapped it on her shoulder.

"See you later," she said.

"Yeah," Juan said.

The intercom buzzed less than a minute after Lisa left the apartment. Juan wondered if Manero had passed Lisa on the street or in the corridor. It wouldn't matter the surgeon had done a great job on her new face. Manero loved New York. He had said that it was the only city in the world where he didn't need his bodyguards. The fool loved the subways and used them many times to travel around the city. He said that the new mayor, an ex-cop, had given the police a chance to do their jobs and that made the city safe again.

"Crazy bastard," Juan said. "Riding the fucking subways." The doorbell rang and Juan took a deep breath and composed himself before answering the door.

"Come in, Chief," Juan said.

"Good to see you, Juan. That was a good tip you gave us. We screwed up at first, but it's all taken care of now."

"I'm glad. That guy was a pain in the neck. What about the money?"

"That's why I'm here. I want you to find Monica."

"She's in a nut house, somewhere upstate," Juan said.

"Not anymore. She checked out of there a few months ago and disappeared. She left the place in a helicopter. Do you have any ideas?"

"What about her place in the village?"

"Checked there. We went in, the place is covered floor to ceiling. You know how they leave a place when they're going away. Nobody's been there for a while but the place had been painted, they're probably selling it."

"I don't know what to tell you. Besides, I wanted to talk to you about getting out," Juan said.

"Out?"

"I have a little money now, a new face, in a sense I'm clean, you know…I can start over," Juan said. Manero didn't react and Juan thought this was a good sign. He looked like he might be considering Juan's suggestion. That was until he spoke.

"I think you're tired. You've had to bounce around since that cop came back on the scene. But that's over and we have work to do. Why don't you take a few days off? Get out and have some fun, buy a new car, a boat, a plane, something to remind you how well you are doing before you think about leaving us."

"With respect, I have more money than I ever dreamed of."

"There is never enough money. We have a plan and you are part of that plan. I would hate to have to say that you didn't like us anymore."

Juan interrupted, waving his hands in an effort to calm Manero.

"Am I really necessary?"

"More than that, you are like my son. Haven't I been good to you? Didn't I take you off the street and send you to school?" Juan nodded his head. "Well, what did you think I was doing all of that for?" Juan shook his head. "Stupido! Who will take my place when I'm gone? Think about it..."

Juan lowered his head.

"I didn't know you thought that much of me. What about your brother?"

"What about him? He's good at what he does, but for the rest I need someone like you. Someone with an education, a modern person who knows computers and things like that. Look at what you've done. Thanks to you we can smuggle much more stuff through, and we're free to send and receive messages to our organization without being afraid of being tapped. You did that."

"You can count on me; forget about what I said."

"Good. We have some good things coming. We already control a major part of the government back home and we have a good toe-hold here in America. We're making something big, something like the world has never seen. Imagine us running things..." Manero said.

Juan smiled and considered the idea.

"I like that," Juan said.

"Good. First thing, that cop had a partner. We have to find out what he knows about the money, then he's got to go," Manero said.

"How do we do that?"

"Easy. He's freaked out after his partner was killed, left his family. He hangs out with hookers, and he's a drunk. The word I get is that the department is going to dump him," Manero said.

"So what's the problem?"

"The problem is he's still looking for us. Drunk or sober, he's dead set on getting even."

"Dead is more like it," Juan said. The two men laughed.

"I want Lisa to set him up, and I want him taken out."

"Why Lisa?"

"Her free ride is over. Either she's with us or she's against us," Manero said

"Okay, I'll take care of it."

"Good. After it's done I want you and Lisa to come down to my place." Juan nodded a yes.

*       *       *

Jess drove slowly across Fiftieth Street from the West Way. He turned right on Ninth Avenue and stopped in the middle of the block. A beefy brown-skinned woman, wearing a blonde wig and not much more, emerged from the shadows and made her way to Jess' car. The closer she got the bigger her hips appeared to be. She stood at least five-feet-nine and had the prettiest body Jess had ever seen. He had watched Sylvia during a stake out once. But that was a time in which he and Debbie were too much in love for him to consider approaching Sylvia. It was a time before Vic was blown away; now, Jess was trying to climb into his partner's grave with him. Jess played the scene of the last time he had seen Vic over and over in his mind until it hurt. No matter how hard he tried he couldn't think of anything he had overlooked the evening he left Vic at the entrance to his house.

"Hey, baby! You back? I can't figure you, I mean, you don't seem to be the type…you know what I mean?"

Sylvia opened the car door and got in. Jess looked at her, smiled and drove to Sylvia's favorite place, an empty spot in the rear of the Javits Center. There was no ceremony, Jess unbuckled his belt, opened his pants and shifted his position on the seat so that his legs were pointed in Sylvia's direction, Sylvia took over from there. In the middle of her energetic facilitation Jess stopped her and told her to take her panties off. Sylvia sat up, smiled and hurriedly removed her panties. Jess used an old tried and true position to make Sylvia comfortable before completing their tryst….

-73-

"I don't believe you," Sylvia said. "What the hell are you doing down here? I don't get it."

Jess removed his gun and shield from the glove compartment, rested them on the seat near the door on his side of the car, took a small box of tissues out and handed it to Sylvia.

"Oh shit, a damn cop, I should have known. But you can't hump me and then lock me up, you know that..." Sylvia said in a questioning manner. Jess made another attempt to give Sylvia a tissue.

"Thanks," Sylvia said. " I still don't get it. Why are you doing this?"

"It's a long story," Jess said.

"You're damn straight about that," Sylvia said and they both laughed.

"My partner was killed and it was my fault. I left him alone and he was killed."

"What happened, did he get shot or something?"

"No. They fucking blew up his house with him in it."

"Shit! That was your friend, I mean, what the hell could you do? If you had been there your ass would have been blown up too." Jess looked at Sylvia. It was almost dark, but he could see the expression on her face. He hadn't considered that fact that he would have been killed.

"You know, you're right. My ass would have been gone too. But I'm here and I have to find those fucks that did it to him."

"Come here, baby," Sylvia said. This time she took on her specialty with a kind of warmth, a personal touch that caused Jess to stir in the seat. It was a new experience, one that blew his mind. At the exact moment a sector car rolled pass and shinned the light into the car. Jess fumbled, his head pinned against the window gasping for breath, for his shield and flashed it over his left shoulder. The light dimmed and the sector rolled on into the distance along with every ounce of tension in Jess' body.

"Whew! I've never been there before," he said.

"Wanna go ag'in?" Sylvia asked. Jess shook his head.

"I didn't think so, you're no freak. You're a stand up guy and you got no business around here."

"Thanks, Sylvia." Jess slipped a wad of bills into her hand. "All of this?"

"You earned it. Here, take this card, if you ever need me call me at this number."

"Thanks, Baby." Jess started the car and took Sylvia back to her spot and dropped her off.

# Chapter *V*

"**S**ee, I told you he wasn't going to let you out of this shit…I told you. Now he wants to get his hooks into me too, damn! What the hell does he want me to do?"

"Its that cop's partner. He wants you to drug him and bring him to this address."

Juan handed Lisa a slip of paper.

"And just how in the hell am I suppose to do that?"

"He's drinking a lot and hanging out with hookers down on the West Side. We want you to go down there and get one of the girls to help you set him up. It'll be easy. He's really fucking up. Manero said they're thinking about firing him. "

"Ain't you a bitch? We…it's we now, right?"

"Manero has big plans for us. He wants us to go down to his place and spend a few days after this is over," Juan said.

"A few days is right. That mother fucker is going to kill us if we go down there."

"No, no, no. He wants me to be second in command."

"You! What about his brother?"

"His brother is a fuck up…"

"Oh, I see. You'd better watch this prick," Lisa said.

"It's cool. Do the job and you'll see. Here, look at what I got for you."

"You expect me to wear that shit?"

"If you can't get one of the girls to do it, I know he'll go for you."

"It's not going to be me wearing that shit. You asked me to do it, let me do it."

"Okay, okay, but you'd better watch your ass."

"Fuck you! You got me in this shit and you're supposed to be worried about me? Fuck you. I'm doing this because I don't have a choice."

Juan threw the outfit onto the sofa and walked out of the room waving his hand in disgust. He mumbled something, but he made sure that Lisa didn't understand it. Lisa's response was a stiff finger towards you know where…

*          *          *

The one thing Lisa had never done was walking the streets to make ends meet. She had on occasion, weaseled a few bucks out of a square to pay the rent, but that was no more than any other single woman had done from one time to another. Alston slowed the limo to almost a walking pace and every girl on the block broke for the curb.

"Anything you want, honey! You name it," a funky looking junkie said. She looked like she hadn't seen a tub since the year of the flood, and her eyes were as empty as her bank account. It was eerie, almost like she wasn't even there. Lisa shuttered and raised the window to a safer height. Later, at the end of the block, the heavier girls emerged from the shadows. The car stopped and Lisa looked Sylvia over, then moved on to a woman wearing a blonde wig. Lisa lowered the window and asked the woman to get in. Sylvia shrugged her shoulders and returned to her place in the shadows.

"Yeah, baby, sixty-five dollars for me and forty-five for the room, its extra for women," the Hooker said.

"Don't flatter yourself. I have a proposition for you. You are seeing a guy, a cop. There's five hundred in it for you if you can get him to come to this address."

"Whoa! Wait a minute, I don't fool around with no cops!"

"All we want you to do is bring him to this address so we can talk to him," Lisa said.

"Yeah, right. Let me out of this mother fucker…"

Lisa handed the Hooker a crisp hundred-dollar bill.

"Okay, let's make it a thousand, keep the hundred for your time and trouble."

The Hooker released the door handle and settled back into the seat.

"You just want me to get him there, right?"

"Yeah."

"Suppose he don't wanna come?"

"We'll work that out after you decide to help us."

The Hooker looked around the car as if she was thinking, hesitated a few moments more and said, " Let me think about it, okay?"

"I'll be back tomorrow night."

The Hooker made an attempt to return the money.

"You keep that as a down payment. One more thing, don't discuss this matter with anyone, we wouldn't like that," Lisa said.

The Hooker nodded, reached for the door and got out of the car.

"Nice talking with you, Sylvia," Lisa said.

The Hooker didn't reply, she nodded her head, puzzled by the woman calling her Sylvia. She didn't correct her. Instead she said, "Sure, baby. Tomorrow night," in a hip whorish manner. Becky waited at the curb until the car turned the corner and ran over to the doorway to tell Sylvia what had just happened.

"I'm getting the fuck out of here, those mother fuckers are serious. If I was you I would get the hell out of here too," Becky said.

"I can't, you said they know my name. It won't take long for them to find me," Sylvia said.

"It's this fucking blonde wig. Every time I borrow it from you somebody thinks I'm you," Becky said.

"You never complained before."

"That was before these dope people came around."

"How do you know they're dope people?" Sylvia asked.

"That woman in the limo. She was dressed to kill, but you could still see the Bronx on her."

"Dressed like shit, huh?" Sylvia said.

"Word. What the fucks are you goin' to do?"

"I'll take care of it. You'd better go home, you know, in case they come back."

"Baby, I'm out of here," Becky said.

Sylvia reached into her purse and searched for Jess' card. It was the last thing she found. She didn't want to be seen calling anyone from the public phone, so she waited until later to call Jess, after finishing a "John" at a motel. She sent the John on his way and called Jess from the motel room. Jess agreed to meet her in Central Park near the boathouse the following afternoon.

*          *          *

"I'm sorry, sir. I don't have that information. Miss Woolford was discharged over a month ago and we don't have any forwarding address for her. You might try her parents. No, Sir, I'm not at liberty to give you their address. I'm sorry, Sir."

Juan listen to the click, followed in a few moments by the dial tone.

"Bitch! She hung up."

"What did she tell you?"

"She said I might try her parents, like I know where the hell they live," Juan said.

"Easy. Send a note to her Fifth Avenue address, I'm sure she'll get it."

"What do you want me to say?"

"Just say you need to see her, and say you're an old friend from Puerto Rico, eh!" Manero said.

"That will work," Juan said.

"Don't forget to give her this phone number."

"But, but."

"It will take them a year to find out who the phone is registered to," Manero said.

*       *       *

Jess entered the park from Lenox Avenue and walked slowly over to the boathouse. A new restaurant sat where the old boathouse used to be. Sylvia was seated at a table facing the water. He didn't recognize her until she shifted her fine body to avoid the sun. Her hair was short, not as short as a man's, but short, and her skin was as smooth as velvet. She looked nothing like the woman he had seen walking Ninth Avenue, she looked more like a teacher.

"Syl-vi-aah?" Jess said.

Sylvia laughed and motioned for him to join her at the table.

"You look so different," Jess said.

"You do too, without a windshield behind you," Sylvia said

"Okay, I deserved that."

They laughed.

"Somebody is after you," Sylvia said.

She searched Jess' eyes for any sign that he already knew what she had just told him. Jess looked at her, palms up, as if to say go on.

"Last night this woman comes around in a limo and gave one of my friends a C-note to help them kidnap you."

Jess nodded his head and said, "How? While we're busy or what?" he asked.

"My friend told them that she had to think it over because she didn't mess with no cops. They're supposed to come back tonight to get her answer."

"Wait a minute, how do you know they are looking for me?"

-80-

"She was wearing my blonde wig last night, we switch around some-times…they thought she was me…the woman called her Sylvia when she got out of the car."

"Well, well, well…the mountain comes to Mohammed. Will your girlfriend help us?"

"No, she's gone. But that's no problem. We all look alike to them, especially in the dark. I can pull it off," Sylvia said.

"These people don't play," Jess said.

"I don't either."

Jess looked at Sylvia, it was a familiar look, one that lets you know you are dealing with someone special.

"Okay, you meet them and I'll take it from there."

"You think so, huh. Well, mister bad policeman there's something else you ought to know. Becky, my friend, recognized the chauffeur. He's one bad dude, a shiv-man. He'll stab you, or throw that knife of his into you, or slice you up before you can pull that gun of yours."

"That bad."

"You'd better fuckin' believe it!" Sylvia said.

"I take it you have a plan…" Jess said.

Sylvia smiled and said "Yeah."

"Okay, let's hear it."

"You watch my back tonight, maybe follow them after we make the deal and see where they go, you know?" Sylvia said.

"Not bad. Not bad at all."

"Okay. I'll tell them some shit about you being a weekend john. Saturday night, yeah, that's good, but make it early, you know a girl has to make a living."

"You're a nut."

"Nobody is after my ass," Sylvia said.

"That's not completely true, but thanks, Sylvia. What can I do for you?"

"Nothing, you're a nice guy. I just want to see you get yourself together. The cops have always been straight with me, you know, no hassles. These drug mother fuckers are another story. They're fucking crazy. One of them killed one of the girls down here one night for the hell of it."

"Do you know who killed her?"

"It was taken care of. You don't have to worry about him," Sylvia said.

"Oh! Good, but I don't want to know the rest."

"What's to know? Hey, are you buying me lunch?" Sylvia said.

"You're damn straight," Jess said.

\*　　　　　　　\*　　　　　　　\*

Sylvia watched the limo turn the corner. She didn't want to appear anxious, so she waited until the car reached her spot before walking out of the shadows. The car stopped and Sylvia waited until the smoky window in the passenger section lowered slowly and a hand beckoned her to the car.

"You're not the woman I'm supposed to meet," Lisa said.

"I'm Sylvia. That's who you're looking for ain't it?"

Lisa didn't speak. She checked Sylvia from head to toe. Sylvia didn't blink, but she knew that this was as close to getting her ticket canceled as she was ever going to be. Lisa closed the window and opened the door.

"Get in," Lisa said.

Sylvia adjusted her tight skirt, leaned forward and got into the car.

"What the hell is going on?" Lisa said.

"My girlfriend and me switch wigs sometimes. She told me what you wanted, so here I am."

"Where's your girlfriend?"

"China by now. You scared the shit out of her."

"And you?"

"I'm about money," Sylvia said.

"Move over here! Alston."

The Chauffeur got out of the car and joined them in the back area.

"Search her."

"What the fuck is goin' on here?"

"I want to make sure you're not wearing a wire."

"Dumb bitch! If I was wearing one your ass would be in deep shit now," Sylvia said.

Alston had his hand in her bra. He asked her to sit on the jump seat and turn around. Sylvia sat on the little seat with its back lowered. The small seat became an exam stool. Alston was obviously enjoying his work when Lisa said. "That's enough." Alston took one more feel in Sylvia's most personal area before opening the door and getting out of the car.

"That's goin' to cost you fucking extra. Nobody touches my shit without paying."

Sylvia turned, moved close to Lisa, and put a straight razor against Lisa's neck.

"You tell that stupid mother fucker if he ever touches me again' I'll cut his balls off. Now you owe me a hundred for the feel…"

Lisa bit her bottom lip and whispered "Okaaay, okay. I'm sorry. We have to be careful." She opened her purse and handed Sylvia some money.

"Take the hundred, okay?"

Sylvia in the best tradition of the street took two. She moved away from Lisa cautiously and folded the razor. "What's on your mind?" Sylvia asked in the same calculating whisper.

"This cop owes us, or at least he knows where there is some money that belongs to us. We want it."

This time Lisa's voice held the threat.

"Okay, so what do you want from me?"

"He's a customer of yours. We want you to take him somewhere we can talk to him," Lisa said.

"You told the other woman there was five hundred in it for her, sounds like it's worth more to me," Sylvia said. Lisa smiled.

"Okay, you call it."

"Well, figuring on what's going to happen to that cop and what I'm gonna have to do, what do you call it? Relocate, I figure it worth at least five grand."

"The other girl was worried about the cop, and what might happen to him."

"Fuck the cop. You have my five grand ready Saturday evening, come by early, and I'll deliver his ass around midnight."

Lisa nodded her head and said, "See you Saturday night."

Sylvia kept the closed razor in her right hand and opened the door with her left hand. She slid across the seat toward the door and stepped out backwards. Once outside she saluted Lisa with the hand that held the razor. Lisa tapped on the partition in front of her and Alston moved the car forward.

Ninth Avenue is one way downtown. Jess was parked at the corner, waiting for Sylvia's signal. The limo pulled away from the curb and Sylvia leaned against the corner lamppost and adjusted her shoe. That was the signal. Jess started his car and followed the limo. He dropped back two cars and followed the limo back to a Seventy-second Street address. Lisa got out of the limo and entered an apartment building. Jess noted the address and followed the limo back to the garage.

*     *     *

The phone rang once and Juan picked it up. "Hello." The phone was silent. Juan knew someone was on the line, still no answer.

"Hello, who the hell is this?"

"You're supposed to be dead."

"Monica, how are you?"

"I thought you were dead. Fangio said he saw you get killed," Monica said.

"Its a long story. I need to see you."

"I can't help you anymore, my father is dead."

"I'm afraid it's not that simple. It seems that there is some money missing and the feeling is that you might be able to help us find it," Juan said.

"What happened, you sound so different?"

"I made an effort to improve myself."

"Uh huh. Why should I help, after all, they screwed me and I ended up in the funny factory. Why the hell should I help?"

"Its business," Juan said. Monica clenched her fist.

"Monica, Monica, are you there?"

"South Street Seaport, tomorrow at noon. I'll be at Nathan's," Monica said.

"Good." Juan closed the phone and gave Manero the high sign.

"That was Monica."

"Good. Let's see what she knows," Manero said.

"She's pissed about the way she was treated."

"We'll work it out."

# Chapter *VI*

---

*D*etective Martinez, volunteered to help Jess with the problem on the West Side, he needed a woman for the job. Martinez parked the black Ford in the shadows of the overpass and took out a pair of night glasses. A few minutes later Jess pulled up and picked up Sylvia. She gave him an address over in Greenpoint and Jess used the cellular phone to pass the information on to Detective Martinez. They had chosen a good spot, an abandoned building behind a large trucking company. The street was a dead-end street, impossible for anyone to enter without being seen. The back and side of the building sat on the edge of a large canal. Detective Martinez arrived well ahead of Sylvia and Jess. She spotted a problem as soon as she saw the building and made a left turn onto the street at the corner just before entering the dead end street. It was dark as hell good cover for her. She found a bushy area near the trucking company fence and hid the car there. Detective Martinez hugged the side of the building and moved slowly towards the abandoned building at the end of the street and found a position close enough to cover Jess in case of trouble. A moment later a car's headlights bounced off the building, almost exposing her.

"This is supposed to be a lovers lane, hot shit, right? Sylvia said.

"What's next?"

"I don't know, but her limo is parked over there. Let's get started and see what happens."

Vic parked and moved back against the window, far enough for Sylvia to bury her head in his lap. This time her head brushed against a .38 Detective's Special.

"Be careful with the fucking gun," she said.

"Yes, grandma," Jess said. The limousine started: the headlights pierced the darkness, the car moved forward, and parked behind Jess' car. Alston, Lisa's driver tapped on the window behind Jess, and Jess looked back into the barrel of a Uzi. Alston motioned with the gun for Jess to open the door. Jess eased his fingers into the trigger slot. Sylvia got up slowly and moved back. Alston pointed to Sylvia and told her to unlock the doors. He snatched the door open and pulled Jess out of the car, Jess' gun fell onto the street.

"Don't move. If you move I'll kill you." Jess did what Alston told him to do. He remained still, lying on his back, his feet resting on the floor of the car. Alston straddled him and reached into the car and blew the horn. From the darkness a glare of headlights blinded Jess as the second limo moved forward. Alston picked up Jess' gun and threw it in under the car. Detective Martinez used the opportunity to get closer. The limo blocked her view for a moment, forcing her to expose herself.

"Police! Drop the gun, now!" Alston dropped his gun and Jess slowly pushed his way from the car. He picked up Alston's Uzi, checked the safety and motioned for Alston to move back. In one swift motion Alston drew his knife and threw it towards Detective Martinez. Detective Martinez screamed and dropped her gun. Alston kicked Jess in the side and ran toward the limo. Jess opened up with the Uzi and sprinkled its load into Alston. His body vibrated with the hits, the last shot hit him in the head, after which his head exploded. Blood and Alston's brains covered the windshield. During the confusion Sylvia sneaked around the limo and gave the driver a close shave, too close. Lisa sat frozen in the back seat.

Jess called for backup and an ambulance.

Detective Martinez sat up, the knife lodged in her shoulder.

"We can't take the knife out," Jess said.

"I know. I'll be all right, you take care of what you have to do." Jess reached into the limo and pulled Lisa out. He put her against the car, cuffed her, and then put her in the back of his car.

"Sylvia can you drive?"

"Yes."

"Good! Take my car and wait for me up near the bridge and make sure she keeps her head down until I get there."

"Okay. By the way," Vic removed a large envelope from the back of the limo and handed it to Sylvia. " Here, you earned this."

"Thanks, baby!"

"Get the hell out of here."

The first sector car and the ambulance arrived at the same time. The EMT guys said they did the right thing by leaving the knife in Martinez's wound. A Sergeant on the scene became inquisitive. He didn't like what he had seen. The question was why did the thug kill his backup man? Jess took him over to the side and gave him a few details to satisfy his curiosity. The Sergeant had heard of the Commissioner's Squad, but this was the first time he had run into the special squad in his precinct. He backed off Jess, but Jess knew he was going to look into the matter long enough to get himself in trouble. A fence of crime scene tape roped off the scene. One of the sector cars offered Jess a lift, but he declined and told the patrolman that he would take his car. The Sergeant took one more shot at Jess, and was really pissed when Jess handed him the phone after calling the Commissioner in the middle of the night. The Sergeant waved Jess off when Jess offered him a chance to speak to the Commissioner. Jess apologized and gave the Commissioner a brief report. The Sergeant had left before Jess completed his call. Jess checked Detective Martinez once more before the ambulance left; he took her car keys and promised to bring her car to the hospital.

*        *        *

Lisa twisted her body in an effort to find a comfortable position but it was hopeless. Sylvia tapped her gently on the head to remind her to keep her head down. She relaxed when she saw Jess coming. Jess opened the door and got into the car.

"Thanks, Sylvia," he said.

"No, it's my time to thank you. That low down Alston is gone, thanks to you. Everybody on the street hated him. He was the one that brought that killer around. What are you going to do with her?"

"Get as much information as I can and take her to jail," Jess said.

"Well, if you don't need me for anything I'd like to go home."

"You got it. Where can I drop you off?"

"West End Avenue and 95th," Sylvia said.

"Good enough."

Jess headed uptown, Sylvia sat with Lisa in the back seat. The night was quiet, so peaceful it was hard to imagine anyone dying."

"You can sit up now," Sylvia said

Lisa stirred a little and sat up.

"These cuffs are hurting me," Lisa said.

"That's not all that's going to hurt if you don't tell me what I want to know," Jess said.

Lisa starred at Sylvia, "You're in big trouble," Lisa said.

Sylvia extended a stiff finger to Lisa.

"Honey, you don't know what trouble is. Fuck with me and you'll find out. Thank you, baby. Let me out here before I kill this bitch."

Jess pulled over and let Sylvia out.

# Chapter *VII*

*J*uan arrived early; he wanted to make sure Monica wasn't setting him up. He ordered a frank and root beer. Juan paid for his order, walked over to the window, dipped some mustard from the tin, and loaded his sandwich with sauerkraut. He took longer than usual. The condiment counter was a perfect spot to observe the street below. He spotted Monica entering the building and watched carefully to see if she was being tailed. He chose a seat facing the river. It was early in the day and the only other customers in the place were tourists. Monica stopped at the counter, and ordered pastrami on rye. She paid for her order and took a seat by the window. Juan waited a few minutes more before moving over to Monica's table. She hadn't noticed him when she entered.

"Hi, Monica."

"Yes?"

"Its me, Juan."

Monica did a double take.

"They did a hella'va job on you. Damn! I wouldn't have recognized you in a million years."

"That's good to know," Juan said.

"You even sound different."

"School does that for you."

"School…if I didn't really know you I would say you're someone else. What's this about?"

"Manero, you know the big boss, said they never received the last shipment from your father. They think you might be able to help them find the money. Its over twenty million."

"Wait a minute. My father never handled that much at one time."

"He must have been holding out on you, he handled that much and more."

Juan removed an envelope from his jacket and handed it to Monica.

"I don't believe it…he was still using me. That bastard," Monica said.

"Hey, that was your father. You shouldn't be saying things like that about him," Juan said.

"What do you know? Nothing, that's what! You don't know a fucking thing about my dear old daddy."

"Hey…hey…easy," Juan said.

He took a look around the room to see if anyone was noticing them, and then continued. "Manero said he only gave you the small stuff."

Monica looked at Juan and shook her head, her mouth wide open.

"The big stuff he had someone else handle. One of the conditions your father insisted on was that only he would deal with the inside man."

"You're putting me on," Monica said.

"No, they think its someone in government; or the head of some financial company. Anyway, on the day your father was killed the courier arrived just after it happened."

"They said you killed him," Monica said.

"Bull shit! I was in a hospital getting my faced fixed."

"Then who killed him?" Monica asked.

"We don't know, but it wasn't us."

"Is it possible for me to talk to the courier?" Monica said.

"Sure, why not? What do you want to know?"

"I want to know if he saw anything the day my father died."

"What do I tell Manero about the money?"

"Tell him I'll work on it."

"Good," Juan said.

"What about the courier?"

"Tomorrow on the Circle Line. Let's say around noon."

"I'll be there."

"Why don't we take a walk outside, there's so much I have to tell you," Juan said.

Monica folded her sandwich into a comfortable grip, poured her beer into a plastic cup, and followed Juan outside.

*          *          *

"Where are you taking me? Oh shit, don't tell me this is going to be one of them rape things?"

"And what's that suppose to mean?"

"You know how you cops are..."

"No, why don't you tell me," Jess said.

"It happened to a friend of mine. They took her to a place like this and fucked her before they took her to the precinct. You guys are all alike," Lisa said.

"Not this time, baby. Your people killed my friend and his wife, and now you're trying to kill me. You have more to worry about than jail. Get out of the fucking car!" Jess said.

Lisa slid to the edge of the seat and stepped out of the limo. She looked around for any signs of life but the only hint of civilization was the dim glow from the water treatment plant in the middle of the island. Lisa screamed at the top of her voice. Jess just stood there waiting for her to stop. That really frightened her.

"Ain't nobody here but us chickens," Jess said.

He grabbed her arm and pulled her towards the rear entrance of their old base. The place hadn't changed. He almost expected Vic or Honey to emerge from the shadows. Jess unlocked the door and hustled

Lisa inside. He turned the lights on and sat Lisa on a chair in the middle of the stark room.

"I don't have much time, and no patience. Who the hell are you, and who sent you after me?"

"Fuck you! I want a lawyer and I want one now," Lisa said.

"Haven't you gotten the picture yet?" Jess said, and slapped Lisa across the face. She hadn't expected him to hit her and caught the full force of the blow. A trickle of blood oozed out of the corner of her mouth. It was in that instance that she realized that she might not live to see the light of day. Beads of perspiration bubbled through her expensive makeup and she suddenly had a strong, almost uncontrollable desire to urinate. The feeling increased when Jess approached her again with his hand raised. Lisa felt a warm wetness leaving her body. She bit her bottom lip and took one more stab at dignity.

"Juan is going to kill you for this," she said, tears rolling down her cheeks. Jess raised his hand to hit Lisa again, but realized that he had broken her, and pulled the punch.

"Juan, who?" he said.

"You know who. He's really going to get your ass for this."

"And just how is he going to do that?"

Jess kicked the chair and moved closer to Lisa, his face less than a half-inch from hers. Lisa turned her head, but he was still there, so close she could smell his last meal. Jess cupped her face in his left hand and turned her head.

"Juan Acevedo? You don't mean Juan Acevedo the son-of-a-bitch that set my partner's wife up?" Jess said in a snake-like hiss. Lisa could feel his hot breath against her face. She nodded her head, turning it to avoid touching Jess. He was closer now, almost kissing her.

"Juan's not big enough to set me up, who's behind it?"

"You know I can't tell you that…if I tell you that they will kill me."

"And I'll fucking kill you if you don't."

"I want a lawyer. I have rights," Lisa said

"Honey had rights too, that was until she was shot down by Manero."

"If you know who's behind this why are you fucking with me!"

Lisa's eyes filled with hate. Jess had seen that look before, in the eyes of Vic before he used that shotgun of his to blow away a killer. Lisa was telling the truth, she had no other option.

"Where's Manero now?"

"I don't know."

"Where's Juan?"

"He's my husband, he's my husband."

"You're going up for murder one, or at least conspiracy to murder one."

"I don't know anything about killing anybody. I'm his wife, I don't know nothing, I'm his wife."

Lisa's harshness faded for a moment.

"There's a way out of this for you," Jess said.

Lisa sniffed and looked up, her face a mask of questions.

"How?"

"We know that you didn't have anything to do with the business in the past, but this thing you tried to pull on me makes that different. It will be hard for me to convince my bosses that you are not part of the operation."

Lisa eased forward on her seat.

"That's what I told Juan. But he said Manero told him my free ride was over. That bastard said I was either in or out."

Lisa stared at Jess her eyes wide open.

"Juan wants to get out too, but that bastard ain't going to let that happen, I told Juan that, but he's stupid. He almost begged me to set you up, that stupid fuck!" Lisa kicked at the space in front or her in disgust.

"We want Manero. Juan has to do time too, but if he helps I think we can get his time reduced and put you both in 'Witness Protection.'"

"You get Manero and that fucking brother of his and we won't need protection," Lisa said.

"Where's Juan?" Jess said.

Lisa hesitated before answering.

"We got a place on Seventy-second Street."

"Okay. Here's the drill. We're going to take you to jail. Detective Martinez will take you in."

Tina Martinez walked from the shadows into the light. Lisa shuddered. The woman hadn't made a sound the whole time they were there.

"Do you think you can forget about this place?"

Lisa nodded her head eagerly.

"Good. Stand up."

Jess eased the tension on Lisa's cuffs and nodded to Detective Martinez.

"Let's go," Detective Martinez said.

Lisa didn't like this silent woman. Where had she come from and what kind of woman was she, letting him slap her around like that. Lisa felt her body stiffen at the thought. In the same instance she felt the power of Detective Martinez's grip. The woman didn't say a word, but Lisa knew better than to try anything stupid. Jess followed them out of the building and watched them get into Detective Martinez's car. They took her to Manhattan South where she would wait until her next stop, arraignment at the Tombs, 100 Center Street.

Jess double-parked in front of the station house until Detective Martinez returned. She had left Lisa with a patrolman; they would meet them later at the ADA's office. There they would go through the time consuming process of writing up the charges, after which they would wait in line with the rest of the cops for their turn at bat.

The Assistant District Attorney argued against the attempt on Jess' life, after all, the two perps were dead, and there was still the question of how the second man at the scene died. Jess and Detective Martinez acquiesced to the superior knowledge of the young ADA. The charge would be conspiracy to abduct a police officer. Jess mentioned Lisa's promise to cooperate, but the ADA wouldn't have any of it until she heard it from Lisa. Detective Martinez asked about her injury, and the ADA's answer was, "The Perp that injured you is dead. I'd call that even."

*       *       *

"Damn! He got Lisa. Alston and Tony are dead!" Juan said.

"Lisa...will she stand up?" Manero asked.

"Yeah, you don't have to worry, but we'd better get the hell out of here. We have a problem."

"What problem? "Manero said.

"How the hell did they get on to our plan, that's the problem."

"Juan, you see, it's like I said, you're the man I need."

Manero used his cellular phone to make a call.

"Where do they have her?" Manero asked.

"The Tombs," Juan said.

"Tombs, yeah downtown, okay. Just get the hell down there and get her out of there." Manero folded the phone.

"Like you said, we' d better get the hell out of here," Manero said.

"What about, Lisa?"

"My lawyer is on the way. We go downtown and wait outside the court, he'll bring her out to us."

"But suppose she can't get out?"

"She will, I promise," Manero said.

*       *       *

"New York, and the County of New York, Vs Lisa Acevedo. One count of conspiracy to abduct a Police Officer for the purpose of doing him bodily harm," The Bailiff shouted.

"How do you plead?" The Judge said.

A voice from the aisle leading to the area in front of the bench interrupted the proceedings.

"Your Honor! If it pleases the court, I would like to confer with my client before a plea is made."

"Are you the attorney of record?" the Judge asked

"I will be as soon as I can confer with her."

The court appointed attorney handed Lisa's papers to the expensively dressed lawyer. The Judge nodded his head and motioned for the bailiff to call the next case. The Correction Officer took Lisa to a room just outside the courtroom. He removed the cuffs and left the room.

"I'm Miles Saunders. What have you told them so far?"

"Nothing," Lisa said.

"You're sure? Don't sandbag me or we could be in a lot of trouble, get my drift?"

Lisa nodded her head. Miles walked over to the door and called the corrections officer.

"All right…. you go back with the Ballif and I will prepare for your release."

"You can get me out?"

"We'll see," Saunders said.

The correction officer cuffed Lisa and led her out of the room.

Back in the courtroom, Miles waited until an available moment and asked to approach the bench. The ADA followed him.

"Your, Honor. I need time to review my client's charges before we continue," He was careful not to say plea. His request surprised the ADA. She had thought that he would show up with a satchel of money and bail Lisa out.

"Your Honor. The case is simple. The Defendant conspired to lead a New York City Detective into a trap. A trap in which one detective was injured and two people were killed," the ADA said.

"What's the problem, Mr. Saunders?"

"Your Honor I just walked into the courtroom, I haven't had time to confer with my client properly," Miles said.

"How much time do you need? This is an arraignment, not the trial, get on with it."

"Your, Honor."

"The task is simple. She pleads guilty, or not guilty. Step back and be ready when you are called again."

Miles moved away from the bench.

"Second call, New York, County of New York, Vs Lisa Acevedo. Charges under Penal Code 105.00: one count of conspiracy in the fourth degree, in abduction of a Police Officer for the purpose doing him bodily harm. Count two: Under Penal Code number 125.10, Criminally negligent homicide, the defendant did cause the death of two people," the Bailiff shouted.

A correction officer, laden with several pairs of cuffs in one hand, holding Lisa with the other hand returned Lisa to the courtroom and stood her in front of the judge. Miles Saunders stood next to Lisa and told her she would have to plead not guilty. He would try to get her released without bail.

"How do you plead, young lady?" The Judge asked. Miles responded.

"Not, guilty, Your Honor. This is the Defendant's first arrest; she has had no previous problems with the law. We respectfully request that she be released without bail."

The ADA took a deep breath and opened her mouth. The Judge waved her off.

"In another world, Mr. Saunders! Bail set at one million dollars."

"Your Honor!"

"Mr. Saunders most of your clients carry that much for pocket change."

"Your Honor, I must protest…"

"Noted, next!" The Judge shouted and motioned for the bailiff to call the next case. Saunders followed Lisa to the door leading to lockup.

"Don't talk to anybody, clear?"

Lisa nodded her head.

Detective Martinez gave a thumbs up to the ADA. She waited for the lawyer to leave and followed him. He crossed the street and walked across the small park near the entrance of the Tombs and got into a limousine. Detective Martinez waited until the lawyer was in the car and walked towards the subway entrance down the block, noting the license plate of the limo in the process. She used a radio to call Jess and gave him the information on the limo. Jess was parked in front of the court. He started the car and drove around the block to get behind the limo.

"Where the fuck is Lisa?" Juan asked.

"Why didn't you tell me she tried to kidnap a cop?" the Lawyer said.

"What! When the hell is it that I have to tell you what my people have done? Can you get her out?" Manero said.

Manero had that strange look in his eyes again. Juan and Miles Saunders moved back a little. "Well can you! What's the problem here?" Manero asked.

"They set her bail at a million dollars," Miles said

"Is that it?" Manero said.

"That's it," Miles said

"How do we arrange it?"

"A cashiers check for the amount made out to the court. I'll take it to the court tomorrow morning and they will release her."

"Okay, but I want you to have our people inside keep an eye on her. If she gives us up, you know what must be done."

"I'll take care of it," Miles said and reached for the door. Juan was silent…. Manero tapped on the partition and the car moved forward. Detective Martinez waited for the car to drive away and for Miles to leave the scene before walking out to the curb. Miles walked right past her on his way back to his car, just as Jess arrived to pick her up.

"Get in!" Jess said.

"Do you think the guys we're after are in that car?"

"Probably."

Jess pushed the accelerator to the floor and the car screamed forward. The limo was dead ahead of them moving at a normal speed down Chambers street heading toward the river. Jess slowed a little, keeping the limo in sight. Suddenly a large truck turned in front of them, stopped, and attempted to back into a narrow space ahead of them. Jess blew the horn, but it was too late, the large semi-trailer had blocked the street. Jess blew the horn frantically the driver ignored him. Jess hit the siren and clamped the red light onto the top of the car and blew again. This time the driver tried to move hastily and in the process rammed his vehicle into a car parked on the other side of the street jamming the front of his truck against the car; the truck was stuck. Jess made a U-turn and raced backed up the block, made a left and took the next available street leading to the river, but it was too late, the limo was nowhere in sight.

"Damn! We had them! I should have just grabbed them!" Jess said.

"Maybe it was them, and if it was, we couldn't' grab them in front of the lawyer," Detective Martinez said.

Jess banged his hand against the dashboard, but he knew Detective Martinez was right.

"I'm sorry. How's the shoulder?"

"I'll make it." Detective Martinez said.

"Tina, thank you for the help last night. I couldn't have pulled it off without you," Jess said.

"The Commissioner is probably going to give me hell."

"No, I'll explain it to him, we couldn't use a man on this one. By the way, when can I have Fuchs?"

"Tomorrow. We think we convinced him to take it easy, and he knows that you are in charge."

"Thanks."

"Hey, beats the hell out of office work," Martinez said.

"Good, one more thing, let's check out the seventy-second street address."

"Why not?"

\*                    \*                    \*

Vic finished his training. The last part of the course had nothing to do with violence; bookkeeping, computers, and paper trails, or as Duke described it, "the roadway to the big guys." Vic held his own and finished with flying colors. He hadn't had time to think about Manero, that was until he read about the shoot-out in Brooklyn. The papers were full of Jess' heroic deeds. Vic didn't recognize the female detective in the picture, but nothing about Jess had changed. Vic was tempted to pick up the phone and call Jess, but the one thing constant in his orientation process was the importance of keeping the fact that he was alive, secret. Duke entered the cafeteria and joined him at his table.

"Have you read the paper?"

"Yeah," Vic said.

"What's up?"

"My old partner is back on the job, he bagged two of the bad guys last night in Brooklyn."

"Good, it's about time we won one," Duke said and took a sip of his coffee. "Well, it's time. We're going to New York. Your man is there, but we want him alive, he's the key to the big man here in the States."

"I didn't bargain for this. If we find him, I'm going to kill him," Vic said

"His number will come up, I promise…"

Vic took a deep breath and looked past Duke.

"I mean it. You can have him once we find out who the inside man is."

"Okay, but don't slip up," Vic said.

"Let's get the hell out of here. We'll bide our time on Mr. Manero. He's under surveillance now. I don't want you to blow your top, but he's with Juan Acevedo."

Duke hesitated a moment to observe Vic's reaction. Vic didn't blink.

"You can have Juan if you want, but there's something else…they have his wife and they're willing to turn her over to us. Handled the right way she might be the key we need. That's if we can turn her," Duke said.

"You do what you have to do, I made a promise. I won't touch Juan until you give me the okay."

"Good, let's get the hell out of here."

*                *                *

Lisa had heard stories about being in jail. Being locked up in a single cell at the precinct was bad enough, but being thrown in with the rest of the population at the courthouse was too much. Something was going on, she could sense it, but she couldn't put her finger on it. Some of the younger women were being hassled, but not her. A Correction Officer opened the pen and motioned for her to come with him. A couple of the hookers in the holding pen gave her a dirty look, but they didn't say anything. They had ragged every new woman they brought into the pen, why not her? The Correction Officer cuffed Lisa and told her to get in line with the other prisoners.

"Where are you taking me?"

"Quiet. All right, everybody follow the officer at the head of the line," The Correction Officer said.

The lead Officer opened a door that led to an alley in a courtyard. She led them to the prison bus and stood aside until the last prisoner entered the bus. Lisa was held back. The lead officer got on the bus, handed her keys to a second officer and closed the doors. Lisa was taken to a car parked behind the bus and placed in the back seat. A wire petition separated her seat from the driver and the Officer who had cuffed her in the holding area. A large metal gate folded open and the two vehicles moved out onto Center Street. The two vehicles made a right turn at the corner onto Third Avenue. They took Third Avenue uptown.

"I got a message for you. Everything will be fine, and if you need anything ask for me. I'm Gregory. If anybody bothers you, I don't care who, just tell him or her Mr.G looks after you. You understand? Mr. G looks after you," Gregory said.

Lisa nodded her head.

"Good."

That was it; the man didn't say another word all the way to Rikers. Lisa was no stranger to Rikers; she had visited Juan there. That was different, this time she was the prisoner, sitting in the back of the car, locked in a cage like an animal. So the man had connections and Gregory was one of them. At least that was in her favor. That was when she understood the treatment back at the holding pen. She thought it was because of the way she was well dressed. Now she realized it was because she had connections. She would use that. Suddenly she felt a chill. It could work two ways. If she talked, she was dead, if she clamed up, her stay would be a picnic.

\*          \*          \*

Miles arrived at the court at ten sharp. He wanted to post Lisa's bond and get her the hell out of custody. Gregory had given him a good report; Lisa had kept her mouth shut. He didn't notice the delay at first. Transportation from Rikers was always slow, but when the clock reached eleven, Miles went out into the corridor and called Gregory. Gregory asked him to hold on while he checked to see if there had been any problems. Gregory checked with the dispatcher, there had been no reports of any problems, he didn't push the issue and attributed the delay to remnants of the rush hour.

"Everything here is okay, they must be stuck in traffic," Gregory said.

"Thanks," Miles said and folded his phone and returned it to his pocket. He returned to the courtroom, nothing had changed there.

*   *   *

The prison bus took the old trolley lane onto the bridge from Queens Plaza; the morning traffic was at its peak. They inched forward, stopping frequently, too frequently for the passengers. The bus crossed the bridge and stopped at the intersection of Delancey and Orchard Streets, stuck half way in the right turn lane. One of the hookers screamed obscenities at the driver, his mother, and his mother's mother.

"Shut the hell up, bitch," from the front of the bus. The woman screamed again, this time she screamed as if her scream would stop the large truck hurling in their direction. The truck had struck two cars in the intersection, and was heading straight for them, full speed. Everything appeared to be in slow motion. At the very last second the bus driver was able to move, just enough to avoid the full impact of the on coming truck. Lisa raised her arms as far as possible, then lowered her chin into her hands, that was the last thing she remembered. Later at the hospital after she regained consciousness, the sting from a needle penetrating her shoulder jolted her back to reality.

"Relax, it's all over, you're going to be all right."

Lisa nodded her head. "We're taking you upstairs for x-rays, you have a nasty bump on your head."

"Thank you," Lisa said.

The loud hooker gave Lisa a—thumbs up—and winked at her. Lisa whispered "Thank you." Lisa counted the ceiling tiles and the lights above her from the moving stretcher. She tilted her head back a little and looked up into the chin of a large orderly.

"We'll take her from here, wait in the corridor," Duke said.

"Who are you, what do you want?" Lisa said.

"We're your friends. We're here to keep you alive."

"I don't need your help."

"So you think. Without our help, it's all over for you; you're going to die."

"What are you talking about? They said everything was okay. Who are you?"

"I already told you. I'm the man who's going to keep you alive.

"All right, all right."

"I arranged this meeting, the truck, the whole bit."

Duke looked down at Lisa and opened his arms in a blessing-like gesture. Lisa could have sworn he made the sign of the cross. The chill was back and Lisa broke out in a cold sweat.

"When you finish here they're gonna take you to court. Your lawyer is there with the bail money. If you keep your promise to us we'll take care of you. Manero isn't the kind of guy who'll trust you. Right now he' s thinking about burning you," Duke said, and let the message settle in.

"What do you want from me?"

"We want you to keep your eyes and ears open, and report anything you hear that can help us find out who Manero's inside man is." Duke said.

"What about Juan?"

"We want the big guy, Juan means nothing to me," Duke said

"Suppose I have something I need to get to you?"

"You shop, we'll have someone at the makeup counter at Bloomindales. Go there when you have information for us, we'll take it from there."

"Who will I report to?"

"Don't worry about it, we'll contact you. Orderly!"

"But?" Lisa said.

The orderly returned and took Lisa into the X-ray room; the knot on her head had diminished, eradicating any signs of the accident.

\*　　　　　　　\*　　　　　　　\*

Miles jumped when his cellular phone rang. The Judge gave him a dirty look and Miles did a fake bow and left the courtroom. It was Gregory, calling him about the accident. He said that there were no serious injuries and that he would bring Lisa to court. Miles thanked him and closed the phone. He reentered the courtroom and made a gesture to indicate that his phone was off. The Judge took a deep breath as if to speak, then used a hand gesture to show his displeasure.

\*　　　　　　　\*　　　　　　　\*

The X-ray Technician assisted Lisa onto the stretcher, called the Orderly, who wheeled Lisa back to the emergency room. Gregory met them at the elevator. He cuffed Lisa and followed the stretcher back to the area where the other prisoners were held. The hooker was admitted, and the rest of the group were bandaged or stuffed with painkillers and sent on to court. Gregory told the relief driver that he would take Lisa to court, that her case had been called and they were waiting for her. The driver shrugged his shoulders and handed him Lisa's papers.

Miles stood when he saw Gregory enter the courtroom and hand the Court Officer the papers.

"The Court calls Lisa Acevedo," the Bailiff shouted.

Miles joined Lisa at the table. Miles stood and petitioned the court.

"Your Honor, the defense is ready to proceed."

"Are you prepared to present bail?" The Judge asked.

"We are, your Honor."

"Approach the bench," the Judge said.

Miles and the ADA met at the edge of the podium.

"May I see the check?" the Judge said. Miles handed the check to the Judge.

"Mr. Saunders, I am amazed by your ability to produce these staggering amounts on such short notice. Be careful. I'd hate to see you coming before me one of these days as a defendant. Step back."

Miles joined Lisa at the table.

"Mrs. Acevedo, you are to surrender your passport and you are not to leave this jurisdiction until your case is settled by this court. Is that understood?"

Miles nudged Lisa and whispered, "Yes, your Honor."

"Yes, your Honor," Lisa said.

"Furthermore, if you leave this jurisdiction you will forfeit your bail and a warrant will be issued for your immediate arrest. Mrs. Acevedo is released on bail of one million dollars. You are to return to this court," the Judge looked at his calendar. "Will two weeks be long enough, Miss Stanley?"

"Yes, your Honor," the Assistant District Attorney said.

"Miss Acevedo, you are to return to this court two weeks from today at ten a.m. Pay the Clerk."

The Judge gave Miles a penetrating look, and said, "Bailiff call the next case."

Miles presented the check to the Court Clerk, obtained a receipt, and returned to Lisa.

"Here, these are for you. You can change in the ladies room," Miles said.

"You mean I can leave," Lisa said.

"Is the Pope Catholic? Juan is waiting for you across the street in the car."

Lisa grabbed the bag and rushed out of the courtroom.

*　　　　　　*　　　　　　*

Duke followed Miles and Lisa at a respectable distance. He stopped just inside the entrance-way and watched a stretch limousine appear, as if by magic, and stop in front of the court house. The heavy tinted windows prevented Duke from seeing who was inside, but he guessed that Manero and Juan were in the limo. He watched Miles Saunders and Lisa get into the car, and waited for the car to move before signaling Vic to pick him up. They followed the car towards the Holland Tunnel. The limo made a sudden surge, ahead of a large truck, into a moving lane of traffic, leaving Vic and Duke stuck in a slow merging lane. Vic slammed his hand against the steering wheel. Duke called the Port Authority Police and gave them the information on the limo and asked them to keep it under surveillance.

"Hey, don't sweat it, they're not getting away." Two minutes later the phone rang, it was the Jersey State Police. They said the limo had exited the tunnel and appeared to be heading for Route 3.

*       *       *

The greeting, in the car, had been warm. The fresh clothes were a blessing, but a nice hot shower was what Lisa needed. The limo proceeded at a normal pace after they left the tunnel, and traffic was heavy until they passed the smelly refineries bordering the New Jersey Turnpike. Manero hadn't said much since Lisa entered the car, but now he was talking to her.

"Hey, you did damn good for a first-timer. You didn't even fucking cry, you got balls Lisa. I like that," Manero said.

"Didn't I tell you?" Juan said.

"Sure, but the proof is in the pudding. Here, have some more champagne."

Manero tipped the bottle and filled Lisa's glass. Lisa thought about what the strange man had said at the hospital, and she knew after what Manero just said that she would never be comfortable with him.

"Miles, you do good work and I appreciate the use of your country place. If things work out all right I might buy a place down there."

"I do what I can," Miles said.

"Yeah, at these prices, I guess you do."

Lisa sipped her champagne, if it was poison; it was the best damn poison she had ever tasted. Manero was nice to her too. He glanced at her once and a while, and made teasing remarks. Maybe that guy was wrong. After all, Juan was good at what he did. Maybe he did want Juan to take over for him…

The limo stopped at the tollbooth, briefly, before following the curving ramp that led to the Garden State Parkway. Thirty minutes later they left the Parkway and took a country road deep into the woods. The ride was short; they made a right turn onto a private road and stopped at the entrance to Miles' Estate. Miles reached out of the car and punched a code into the security pad and the gate opened. Ahead of them in the distance between giant cedars, sat an old English Manor House.

"I think I'm in the wrong business," Manero said. The limo filled with laughter. A copter with the distinct markings of the New Jersey State Police hovered quietly above them. The pilot called Duke's car and gave them the location of the limo. Duke checked his laptop and punched in the location.

"Hey, according to this, this location checks out to be the lawyer's address."

"So?" Vic said.

"We'd better back off for now. All we need to do is give away our advantage," Duke said.

"Yeah," Vic said.

Duke called Washington and arranged for a surveillance team. They would keep an eye on the place until the backup team arrived.

*       *       *

"Jess, this is Johnny Fuchs," the Commissioner said.

"Pleased to meet you. I've heard a lot about you," Fuchs said.

"Good, I hope?"

Fuchs nodded his head.

"I'm sorry about your partner," Fuchs said.

"Hey, shit happens," Jess said.

"Yeah,"

"Now that the introductions are over there's something I want to discuss with you, Jess," the Commissioner said.

"Its about Detective Martinez, right?"

"You're damned right it is.

"Commissioner, you said anything I needed. Well..." the Commissioner interrupted.

"I...er, well. Look, she's not a street cop, she could have been killed."

"She's a cop, Sir. And she saved my life, damn good cop, I might add."

The Commissioner bit his bottom lip softly, and looked Jess in the eye.

"Be that as it may, Fuchs is your new partner, get me? If you want anyone else, particularly a woman, you call me."

"Yes, sir."

"I mean it, Jess. The next thing I know you'll have Bee out there on the street."

"No, sir," Jess said.

"Well, I just want to be damn sure. What do you have on the case?"

"We turned Lisa Acevedo. She's gonna help us."

"How can you be sure of her?"

Jess shrugged his shoulders.

"I can't, but I gave her my card and she promised to call me when she gets something."

"Where is she now?"

"They bailed her out."

"Posted a million dollars for her?" The Commissioner asked.

"Yes, sir," Jess said.

"She's dog meat now, or they need her for some reason," the Commissioner said.

"You mean they would let that bail money go?" Jess said.

"If they produce a body they don't loose the bail money," Fuchs said.

"Where are they now?" the Commissioner asked.

"I don't know. They moved from the seventy-second street address bag and baggage. The good news is she has a return date at the Tombs next Monday at ten in the morning," Jess said.

"Well, let's hope she shows up. What's your next move?" The Commissioner said.

"Find them."

"That's what I like about you gold shield guys, you're so damn smart."

"We're out of here, if that's all right with you, Sir?" Jess said.

"See, I told you were smart." The Commissioner smiled and focused his attention on the paper work on his desk.

           *            *            *

"You think they're gonna kill her?" Fuchs asked

"Naw, she's married to one of the principals. If they kill her they'll have to kill him too."

"So, what's so special about him?"

"I don't know, but Manero visited him in person, so he must be important to the organization," Jess said.

"Where do we start?" Fuchs asked.

"My cousin works over at Beth Israel. He called me this morning and said he had something to tell me. Said he didn't want to tell me on the phone. I want to stop by there and see what he wants. You know the bit, now and then he spots something he thinks is important to us."

"Don't tell me you have one in your family too?"

"Yeah, they don't mean any harm, but to them everything is a federal case," Jess said.

"Tell me about it. If it's not your family, it's a neighbor," Fuchs said.

Jess opened the car and unlocked the door for Fuchs. It was a little past noon and the traffic was light on the way uptown. Jess had heard the call about the accident near the bridge, but passed it off as just another accident. Jess parked next to a fire hydrant and popped his vehicle ID on the sun visor and dropped it so the plate would show. The two detectives entered the hospital and took the elevator to the second floor. Billy saw them coming and asked his supervisor for a few minutes off. The supervisor waved at Jess and Jess returned the gesture.

"Yo, Jess! Sup?" Billy said.

"Billy this is my new partner, Johnny Fuchs."

"Pleased to meet you. Hey! This is important, let's go downstairs to the deli, I can't talk here."

Jess knew the routine he winked at Fuchs. Billy wanted everybody to see him talking to his cousin the cop. It made him feel important and to the bad guys in the neighborhood it meant don't screw around with him. The Bad Guys were used to his routine, but Billy had never caused them any problems so why start anything. The small deli was crowded. Fuchs suggested a place on Twenty-third Street. Billy jumped at a chance to ride in Jess' car. It was a good idea, one that made Jess take another look at his new partner. Billy sat in the front seat with Jess.

"So, what you got?"

"I don't know how important this is but you know that accident the this morning, you know, the one where that prison van was hit?" Billy said.

"Yeah, so?"

"Well I was taking one of the prisoners, a woman. Wait a minute I got her name written down." Billy shifted in his seat and fumbled for the information. In his excitement he panicked when he didn't find it the first time. He took a deep sigh and produced the napkin he had scribbled the information on. "Yeah, her name was Lisa Acevedo." Jess snapped his head in Billy's direction, then turned to Fuchs.

"Is it important?"

"Why did you take her name?"

"Is it really important, you know, most of the time when I give you stuff you don't seem to be interested," Billy asked.

"It's important, okay, its important."

"Well, I was taking her to be examined when a man stopped me. He was already there waiting for her, that's what made me take her name. To me it looked like he knew she was coming."

"Go ahead," Jess said.

"Well, before we got to the examining room he took her to another room and told me to wait outside."

"What did you do?"

"That's the other thing. One of the administrators was with him and he just kind'a nodded his head to let me know it was okay."

"What did this man look like?"

"Nothing special, he was a big man, that's about all I noticed about him."

"What did he do with the woman?" Fuchs asked.

"They talked for a little while, and then he called me to take her on to the examination."

"That was it?" Jess asked.

"Yeah, except the woman looked like she was scared after he left."

"Good work, Billy. I'm proud of you."

"You mean I really helped? I mean, I know I bug you sometimes."

"No, I really mean it, this is good information."

"Er...I got his license plate number."

"You're kidding!"

Billy handed him the napkin. Jess handed it to Fuchs along with the car phone. Jess found another hydrant near a small candy store a few doors from the deli and parked. Fuchs handed Jess the phone and told him the car was from a rental agency located at Kennedy Airport.

"Hey, it's time for lunch. Today it's on me and the sky is the limit," Jess said.

"What I gave you must be really important," Billy said.

   *      *      *

Monica asked her mother to take her shopping Helen was thrilled. It had been a long time since they had done anything together. They would visit their favorite stores before shopping on Madison Avenue. Helen had said once, it's the fine old institutions that provide the best service. Monica teased her about the first time Helen had taken her to Bergdorfs, and how she had preferred FAO Schwartz, it was natural for her the choose the kid's paradise. Two hours at Bergdorf Goodman, another hour at Saks, Bendel's, Harry Winston's to repair a ring, then onto lunch. The Head Waiter at Le Cirque promised to prepare Helen's favorite lunch, and to hold her favorite table just inside the door near the Park Avenue Wall, as she had designated it, so she could see the strivers parade. Helen loved the parade, television personalities, executives on their way up, all vying for what was considered the best location in the restaurant. What Helen loved most of all was the trouble and expense these people went to in an effort to show their position.

"Mother...I don't know if you want to talk about it, but what happened to the boat?"

"I don't mind. I considered selling it for a while, but the market was bad so I had it put in dry dock."

"Isn't that expensive?"

"No. That was one of the few things you father did right. We own the boat yard and believe it or not it turns a good profit. It seems there's a lot of new money out there and they all have a boat of some kind. Why do you ask?"

"Well, since he's gone I thought I might spend some time on it, maybe write a book."

"Monica! That would be wonderful. What about the apartment in town?" Helen asked.

"I think I'm ready to move in. I'll keep the apartment and use the boat when I want to get away," Monica said.

"That's really wonderful, may I come along?"

Monica hadn't anticipated Helen's interest. She paused before answering. Helen looked at her with anticipation.

"Of course, Mother."

"Good. Whenever you're ready I'll call Mike at the basin and he'll prepare the boat for you. You'll need a crew; too bad about the last crew. We don't know what happened to them, one of them was killed and the others disappeared, just vanished," Helen said.

Monica thoughts turned to the money. Was it possible, did the missing crewmembers take the money? One thing was for certain, she would have to find Wayne's hiding place. She knew he had secret panels on the yacht, a panel somewhere in which he hid his dirty tapes.

*　　　*　　　*

Jess parked in front of the rental agency. The Clerk behind the counter tried to wave him to the parking area around the corner, but Jess flashed his shield and the Clerk threw up her hands and returned to the counter. There must have been a lull because the place was empty.

"Yes?" the Clerk said.

"I'm Detective Jess Norman and this is Detective Fuchs. We want to see if you can help us identify the customers who rented this vehicle. Jess gave the Clerk the number and the date of the rental. The Clerk took the slip and punched the information into their computer. She turned and said.

"So what's the problem, it was rented by one of your people."

"What do you mean?"

"Its one of the specials we keep for you guys, you know, with the radio and siren. This one was for one of the government agencies."

Jess looked at Fuchs.

"Which one?"

The clerk scrolled through the page.

"Justice Department."

"That covers a lot of ground. Which department, FBI, Marshals, what?"

"Look, it just says Justice Department, what do you want from me?"

"A personality," Jess said.

"Not at these prices," the Clerk said.

"I know the feeling," Jess said.

"Don't give me that crap, you guys make big bucks," the Clerk said.

"So why don't you join us?" Fuchs said.

"No balls," the Clerk said, and they all laughed.

"Hey, got something that might help you," the Clerk said.

"What?"

"How about a photo of the guys who took the car?"

"You're kidding!" The Clerk hit a couple of keys and a black and white image emerged. It was a long shot but clear enough to identify the subjects. She punched the print button and the printer buzzed and spat out a slow moving photo.

"What's your name?" Jess asked.

"Candy."

"Well, Candy...take this card and if you ever need help call me."

"Right! That's cool. Like if I get a ticket, right?"

"No, baby, like if someone is trying to kick your butt."

"Now that's really cool," Candy said.

"Hey, are you married?" Fuchs said.

"Come on, man," Jess said.

"Nope, " Candy said.

"Maybe you have a card?" Fuchs said.

"How about a phone number?"

Candy jotted down her phone number and gave it to Fuchs.

"I'm Johnny."

"Yeah," Candy said.

"Thanks, Candy. I hate to break this up but we have work to do," Jess said.

"Yeah," Candy said.

Jess studied the photograph carefully; there was something about one of the men in the photograph that looked familiar. It hit him like a ton of bricks, the face was wrong but the eyes looked like Vic. Jess stood there in the doorway, Fuchs looked back at Candy and shrugged his shoulders.

"I thought we were in a hurry?" Fuchs said.

"We are, but this picture…. one of the guys looks a little like my old partner."

"You're kidding. Didn't you say he is dead?"

"He is dead, but this guy is so much like him. It's not him, but damn he's really close. Let's go visit the Feds and see what we can dig up," Jess said.

Fuchs waved to Candy and followed Jess to the car.

It was a pleasant time of day, mid afternoon. The Van Wyck was empty going into the city. Fuchs was at the wheel with his foot heavy on the gas petal.

"What's the hurry?" Jess asked.

"No hurry. Didn't they tell you that I came out of Motorcycle One?"

"Oh shit! That explains it. You must have gone over on your bike and hit your head."

"Lots of times," Fuchs said and nudged the car up to eighty.

He rolled up on a guy in a hot little Mustang doing seventy and floored the unmarked police car past him like he was standing still. Jess laughed when he turned to look at the kid. The kid actually looked down at his speedometer. Traffic slowed on the hill leading to the Triborough Bridge and Fuchs was forced to slow down. Jess sat quietly planning his mischief for the next time he took the wheel. They parked on Broadway, outside of the Federal Building. Jess and Fuchs filled out the forms at the entrance and walked around the detection devices in the lobby. They were directed to the Justice Department office where they entered a plush reception area. They presented their identification for a second time and waited about five minutes, after which, a young man appeared from one of the offices and took them to a conference room.

"Gentlemen, how can I help you?"

"We're working a homicide, the case where the cop was blown to bits up in the Bronx. We have information that some of your people are interested in one of our suspects."

"Interesting. And where did you get this information?"

"The information came to us from a vehicle registration. We checked it out and found out that it had been rented to the Justice Department. We thought we might be covering the same ground, or that we might be able to help each other," Jess said.

"I see. What case are we talking about?"

"Manero," Fuchs blurted out. The Agent didn't say anything but this eyes narrowed for a split second.

"You are familiar with the case?" Jess said.

"No, I'm afraid not."

The Agent was lying, but why…. Jess glanced at Fuchs.

"Look, this is not one of those competition things, is it?" Jess said.

"What makes you think that?" the Agent said.

"You know the drill. It's obvious that you are familiar with Manero, so what gives?"

"As I said. I don't know this Manero."

"Yeah," Fuchs said.

This time there was a hint of threat in his voice. Jess looked at him, tilting his head in a "Cool it" manner. Fuchs backed off.

"Look, the cop that was killed was my partner, this is personal. I would appreciate any help you can give us."

"As I said before, we don't have any knowledge of your Mr. Manero, but I will take the plate number and see if I can locate the persons you are seeking. Maybe they can help you. And, if I do so you won't divulge where you got the information from, right?"

"Right," Jess said.

"Good. Give me the plate number. I'll see what I can come up with. How can I reach you?" Jess handed the Agent a card.

"I'm Jerry Mulligan. That's all you need to know right now. Don't call me I'll call you. That's important. I lost a partner once, I know the feeling."

"Cool," Jess said.

"Thanks," Fuchs said. The men stood and shook hands the meeting was over. Outside, Fuchs asked, "Do you think we can trust him?" Jess nodded a yes and Fuchs said, "Okay…"

# Chapter *VIII*

---

*T*he call was from Mike at the boat yard. Someone had entered the boat and ransacked the interior. He apologized and said that it would take a little while to get the boat ready. Helen was furious, but Monica convinced her to keep Mike on. Helen agreed, but said that she wouldn't put a foot on the yacht until it was ready.

"Mother, the boat is covered by insurance. Why don't we redecorate it to suit us? In the meantime I can move in."

"That's a splendid idea. Who will we get to do it?"

"Antonio, of course."

"Yes! Are you sure that it is safe for you to work there? After all, who-ever these people are, they might come back," Helen said.

"I can take care of myself," Monica said.

"Of course you can, what am I thinking?"

"Then it's settled?"

"Yes. I'll call Mike and tell him to get a cabin ready for you."

"One with a computer. Tell him I want to use Wayne's old computer, and tell him I will hook it up, Mother."

"Consider it done," Helen said.

Monica stood, walked across the room and hugged her mother. She had many things to do, one of them was to find the money and the other was to get rid of Manero once and for all. He had to pay for the time she spent at the funny factory.

"Monica, dear…are you all right?"

"Yes, mother, why?"

"Oh nothing. I just asked you where did you want to have dinner and you didn't answer me. I hope those were good thoughts," Helen said.

"The very best, Mother."

"Good! For a moment you had me worried. Shall we go into the city and look at the apartment?"

"That's a great idea, Mother."

✳       ✳       ✳

"No luck, not a fucking thing! We took that boat apart, everything!" Juan said.

"Well it was worth a try. Where do you think our money is?" Manero asked.

"I don't know, but if we find it, it will be with Monica's help," Juan said.

"I don't trust her. Remember what she said about being in the hospital. We'd better keep a close eye on her."

Juan was silent.

"What is it? Manero said.

"Well…"

"Yes, go ahead."

"We can't crowd her. I think we'd be better off if we left her alone for a while. If she doesn't come up with something in a few days we'll do what you suggested."

"Okay, that works for me," Manero said.

"Thanks, Senior. Manero. She'll come through," Juan said.

"Hey you guys! Lisa shouted from the kitchen. "I made some lunch. Enjoy it; I'm going shopping…Mr. Manero is it all right if your driver takes me?" Lisa said.

"Sure, I'll call downstairs and tell him. Where do you want to go?"

"Bloomindales," Lisa said.

"Of course."

"Thank you," Lisa said.

Manero nodded his head, picked up the phone and called his driver.

*       *       *

Lisa entered Bloomindales from Third Avenue. She entered the building walked through the men's department and down the stairs that led to the makeup area. A young woman approached her and sprayed her with a fragrance.

"It's Passion, fabulous for attracting the persons of your choice."

Lisa broke her stride for a moment, caught in the woman's choice of words.

"Persons of my choice, what the…."

"Take a seat at the Max counter."

Lisa shook her head to ward off the nightmare she was in, but it didn't go away. Ahead of her at the Max counter stood a massive woman beckoning her to a seat.

"Glad you could make it. Everything you say will be recorded. Do you wish to continue?"

Lisa shook her head, they had her by the balls; what could she do?

"Good. What do you have for us?"

"They're missing twenty million dollars. They don't know where it is but they think Monica Woolford can help them find it. They went to her father's boat looking for the money. It seems that he used to laundry money for them."

"Was Monica part of all this?"

"I guess so, my husband knows her," Lisa said.

"Good. Now that we know we can depend on you, we'll protect you. We are watching them. If you ever feel that you are in danger we want you to get to us. There will always be a black Ford parked near nearby.

We were just outside the gate in Jersey, did you see the road crew working up the road from the place?"

Lisa nodded her head.

"To make sure it's the right car there to pick you up will have a Garfield on the dash board. Garfield the cat will be wearing a policeman's cap. Just say, my name is Lisa and the driver will take you to safety," the Agent said.

"You think its that easy, huh? Well let me tell you. He's got people everywhere, some of your own people are probably working for him…"

The woman interrupted. "No way. We're a special unit, no bad apples in our barrel."

"Don't count on it," Lisa said.

"Is that it?" The Agent asked.

"Yeah," Lisa said.

"We move our locations every few weeks. If you have something for us we'll be at Macys on Thirty-fourth Street, second floor, better dresses. We figure your people won't buy us meeting you at makeup counters anymore."

"I came alone. The chauffeur is waiting outside."

"Rule number one. Always assume that someone is watching you. Now, thank me and shop around a while before leaving."

Lisa stood, thanked the Agent and walked towards the up escalator. A woman, about thirty followed her. She was average, so average the Agent didn't notice her.

*     *     *

"There's a problem," Manero said.

"What?" Juan asked.

"You know the story, when the cat's away the mice will play."

Juan nodded his head.

"Skippy up in the Bronx is spreading the word that we are not up to the job. He told Angelo to go fuck himself when it was time to pay for his delivery."

Juan shook his head and pounded the table with his fist.

"You see why I need you. I got so caught up in this money thing, the rest of the operation is falling a part. I want my money. Don't ever let the idea of me not getting it enter your mind. It's my fucking money! I'm giving you the job of finding it, get it done." Manero said and looked Juan dead in the eye. Juan nodded his head.

"Don't worry about Lisa, my people at the court will take care of her. Tell her it's all over. Make her appearance at court and the charges will be dropped," Manero said.

"Thanks, Boss."

"Juan…you're my partner now. Why don't you call me Manny?" Juan swallowed and said "Okay, Manny." Manero stood and hugged Juan.

"Miles, can one of your people take us up to New York?"

"Sure."

"Good. I'll call Ricardo and tell him to meet us there. When we get there I want you to look up Monica."

"Right," Juan said.

*       *       *

"Unit two. We got one on the move heading in your direction. BMW sedan, three occupants."

"10-4, unit one, we have it in sight."

"Unit, three, move up to two's position. We'll hold here until unit five gets back."

"10-4, unit one."

Once on the turnpike the cars worked in relay teams, one car a quarter of a mile ahead of the car Manero and Juan rode in, traveling at the same speed, and another car three miles behind Manero's car.

They followed the car into the city, where Manero got out on Canal Street, and took the subway uptown. One of the agents made it to the train just as the doors were closing. One of the cars rushed, siren wide open to the next stop to drop off two more members of the team. Juan watched the car speed away and shrugged his shoulders; he didn't notice the car following the car he rode in. The agents made it to the station just as the target train entered the station. They stood at different spots on the platform. One of the agents spotted his partner on the train and gave a hand signal to the rest of the crew. Now they had Manero covered.

Manero sat quietly reading a newspaper. He gave no indication that he had spotted them. The three cars continued along the route of the train until it reached Forty-second Street. At that point one of the cars headed for the West Side Highway and the other to the East River Drive and raced uptown to 125th Street, the train's next stop after 59th Street. If they didn't hear from one of the agents on the train they would continue uptown. The East Side Car would exit the Deagan at Yankee station and take Grand Concourse, if necessary. The West Side car would exit the West Side Highway at the Cross Bronx Expressway and wait at Amsterdam Avenue for instructions.

At Fifty-ninth Street a horde of passengers entered the train. Manero got up and left the train. The agent in his car pressed the button on his radio, held the button down and tapped the radio three times. The agent in the first car moved closer to the door and waited. An instance before the doors closed Manero stepped back into the train and into the car the second Agent was in. He looked back to see if anyone was following him. Satisfied, he smiled and moved to a spot where he could rest against one of the stanchions that anchored the seats to the floor of the train. The second Agent pressed the button on his radio, held it down, and clicked two times.

The train became a local after 145th Street and lumbered its way towards the end of the line. When it became obvious that Manero was taking the train to the end of the line, two of the agents got off the train and called the cars in. The train entered the Fordham Road station, the last stop, and all of the passengers got off. The last agent off the train made sure he was one of the first passengers to leave the station. He rushed past the other passengers and when he reached street level he hailed a Gypsy cab. The cab made a treacherous turn and stopped right in front of him. A car pulled up behind his taxi and picked up Manero. The Agent in the gypsy cab delayed his taxi until everyone was in place. The Cab driver became impatient and told him he would have to tell him where he was going, or get out of his taxi. The Agent said, "When I know where I'm going I'll tell you," and an argument commenced

"Chief! Good to see you! I don't know why you ride the fucking train," Luis said.

"Did you see anybody following me?"

"No," Luis said.

"Hey that's cool and that's why he's boss," Jose said.

"Let's get this thing over with," Manero said.

Luis honked his horn at the gypsy cab. The driver and the passenger were arguing about something. Luis honked the horn once more and the cab driver gave him the finger. Luis twisted his huge muscular frame out of the car and stood. The car in front of them sped off.

"Medicon!" Luis shouted and returned to the car. Luis made a U-turn and drove across Fordham Road to Southern Boulevard. The three cars tailing them kept a respectable distance. At the edge of the Bronx Zoo, on the Southern Boulevard side, Luis made a left turn and drove half way down the block and double-parked. One of the team cars drove past them and parked around the corner. The other two cars parked on Southern Boulevard. The Southern Boulevard car watched Manero and Luis get out of the car and enter a building.

The door buzzed and they entered the smelly hallway.

"You'd think the money he makes with us he'd clean up this place," Manero said.

"I talked to him about that. He said if he cleaned it up his customers wouldn't come here," Luis said. Manero pointed to the door. Luis took his gun out and hugged the wall near the door. Manero rang the bell and the peep hole opened emitting a penetrating sliver of light into the darkened hallway for an instance, followed by the sound of locks opening, the sound of a clanking chain, and the door opening slowly.

"Shit! It's the man himself," Skippy said and gave the okay sign to his bodyguard. The young black man shouldered his Uzi and returned to the table where Skippy's wife sat holding their young baby. She held the baby with one hand and stuffed dope into the envelopes with the other. Manero took out his gun and covered the bodyguard. Luis filled the hallway before Skippy realized what was going on. He grabbed Skippy, lifted him by his jacket and held him suspended in the air. Manero checked the other rooms. Two sickening hisses broke the silence followed by the sound of two bodies hitting the floor.

"Manero! I was wrong! Hey man don't do this!" Skippy shouted.

Manero turned his gun on Skippy's bodyguard and shot him between the eyes. Skippy's wife screamed and he shot her twice; one of the bullets killed the child she was holding..

"Mother fucker!" Skippy screamed and broke away from Luis. Manero shot him in the hip and Skippy fell. He made an effort to get to his gun, but Luis had recovered enough to catch his arm and wrench the gun away.

"Finish the job, you prick!" Skippy shouted.

"That's just what I'm going to do. But before I do it I want you to know what's coming. I want everybody to know what happens if they cross me. Put this bastard on the table and pull his pants down."

"You dirty bastard!"

Skippy fought with all of his energy, but he was no match for Luis. Luis gripped Skippy tightly and turned his head when Manero took out the knife. He had seen Manero operate before and it still made him sick. Manero left the room and returned with a pillow, and told Luis to cover

Skippy's face with the pillow. Luis put pillow on Skippy's face, pushed down hard, and closed his eyes. Manero smiled and slowly castrated Skippy. He let Skippy suffer a while before putting the gun to his head and pulling the trigger. Skippy crumbled into a bloody puddle of his own making.

"Let's get the hell out of here," Manero said.

Back in the car Luis looked at Manero and said "You do that and you don't even get a drop of blood on yourself."

"I'm not the one who's bleeding," Manero said and smiled.

"You taking the subway back?"

"Yeah," Manero said. Luis shook his head. The shadow team kept Manero's car in sight. At the subway one of the agents took the train, the second team hurried to stops ahead of the train and waited there.

*         *         *

"Miss Woolford there's a gentleman here to see you. A mister Acevedo," The Doorman said.

"Tell him I'll be right down,"

"Yes, ma'am."

The intercom clicked off, followed by a small buzz, then silence.

"Who is it, Monica?"

"A person I used to work with. I'll take him somewhere and buy him a drink."

"How did he know you were here?" Helen asked.

"Probably happen-chance, you know, looking for some kind of help."

"Oh. Don't be too long, you know we're supposed to check out your new cabin."

"Yes, Mother."

Monica walked across the room and kissed her mother on the cheek. She checked her purse for keys, after which she left. Juan was waiting in the lobby. He stood when he saw Monica approaching.

"Thank you, Carl," she said.

"You're welcome, Miss Woolford."

"Mr. Acevedo, so nice to see you." Monica extended her hand to Juan. Juan smiled and shook her hand. "I know an excellent little place around the corner where we can have a drink. Would you care to go there?"

"Anything you say, Miss Woolford."

Carl had been standing inside the door at the entrance. He walked outside when Monica shook Juan's hand, opened the door and stood aside. Juan slipped him a buck.

"Thank you, Sir," Carl said.

The bar-restaurant around the corner was crowded with afternoon shoppers basking in their giant fried onions and thickly sauced ribs. It was noisy, a perfect place for their purpose.

"What the hell do you mean coming to my place asking for me!"

"It's better for me to come than Manero," Juan said.

Monica was silent, she knew Juan was right but she didn't want to loose her edge.

"Didn't I tell you I would call you when I had something to tell you?"

"Yes. And that's why I'm here instead of Manero."

"Was that his work on the boat?" Juan nodded his head. Monica studied him carefully. Her bet was that Juan had done the dirty work.

"You didn't find anything or you wouldn't be here."

"No."

"So it was you…after me telling you that I would take care of it, damn!"

"Twenty million is a lot of money, and you say you didn't know your father was handling that kind of money."

"I didn't, and I didn't believe you until I found some paper work he left at the house. It wasn't anything special to anyone but us, just a lot of figures. I hate to admit it but you were right."

"What did the courier tell you?" Juan asked.

"He wasn't any help," Monica said. Monica watched Juan carefully looking for any hint that he might recognize she was lying.

"Sorry. We thought he might get with you and reveal something we missed. I want you to understand something. Manero is like a madman about this money."

Juan paused and looked around the room.

"The two crewmen were living high so we found them. Manero had them picked up and they fessed up before he killed them. The poor bastards had stole some of your father's jewelry and some electronic equipment, you know, some of the navigation equipment," Juan said.

Monica shook her head and looked Juan.

"That's where they got the money they were spending. When they heard the shots they took off in one of the small boats. And I can guarantee you one thing, they didn't know anything or else they would have told Manero. I'm telling you this because I don't want to see the same thing happen to you. "

"Thanks. I'll do what I can," Monica said.

"Damn, Monica. You've changed, there's something different about you. Shit, you're just like Manero." Monica smiled.

"Go back to Mr. Manero and tell him I will do my best to find the money. And tell him after I find it I don't want to see any of you near me again. I will call you. Do you have a way I can reach you?" Monica waited for an answer, then said," Don't tell me you're still using the same system?"

Juan nodded his head. Monica laughed and raised her glass in a toast.

"Here's to the return of your money and the last of your Mr. Manero," Monica said.

"Here's to you, Monica."

Juan signaled for the check. He dropped a fifty on the table and walked out into the sunlight. Monica picked up the fifty and replaced it with a ten. She stuck the fifty in her purse.

*      *      *

The train stopped at 59th Street, Manero got off and ran for the stairs. He stopped just long enough to see the men tailing him charge out of the train and run after him. He counted to five and ran back down the stairs on the opposite side of the staircase passing one of the agents in the process. The chimes warning that the doors were about to close sounded and Manero made it to the train and slid between the closing doors without the possibility of anyone following him. He watched the two agents throw up their hands and run up the stairs again. At the next station he followed the crowd moving towards the exit. He stopped at a flower stand and purchased a bouquet of flowers and held them close to his face. Two of the agents rushed towards the train, one agent stayed behind. Manero removed his jacket, folded it across his arm, and removed his tie. He cradled the flowers lovingly, headed towards the uptown staircase, walked casually down to the platform and took the next train.

"We lost him..." The Agent yelled into his radio.

"How?" Vic asked.

"In the subway."

"They told me you guys were the best!"

"I'm sorry, sir. We'll canvass the area." Vic hung up.

Manero took the R train to Fifth Avenue. He got off the train there and walked upstairs. Ricardo got out of the limo, opened the door and waited for Manero to get into the car.

"These fucking Feds never give up. I think they have a team assigned to me," Manero said.

Ricardo laughed. "Boss, I think it's time for us to go home."

"You're right, Ricardo."

Manero used the car phone to call Juan.

"Juan, it's time for me to take a trip. That problem we had has been taken care of. How are things on your end?"

"I met with our friend. You were right about her, but all she wants is to leave us. She'll help us with our problem, then she wants to go home," Juan said.

"Sometimes I think people don't like me. Lately it seems everyone wants to leave me. Am I that bad of a guy?"

"Not with me. Tell me what you want."

"Good. Make sure she delivers."

"Consider it done, or what will be, will be."

"I knew you were the right man for the job," Manero said and broke the connection. Juan stood there with the phone in his hand thinking about what Lisa had said, "He's going to kill us."

*       *       *

The papers had a field day with the murders. Jess had seen a lot of crimes in his day, but the scene in that apartment was too much for him. Cop or no cop, no one ever gets used to children dying. Mulligan had given them the tip; otherwise they would have dismissed the case as another drug related mass murder. The big detective in the car rental office photo was there in the apartment, but his partner, Vic's double, wasn't. Jess couldn't get a thing out of him, and the agency he worked for had so much clout Jess was told "Hands off." Jess swallowed the bitter pill, but in his heart he swore he would nail Manero. That was until the Commissioner called them into the office.

"Jess, Fuchs, I'm pulling you off the Manero case."

The Commissioner waited for the news to sink in before continuing.

"Manero is tied to a larger case, one that involves a larger interest. He will be dealt with, I promise you. But for now I want you to take a few days off, get some rest. When the Feds finish with him, he's all yours."

"I don't understand," Jess said.

"I know, and I can't tell you anymore. Take the time off, the case is in good hands, I promise."

Jess looked at Fuchs, Fuchs shrugged his shoulders. Jess' face was like a road map into his soul. The Commissioner watched Jess struggle with the pain, he wanted to tell him more but his hands were tied. Jess took out his badge and dropped it on the desk.

"Now, now, Jess…you know better than that. Take some time off you've earned it. When the time comes I promise to bring you guys into the case again."

The Commissioner read Jess' face again. This time he could see a ray of understanding. Jess picked up his shield and stuck it in his pocket.

"Is that all, Sir?"

"Yes. And thank you for taking this so well, I know how you must feel"

"Yes, Sir."

Jess and Fuchs left the Commissioner's Office. Bee stopped them at the desk and offered them some coffee. She pointed to the small area in the corner of the office.

"Jess, the Feds have a special task force on Manero. They're trying to find out who his legitimate source is. They know its someone big, but they don't know how big, so they put everyone on their list."

"What's that got to do with what we are doing?"

"You're getting too close to finding Manero and they want him in circulation a little longer," Bee said.

"So that's it. They think I'm going to kill him."

"Well…" Bee said.

"Come on, Bee! I'm still a cop."

"I know, but it's a hard one to call. This is the man that killed my sister and Vic. I know I would kill him if I had the chance."

"I don't plan to kill him. He might be bruised, but he won't be dead."

"Give them time, Jess. If you arrest him or hurt him, they won't like it, and you know how it is when they want something."

"Yeah…you're right."

"Go somewhere away from here. Tie one on and have a little fun. There's a woman out there I know who will be glad to see you."

"Bull!" Jess said.

"How much do you want to bet?"

"Bull," Jess said.

"Put your money where your mouth is," Bee said.

✳       ✳       ✳

Debbie's heart skipped a beat when she heard the music coming from the apartment. Bee had called her and told her Jess was coming home, but she didn't believe her. She stopped and adjusted her clothes. She wanted to check her makeup, but decided to forget about it. She didn't have a game plan, but one thing for sure was that he had to make the first move. Debbie inserted the key in the door. The door opened and Jess was standing there. He reached out to her and took her into his arms before she could execute her game plan. The feeling was mutual and they gravitated to the bedroom, shedding their clothes in the process. The thing that had worked for them throughout their marriage was their love for each other. Her knowledge of psychology helped, but it was their love that sustained them. Debbie took a deep breath and said "Sooo, you're back?"

"I never left," Jess said

"You could have fooled me. Are you all right? I mean I know you're healthy."

They laughed.

"And so are you," Jess said.

Debbie hit Jess with a pillow, wrapped a sheet around her body and sat on the edge of the bed.

"I'm fine now," Jess said.

Debbie nodded her head and said, "Tell me anything."

She put a finger to her lips and shushed him, she knew what he was about to say, but she couldn't stop him.

"I'm sorry, honey. I should have taken your advice and let them handle the case…but he was my partner. I just couldn't just walk away. About that other business, I'm through with drinking. Today I learned that there are things more serious that loosing a partner. That case in the Bronx…"

Debbie put her finger to his lips and said "shhhhh." She let the sheet fall, after which she melted into his hungry arms. Soon the pain would be gone and Jess would be asleep. And, when he awoke again he would awaken to familiar surroundings, with Debbie lying silent next to him.

*                  *                  *

"Well, Duke, how's my old partner?"

"Savvy as ever. Man was he pissed off when I wouldn't tell him anything."

"That's my old partner all right," Vic said.

"He rattled Mulligan, and Mulligan gave them the lead. I found out that Mulligan had lost a partner as well, you know the bit, sympathetic, one cop to another."

"At least it didn't hurt us. I knew this bastard Manero was mean, but not this mean. Did he do the shooting?"

"According to the wife," Duke said. She wrote his name in blood on the table just before she died. The bastard shot her in the stomach. Killed them both with one shot…mother and child."

"How long are we going to stand for this?" Vic asked.

"Until we get the green light," Duke said.

"How many more people have to die in the meantime?"

"I don't like to see children hurt in this business but that's the way it is. The baby was innocent but the mother wasn't. She was sitting at the

fucking table packaging dope, dope for children in her own neighborhood to use."

"Yeah, you're right, but I want this bastard."

"Be patient, you'll get your chance," Duke said.

"Not if your guys can't find him."

Duke lowered his head and looked away.

*   *   *

The games at Le Cirque were in full swing, but Helen had had
enough, she signed the check and they left the restaurant. Helen's car
was parked at the hotel next door. They entered the limousine and took
it to the Boat Basin. The ride to the Bronx was just what they needed to
change the pace. When they crossed the bridge to City Island Monica
caught a glimpse of the yacht at the end of the dock. They drove into the
boat yard and Mike met them at the entrance.

"Mrs. Woolford, Miss Woolford."

"Afternoon, Mike. Are you making any progress?" Monica said.

"Yes we are. I have the cabin you requested completed, and managed
to prepare one for you as well, Mrs. Woolford."

"Thank you, I am relieved. Mike what happened here?"

"Mrs. Woolford, it doesn't make any sense. I can tell you this much,
they didn't come in through the gate. And no one heard them the night
it happened. It was as if a Ninja had sneaked into the yard and ransacked the boat, but why? The missing crew members had already taken
anything of value." Mike said.

Helen's eyes were fixed on Mike. Monica had the same deadpan
expression she had before hearing about the vandals. She excused herself and walked toward the boat.

"Miss, Woolford...the cabin in the aft compartment is ready. The
one next to it is for your mother."

"Thank you, Mike," Monica said.

Monica left Helen with Mike. She stood on the main deck and looked inside the bar, everything that looked like a hiding place had been opened. Monica turned and walked towards her cabin at the rear of the boat. Antonio had done an excellent job; the room was decorated in gray glove leather, trimmed in a grained cherry wood. She booted up the computer and started a search of her father's files. If Wayne had the money, the hiding place would be somewhere in the computer's database. The screen flickered and a list of files danced down the computer screen. She stopped the scan and highlighted a file named Blue Beard. Walla! Wayne Woolford's hiding place filled the screen. It was so obvious; Monica was puzzled, why didn't Juan see it? She printed out the account number, folded the page and put it in her purse, after which she phoned Juan.

"You know who this is."

"Yes," Juan said.

"Tell the man I will deliver the package to him, and him alone. Tell him I will call you again in one hour to give him instructions on the meet." Monica said.

Juan heard the phone click, followed by the dial tone, but shouted into the phone anyway.

"Wait a minute! Just a fucking minute…Hello, hello?" Juan pressed the phone's memory button and called Manero.

*          *          *

"Hey Jess! He's on the move again, just got the AWAC's report. He's a smart one this time he's using a charter. You won't believe this he's headed to Westchester Airport!"

"That's just like our boy, you never know what he's going to do next."

"Chop, chop, buddy!" Duke said.

The drive to the airport would get them there a half hour before Manero. Vic had suggested that they leave the surveillance vehicles

North and South of the airport exit, they didn't want to spook anyone that might be meeting Manero. Monica had arrived at the airport early. She waited patiently for Manero's plane to land. A figure stepped off the plane and headed for a waiting limousine. Monica watched the surveillance vehicles take off behind the limousine and laughed. Manero waited until the cars had left before he stepped off the plane and walked across the tarmac to Monica's plane. He wore a custom made pilot's uniform and carried a flight bag. One minute later another figure dressed in a uniform left Monica's plane and entered Manero's chartered craft. Monica's plane taxied towards the runway and waited its turn to take off. The small chartered aircraft buzzed past their plane and climbed into the evening sky. Shortly afterwards Monica's plane took off. Helen thought it was strange and mentioned to Monica, that it seemed they had a new crewman.

"It's all right, Mother, we're giving him a ride home, he lives in Bern."

"Oh…I thought it was strange, that's all."

"Yes, Mother."

Monica opened a magazine, Helen put on the headset and tuned into a classical music channel. Monica waited until her mother had fallen asleep before joining Manero in the pilot's lounge.

"It's good to see you, Monica. Why are we going to so much trouble?"

"The money is in a Swiss bank account. As heir to this money it will be necessary for me to go there and claim it. I have all the necessary paper work. How do you want to handle it?"

"In the usual manner, we'll make a transfer. What's this about you wanting out? Didn't we treat you well?"

"Let's not get into that. You'll have your money and I'll be rid you, right?"

Manero nodded his head. Monica weighed the gesture. It was meaningless; the bastard was going to kill her.

"We have a deal, right?" Monica said.

"Yes. What about your mother?"

"I convinced her that this trip was for relaxation. We are going to one of the spas, and once she's settled in I'll meet you. Let's plan for noon tomorrow."

Monica wrote down the address of their meeting place, a villa on the edge of town.

"Until tomorrow," she said. "By the way I'm taking five percent in cash."

"Fine, you've earned it." Monica smiled. Manero had no intentions of giving her anything. Not when he could solve his problem with his knife.

"Well that's it until we meet at the villa, unless you have something else on your mind."

"I just wanted to say you were important to us and we didn't want to hurt you."

"What is this we business?"

"There are many things to consider in this business; man does not live by bread alone."

"Bull shit! You're the boss. Don't hand me that crap."

"You're right. I am the boss but there are others. This is a 438 billion dollars a year business and I damn sure don't get it all. What I'm trying to say is it was I who said put you away rather than kill you."

Monica stared at Manero.

"So I guess I should thank you for drugging me and dumping me in a mental institution?"

"You're fucking right. If it hadn't been for me your ass would have been gone," Manero said.

"Thanks."

"That's no way to be. Be straight with me about this money and I'll make sure you get out clean."

"Okay, I won't take the five percent. I'll leave my commission up to you," Monica said.

"That's better. Everything will be fine, until tomorrow then."

Monica returned to the main cabin.

"Would you like a pillow, Ma'am?" The Attendant asked.

"Thank you," Monica said.

The Attendant fluffed the pillow and tucked it under Monica's head.

*       *       *

"Shit! That's not Manero! We've been had," Duke said and pounded on the dashboard.

"Cool it. Let's review the events at the airport. Manero's plane landed and the decoy got out and entered the limousine," Vic said.

"So," Duke said.

"So, isn't it strange that we didn't see anyone else?"

"What do you mean?"

"Manero got off and that was it. No pilot, no flight attendant, nothing. You would think after a flight like that everybody would get off and stretch their legs. Or at least the pilot would check the plane before taking off. Let's go back to the airport and see if anyone noticed any thing strange," Vic said.

"All right, what the hell?" Duke said.

"The flight originated in San Juan so customs wouldn't have to get involved, but everyone has to file a flight plan, right?" Vic said.

At the airport Duke went to the tower, while Vic questioned the ground personnel. The driver of the fuel truck had noticed a pilot leaving the charter plane and entering the Woolford Corporation's jet. Vic joined Duke in the control tower and coordinated their information.

The chartered planed refueled and returned to San Juan, the larger jet registered to the Woolford Corporations departed within minutes of the charter plane, destination was Bern, Switzerland.

"Bingo!" Vic shouted."

"Yeah, our stew is beginning to boil, it seems our Mr. Manero is still chasing the lost money and our little Monica is helping him. Just think Honey had to die because he thought I took the money…" Vic said.

"She didn't die in vain. Her death upset enough people to give us the support we needed to go after these bastards. And don't forget, there's someone else in this pulling the strings."

"Yeah. Do we go to Switzerland?" Vic said.

"No, we'll stay here and wait for our young Miss Woolford."

*     *     *

The Villa was impressive, gate, private road, and seclusion. Manero waited while the Security Guard called Monica for clearance. The Guard thanked Monica and opened the two large gates. Manero thanked the Guard and followed the road leading to the main residence. Monica watched the car from a second floor window. She tucked her PPK into a garter holster, lowered her dress, checked her appearance in the floor length mirror and turned in a complete circle for one last look. She was pleased and knew that she looked good. She left the room and went downstairs to meet Manero. She was halfway down the staircase when Manero entered the house.

"Mr. Manero…so nice to see you."

"You too, Miss Woolford."

"Helga, we don't want to be disturbed."

"Ma'am," Helga said.

"Some place you have here!" Manero said.

"Leased for the summer," Monica said.

"Oh, I see."

"Shall we go into the game room?"

"This is just fine. Do you have my papers?"

"Of course, in the game room."

Manero tensed and looked at Monica.

"What's this, the great Mr. Manero afraid of little ole me?"

"Cut the crap. Go ahead."

Manero followed Monica down a long corridor. At the end of the corridor a flight of stairs led to the basement. The room at the bottom of the stairs was equipped with card tables, a bar, and a billiard table, which sat in the middle of the room.

"How about a drink?"

"Good, I could use one," Manero said.

"Scotch, okay?" Manero nodded yes.

Monica poured two drinks and put them on the bar. Manero finished his drink, after which Monica refilled his glass and made a toast. Manero was too busy looking at Monica's cleavage to see her flip the poison into his glass.

"There's been a problem. We'll have to wait one more day for the money to clear."

"Couldn't you tell me that on the phone?"

"You know you wouldn't have settled for that," Monica said.

Manero smiled and nodded his head again.

"Yeah. I would have blown my cool, you're right," Manero, said. He shook his head as if he was trying to compose himself. Monica watched him clinch his stomach, she had deliberately given him a smaller dose, she wanted him to die slowly.

"Bitch," Manero whispered and tried to lift his hand.

"Well, that's that. It was so uncomfortable with this gun strapped to my leg. Thank you for being so cooperative," Monica said.

Manero held on with every ounce of energy he could muster. He fell forward, arm extended, trying to reach for Monica. Monica pushed a button behind the bar and two men rushed into the room.

"Is the car ready?"

"Yes."

Monica removed an envelope from her purse and handed it to one of the men.

"Thank you for your help. You know what to do with him."

"Yes, It was a pleasure to see you again," the man said.

The ride back into town was pleasant, Monica had evened the score.

\* \* \*

"Mr. Acevedo there's a phone call for you," The Butler said.

"For me?"

"Yes." Juan looked at Lisa, puzzled.

"Why you lookin' at me?" Lisa said.

"Who would call me here, I mean Manero would call me on the cell phone."

"Answer it, man. Don't stand there looking at me," Lisa said.

Juan took the phone from the butler.

"Hello…"

"Mr. Acevedo we need to meet. I'll have someone pick you up. There will be a helicopter at your location in the next five minutes. Make sure you are on it and come alone."

"Who is this?" Juan said.

"Five minutes, Mr. Acevedo." There was a faint click and the phone was dead.

"So," Lisa said.

"A helicopter is coming to pick me up."

"Where?" Lisa asked.

"Here."

"Here?" Lisa asked.

"Yeah, in a couple of minutes. Don't ask me anything else; I don't know anymore than you do about this. But, I can tell you one thing, I'd better go."

"Man, listen to you. You gonna get on some helicopter with somebody you don't even know. Are you crazy?" Lisa said.

"No I'm not fucking crazy. Whoever it is knew that we were here and how to call us, that's good enough for me. Anyway if he's sending a helicopter he has to be connected to something big."

"You talking about the mob, come on..." Lisa said.

A thundering sound of a helicopter approaching Miles' estate grew louder; soon they could see the olive drab vehicle approaching in the distance.

"See what I mean, that's a government copter. I'm not fucking around with those people. You stay here and I'll call you when I can. Call Miles and let him know what's happening, okay?" Juan said.

"Okay. You be careful, Juan."

"You know me. I got my shit with me."

"Good." Juan kissed Lisa and hurried out to the waiting vehicle. Lisa watched the door of the craft slide open and Juan climb aboard. The craft lifted off immediately, with the crewman struggling to close the door.

# Chapter *IX*

---

*T*he room filled with automatic fire and one of the men standing over Manero dropped, and landed on Manero's body. The force of the automatic weapon pushed the other man half way across the room. Manero's face was pale, his eye almost lifeless. He struggled to breathe, but maintained enough energy to point to the glass on the bar.

"Leche, leche…" he whispered.

The gunman hurried to the refrigerator and removed a carton of milk. He sat Manero up and gave him a drink from the carton. Two lines of milk trailed down from Manero's lips as he struggled to swallow. He dropped his head for a moment, raised it and said " Dr.Fjelde…"

The gunman lifted him to his shoulder, automatic weapon in one hand and his arm around Manero's legs balancing him with the other. He made it to the car just ahead of the backup team. He put Manero into the back seat, closed the door, and hurled a grenade at the three men approaching the vehicle. They dropped to the ground, firing in his direction. A loud whump interrupted the gunfire, and then all was silent. The exception was the sound of Manero's car speeding towards the main gate.

*        *        *

"Duke, her plane has entered our airspace," Vic said.

"Good, we'll nail Manero when he steps off the plane," Duke said.

"Damn that Jess, he's shaking the leaves again," Duke said.

"What do you mean?"

"Last night he pushed Fangio around. Fangio pulled a gun on him and Jess shot him."

"Kill him?" Duke said.

"No. That's the fucking problem. Fangio's lawyer filed a six million dollar lawsuit against the City of New York. We wanted Manero and his people to think that we had dropped the investigation, now this."

"What's the problem? We'll have some of our people intervene and process Jess as a traumatized policeman, you know the bit, his partner was killed, bla, bla, blah."

"Think it will work?" Vic said.

"Don't know, but it won't hurt to try it," Duke said.

What are we really up against?"

"Money, you know that...there's so much money out there nobody wants this thing to end. That's why the Chief organized our unit. Why do you think he's getting so much flack up on the hill? They nit-pick at everything they can get their hands on. Fortunately their schemes fall apart, but look at how the country is tied up as a result. They hope the people will get fed up and ask for the President's resignation, and then their man can get in. Ain't gonna happen, but that's their plan."

"Come on...you don't mean the Congress?"

"If they give a street cop a million, what do you think they lay out for real protection?"

"I think we're in trouble," Vic said.

"We don't exist, how can we be in trouble?" Duke said.

"You too, but...?"

"I told you about how they got my family, what I didn't tell you is they thought they got me too."

"I'll be damn."

"Everyone in the special squad has been victimized. For all intent and purpose none of us exist. I hope one day this will be over and we can resume normal lives, but I don't think so. These people multiply just like the coca leaves they push."

"We have thirty people in our squad! All of thought to be dead."

"Hell, they kill judges and politicians in their country?"

"Yeah. They kill judges, and they killed Honey."

"Now you're getting the picture. We have to stop them before we have the same thing happening here in America."

Vic nodded his head. His facial expression told the story, he finally knew who the real enemies were.

*        *        *

The helicopter landed in a field located in the middle of nowhere. A crewman opened the door and told Juan to get out. Juan stepped down from the craft and the engines roared, and the copter took off. Juan ducked his head instinctively and moved toward safety. A four-wheeled vehicle emerged from the bushes and sped towards him. The rear door opened. Juan walked over to the off road vehicle and got in, closed the door and sat back in the seat. Two men sat in the front seat, neither looked at him. They rode about a mile into the Forrest and stopped at a large cabin. The larger man got out of the vehicle, opened the door for Juan, and pointed to the cabin. Juan saw the grease gun rigged to the door, and he didn't hesitate. Juan did a half nod and moved towards the cabin.

A younger man removed a glass from the table next to the man sitting in a recliner facing the television, and pointed to a chair near the recliner. He would have recognized the man anywhere; it was the perfect haircut, and years of news clips that had made his host's hair as identifiable as his face.

"Have a seat, Juan."

"Yes, sir…"

"Bring Mr. Acevedo a drink, Harvey's on the rocks with a touch of lemon," the man said.

Juan shifted in his seat.

"Don't be alarmed, Juan. I like to know everything about the people involved in our business. I have some bad news for you. Manero is in a bad way Monica tried to kill him. His brother is good for only one thing, so that leaves you."

"I don't understand, I mean you're..."

"Yes I am. You see, Juan, this thing is so big we can't stop it, so why not see that it is managed properly."

"But you're..."

"I know, I know."

"You work for the President."

"Many of us work for the President. Now...now.... don't be upset, he doesn't know anything about us. Presidents come and go, but we are a permanent organization. Let's get down to business. Manero told me about your desire to get out of the business, maybe we can change your mind, at least for a while."

"Sir?"

"We need someone with a level head, someone who knows how to live a quiet life, someone like you. You've come a long way from the Bronx."

Juan looked at the distinguished man and wondered how much he knew about him. That was settled in the next breath.

"I like what you did for your mother and the way you took care of the woman caring for your house in San Juan. How would you like to go back there and live?"

Juan smiled.

"I thought so. We have a little cleaning up to do down there, straighten out a few people, then you are free to go home. But first I want you to go to Columbia and take over Manero's job. Build yourself a nice house, nothing ostentatious, comfortable. We will train you on processing and shipping. The financial end of the business will come later."

"What about the cops in San Juan?"

"That's the matter we have to take care of. Can I depend on you?"

"Yes, sir."

"No more talk about getting out?" Juan shook his head, indicating no. "Good. We won't see each other again, but if you really need me call this number and leave a number where you can be reached."

The man stood and extended his hand to Juan. The door behind them opened and the huge man from the vehicle stood near the door.

"He'll take you back," The Man said.

"Yes, Sir."

Juan followed the huge figure of the man out of the house and back into the four-wheeled vehicle.

*         *         *

"Hey, pull over," Jess said.

Fuchs maneuvered the car close to the curb and stopped.

"What is it?" Fuchs said.

"Look who's coming out of the building across the street."

"Who?"

"Remember me telling you about the rich woman involved in the case Vic and I were working on?"

"Yeah," Fuchs said.

"Well, that's her coming out of that fancy apartment building over there. She disappeared for a while. Just vanished off the face of the earth."

"So?"

"She was into the deal up to her neck. If she's back she's involved again. Let's tail her," Jess said.

"Hey, it beats the hell out of what they have us doing."

"Well, well, well Miss Woolford, Let's see where you take us this time."

Monica's taxis turned out of the circular drive way and headed downtown. A car parked at the curb pulled out and followed Monica's taxi. Vic looked at Fuchs, twisting his face into a "how about that expression." Monica's taxi made a left turn onto Mc Dougal Street and drove toward Houston Street. The car following her taxi cut her taxi off and a man got out.

"Move it, Fuchs!"

Fuchs hit the siren and pushed the pedal to the floor. The gunman heard the siren, fired one shot at Monica and ran towards West Broadway. Fuchs bumped across the curb, narrowly missing two people and followed the car; Jess followed the gunman on foot. The gunman fired at Jess and Jess dropped down to one knee and fired two shots. The gunman fell, after which Jess whispered, "Stop police, drop the gun." The first bullet hit the gunman in the chest and penetrated his heart; the second bullet went through his neck. Jess turned around and watched Monica walk calmly across the park towards her house on the other side of the park. A uniformed officer ran out of the park, gun in hand shouting for Jess to drop the gun. Jess put the gun down and flashed his shield.

"What's up, Detective?"

"See the woman in the blue dress?"

"Yes."

"Get her and bring her back here, she was the intended victim."

"Right!"

The Uniformed Officer ran across the park and stopped Monica. He grasped her arm and headed back to the crime scene, Monica in tow. In less than two minutes the area was overwhelmed with police cars. A Uniformed officer moved onlookers back while his Partner marked the crime scene with yellow crime-scene tape. An ambulance arrived and parked on the curb near the gunman's body. The EMT Tech lifted the crime scene tape, passed the stretcher to his partner, and kneeled near the body.

"303,K."

"This is 303,K."

"303 meet your partner at Prince and West Broadway, K."

"Ten, four, Central."

"Ten, four. Central to 427,K."

Jess put the radio back into his pocket. He watched the Internal Affairs Officer check the Perp.

"Looks clean to me."

"Did you order him to drop the gun?"

"Yeah, did it by the book," Jess said.

"As long as you told him to drop the gun, you're clear," The Detective said.

"You IAD boys don't miss a trick," Jess said.

"You do your job and we do ours."

"Yeah. Hey Patrolman! How about a lift to Prince and West Broadway?" Jess Yelled.

"Sure thing, Detective."

"Mind if I tag along?" The IAD Detective said.

"Do I have a choice?" The Internal Affairs Detective laughed.

The ride was short. Fuchs had cut the shooter's car off, forcing it up on the curb.

"Hey, there they are, thanks Officer."

"Anytime. You guys have sure livened things up around here," the Uniformed Officer said and let Jess out of the sector car.

Jess smiled.

"Who's your friend?" Fuchs asked.

"Internal Affairs Division."

"Damn, already. You won't believe what I have, our Perp is Federal."

"Come on…"

"According to him, he's deep cover," Fuchs said

"He'd better be telling the truth," Jess said.

"What's up, Detective?"

"We got a situation here. Our perp is working for the Feds. My partner checked him out and they want us to bring him home," Jess said.

"So?"

"We have to baby sit him and take him home. I don't like it, but orders are orders."

"I've done some checking of my own. You two are suppose to be working missing persons. How did you get involved in a shooting?" The IAD Detective said.

"What the hell are we suppose to do, we see a shooting right in front of us, what are we suppose to do, call a cop?"

"Don't wise ass me? The target is part of a case you were told to lay off."

"Coincidence. We turn the corner and see this fuck with a gun pointing into a taxi."

"All right, that had better be the way it is. Your boss wants to see you at headquarters, forthwith!"

"We love you too, baby."

"Detective, Norman."

"Yes?"

"Your gun..."

Jess took his gun out, popped the clip out, cleared the chamber, and handed it to the IAD Detective.

"If this incident checks out, you'll get your gun back in a couple of days. I hope we don't meet again in a similar incident before you get it back."

"You're all heart, "Jess said.

"Jess you have a call. The Cop on the scene wants to know what you want to do with you-know –who," Fuchs said.

"Tell him to take you-know-who home and stick with her," Jess said.

"What's that all about?" The IAD Detective asked.

"Teenage runaway, nothing important."

"Bull shit! "

"Don't know what you mean, Detective."

"If…" The IAD Detective said.

"If fucking what! I just killed a man. You'd think you guys would give me a little slack! Fuck what you think!"

"The IAD Detective motioned with his head for Fuchs to take Jess away. Fuchs touched Jess on the arm and pulled him towards their car.

"Easy, man. You know these fucks…besides he's got a job to do too."

"I know, but can't it fucking wait?"

"Come on, the Commissioner is waiting to give us hell too.'

"We will see who's going to give who hell, " Jess said.

Fuchs pushed Jess' head down gently to protect him from bumping it as he entered the car.

*           *           *

Bee shook her hand frantically to indicate the man was pissed. She looked at Jess and whispered, "What did you do?" Jess shrugged his shoulders.

"Jess, Jess…I asked you personally to leave this case alone, to forget about it…now as I see it that should be enough. I mean, after all, I am the Commissioner."

Jess parted his lips to speak but the Commissioner waved him off. "Doesn't the word, "No" mean anything to you? I got a call from Washington, a personal call from Washington from the Justice Department wanting to know what are we doing meddling in their case! You, you…."

The Commissioner turned his chair towards the window for a moment as if to compose himself.

"I should put you back in uniform, right now! What the hell were you thinking?"

"We weren't interfering with the case, Commissioner. We were on our way back here and the whole thing blew up in front of us."

"Do you have any Brooklyn Bridge stock?" The Commissioner held his hand in a stop position. "If you do, you have a better chance of selling me that stock than what you are telling me."

"That's just the way it happened, Sir." Fuchs said.

"Screw up number one supporting Screw up number two, huh? Fuchs lowered his head.

"Commissioner, we turned down Mc Dougal Street, and right in front of us in broad daylight a car cuts off a taxi, and a man gets out with a gun in his hand. We thought it was a robbery or a fight about driving. Fuchs hit the siren, the man fired one shot into the taxi, then turned on us."

"I tell you this much. This had better be on the level, or Vic or no Vic you're in deep crap. You understand me!" Jess nodded his head.

"And you, mister wise guy, your word isn't worth doodle when it comes to close calls, do you get me?" Fuchs nodded his head.

"What's the problem?" Jess asked and the Commissioner gave him a dirty look.

"What's wrong? I'll give you a what's wrong! You have Monica Woolford under house arrest and you ask me what's wrong. What the hell does Miss Woolford have to do with this?"

"She was the intended victim, and she's part of the Cartel," Jess said.

"You're out of your fucking mind," The Commissioner said. "Her family is one of the oldest families in this City. I want you to go to her place, apologize, and get the hell out of her place as fast as possible."

"She's part of the case, Sir." Jess said.

"The hell she is! Go up to her place and clean your mess up. Then I want you back here. I have a job for you and Mr.Fuck up here."

"She was the target, Commissioner," Jess said.

The Commissioner hesitated a moment, as if he was considering what Jess had told him, but when he spoke….

"Then give the Feds what you have and drop it. Did you hear me?
"Yes, Sir." Jess said.

"Good. I want the two of you to go to Miami and pick up a prisoner. He's supposed to have some information on a shipment coming in from Columbia. Watch yourselves he has a contract out on him."

"Yes, Sir," Jess and Fuchs said.

"Bee has your paper work. If you two cops listen to me you might get what you are looking for."

"This prisoner, he's part…" Fuchs elbowed Jess.

The Commissioner pointed to the door. Fuchs touched Jess' elbow again and pointed to the outer office.

"Keep your noses clean," the Commissioner said.

"He's telling you right, the Feds will handle it from here on in," Bee said.

"Whatever you say, Bee. But I don't have to like it, we had her."

"Just bring this guy back in one piece and maybe you'll have what you're looking for," Bee said.

"What gives, Bee?"

"I don't know but some kind of special unit has taken over the case. They're Feds, but not regular Feds. I don't know who they are and I can't get a line on them. You know what that means."

"Yeah, The Company," Jess said.

"Maybe, but I don't think so. These people don't seem to exist." Bee said.

"These are my notes. Give them to the glory boys and we'll see you when we get back," Jess said…

"Yeah," Bee said.

*       *       *

"Who are you and where are you taking me?"

"Monica you're quite a lady. I wouldn't have a drink with you, but you're quite a lady," Duke said.

Monica shifted in her seat. The car entered the Holland Tunnel and drove towards New Jersey. Duke instructed the driver to take them to Avitat. The driver nodded his head.

"Look at it this way. You help us and we get you out of this mess once and for all."

"And how can you do that?"

"We're a special force and our job is to find someone. There's some people helping your organization from our side and we want them. We know about your friendship with the Assistant."

"If you know that much, you know he was my only contact. By the way, he didn't have a heart attack, he was healthy as a horse," Monica said.

"Maybe. That was one friend; the dirt bag we are after is larger than your old boss. We want you to contact Juan Acevedo. Give him some cock and bull story of how you were holding up until you thought it was safe to call him. Tell him someone is trying to kill you."

"It was Juan who tried to have me killed," Monica said.

"We don't think so. We think it was our guy who sent the killers after you."

"What makes you think that?"

"We captured one of the people who tried to kill you and he was killed in jail. Killed with a man posted outside his cell. The guard on duty that night disappeared. They must have paid him a bundle, or…"

"Or they killed him," Monica said.

"Right."

"What's in it for me?"

"Work it right and you can walk," Duke said.

Monica nodded her head slowly.

"Good."

"Your boy is in Columbia, but we have a way for you to reach out to him. Tell him you still have the money and want him to deliver it," Duke said.

"Whatever you say, officer."

"Get her out of here. Take her back to the city, then call the hospital and tell that idiot I'm coming to see him."

"What about his lawyer?"

"I think it's time for someone to pick his lawyer up for possession," Duke said.

"You got it," the Agent said.

Duke picked up the phone and called Vic. Vic's filled Duke in on Juan's movements. He had left the lawyer's house in New Jersey covered and was on his way back to the city.

"Good! Meet me at the hospital prison ward and don't worry about Fangio's lawyer, we' re going to turn him, and he'll advise Fangio on what's best for him." Duke said and closed the phone.

*      *      *

"Take a break and leave the key with me."

"Yes, sir."

The Guard handed the key to Duke, he looked at Fangio, smiled and left the room.

"I ain' t saying nothing until my lawyer gets here," Fangio said.

"Oh, just a minute, he asked me to call him when I got here," Duke said.

He removed the cellular phone from his jacket and dialed Miles' number.

"Just a moment."

Duke handed the phone to Fangio. The conversation was short, Fangio listen and at the end of the call said, "shit!"

"Problem?" Duke asked

"I don't get this crap. One of your gun-happy cops shoots me and my lawyer tells me to cooperate with you. I need another lawyer!"

"I'm gonna make this quick. Sooner or later Juan is going to contact you. When he does we want you to let us know," Duke said

"You must be crazy," Fangio said. " I'm firing my lawyer, get the hell out of here!"

At that moment the door of the unit opened and Vic entered the cell.

"Who the hell is this?" Fangio asked.

"The man who's going to stick a knife in that bullet wound of yours if you don't cooperate," Vic said.

"Cool it, Vic," Duke said. Vic moved closer to the Juan's bed and stood too close to him.

"Vic, cool it. I gotta tell you, Fangio. The woman they killed down in Puerto Rico was Vic's wife, but you know that already."

"What woman?"

"You remember San Juan. Juan set up the hit," Duke said.

"I didn't have anything to do with them killing that woman."

"You might as well have pulled the trigger, you helped Juan get away," Duke said

Vic stepped a little closer to Fangio and raised the covers.

"Hey, man, hey! You just tell me what you want and I'll do it! Just tell this guy to get away from me, okay?" Duke motioned with his head for Vic to move away from the bed. Vic stepped back from the bed; at the very last moment he tapped Fangio once on his injury.

"Damn, damn, man! I told you I would help! Why did you do that?"

"That's just a sample of what you're going to get if you don't deliver," Vic said.

"Vic, Vic, cool it. The man is going to help us."

"All right, all right, but remember," Vic said.

"Here's the game plan. When Juan calls you. You call us, or your ass is gone. That means as soon as you hear from him you call us. If he's in town you give us the location of the meet, clear?"

"Yes, sir."

"Good."

Fangio nodded his head. Vic and Duke left the room. On the way out Duke asked the guard to keep a special eye on the prisoners.

"If anyone tries to move him let us know. I don't care if it's the Commander in Chief; Call us."

"Yes, sir."

"Let's get the hell out our here, Vic."

"Right."

*         *         *

The prisoner pickup in Miami was quick. It was as if they wanted no part of the prisoner. It was Jess' idea to take the prisoner to the airport in a taxi. This didn't make the SWAT Team happy, but they settled on a compromise. They would escort them to the airport in unmarked cars. The ride to the airport was uneventful. The Miami Police had arranged a lift to New York on a U.S Marshal's plane. That was a great help, but Jess and Fuchs didn't relax until the plane taxied to the runway and took off.

"So, Phillippe…what do you have for us?" Jess said.

"Who the hell are you guys?" Jess showed Phillippe his identification.

"We're the people you're suppose to meet," Jess said.

"Let's see your identification again," Phillippe said.

"What?" Jess said and handed Phillippe his shield case.

"Okay, you're who you're supposed to be," Phillippe said

"If we weren't you'd be dead," Fuchs said. Jess smiled

"Hadn't thought of that," Phillippe said.

"So what do you have for us?" Jess asked.

"There's a shipment coming in. It's the biggest shipment ever sent out of Columbia. The feeling is things are getting too hot so they came up with this new idea. The Cartel gathered up several crops, crops from all over the place, even from some of their competition. They plan to lay off for a while after the shipment clears, you know, let things cool off."

"And just how are they going to move this large shipment, we have the whole area covered," Jess said.

"That's the beauty of the plan...your people are bringing it over."

"What the hell are you talking about?"

"One of your navy's ships is bringing it over," Phillippe said and looked at Jess and Fuchs with a smart-ass expression on his face.

"Bull shit!"

"Its already at sea."

"No way," Jess said.

"There's a way, and they found it."

"What the hell are you talking about? Impossible...the whole damn crew would have to be involved," Fuchs said.

"That's the beauty of the plan. The ship brought supplies over to help the hurricane victims, and while it was there they loaded the shipment onto the trucks returning to the ship. Somewhere near Home Port the ship will loose its propellers. A small device planted in a strategic spot will cause the damage. The ship will have to be towed in for repairs, and that's when they will recover the stuff."

"The only thing wrong with that plan is the trucks will remain on the ship," Jess said.

"That works for me," Phillippe said.

"Come on..." Fuchs said.

"I don't believe you," Jess said.

"Believe what you want, I've given you what I promised," Phillippe said.

"You've given us nothing. What's the name of the ship?" Jess said.

"I'll give you the number and tell you where the crap will hit the fan, and that's all."

"Here, write it down and we'll check," Jess said.

"I'd be careful where you check if I were you. There are some powerful people involved is this operation."

"Who for instance?" Fuchs asked.

"All I heard is that we were protected, and they wouldn't be stopped," Phillippe said.

"Why are you being so good to us?" Jess said.

"Your government pays well, and they promised me a new identity." Jess looked at Fuchs puzzled. Fuchs nodded his head a couple of times.

"You thinking what I'm thinking," Jess said.

"Yeah," Fuchs said.

"We're in trouble, Phillippe, but I think we have a away out. Relax and I'll be right back," Jess said. Jess went forward towards the cockpit. One of the Marshals stopped him near the cockpit door.

"Sorry, Sir, no one is permitted in the cockpit area."

"Do you want to live to see tomorrow?"

"Pardon, Sir?" The Marshall said and placed his hand on his gun."

"Relax, I'm not going to cause a problem. Listen carefully. We are all going to die unless you let me speak to the pilot," Jess said.

"What do you mean, what's going on?" the Marshall said.

"The Prisoner we brought on board is a member of a Colombian Drug Cartel. He just gave us some information that is so dangerous I'm sure this plane is going to crash before we get to New York. I don't know how it is going to happen, but it will happen…If I don't speak to the pilot right now."

The Marshall studied Jess for a moment.

"You can't go in, but I will ask him to come out here."

"Good enough."

The Marshall left Jess standing at the partition and used the phone to contact the pilot. The cockpit door opened and the Marshal went inside. A few moments later he returned with the pilot.

"I'm Captain Carson, what the hell is going on?" It took ten minutes for Jess to convince the Captain, but he promised to do as Jess asked. He also said that would explain the instructions they had just received. They were instructed to fly east of New York and hold for further instructions. If Jess' plan worked they would cripple any plans for their destruction. The Captain returned to the cockpit and Jess returned to their seats.

"Here, I got something for you," Jess said and handed Phillippe army issued coveralls and a cap.

"Put these on now. In a few moments the pilot is going to declare and emergency and we are going to land in Philadelphia. I want you to get off the plane and walk a head of us carrying this case. Once inside the building wait for us, clear?"

"Yes," Phillippe said.

*        *        *

"May day! May day! Special 3925 May day! Engine out, remaining engine showing pressure problems. Request immediate permission to land Philly International."

"Copy, SPECIAL 3925. Come right to 285, maintain a flight level of 2500 feet to final. Do you need assistance otherwise?"

"Roger, Philly control, emergency equipment please. We do not know the extent of our problem, over."

"Roger SPECIAL 3925, you are thirty—five miles east of glide path begin your descent into runway 22, land on visual, over."

"Roger control, thank you."

The passengers and crew were instructed to prepare for an emergency landing. Phillippe returned to his seat dressed in the army clothing. He adjusted his cap and strapped himself into his seat.

# Chapter *X*

*J*ames Latten picked up his phone, listen for a few moments and replaced the phone on its cradle. He looked at his assistant and sighed.

"We have a problem," he said.

"Sir?"

"Our plane has diverted to Philadelphia. You know the saying; best laid plans, and all that crap. Get someone in Philly to take care of the matter," Latten said.

"How much time do we have?"

"None."

"Yes, sir. Will the plane?"

"You have forty-five minutes. Have one of our people in Philadelphia deactivate the instrument and remove it. By the way if the opportunity presents itself, have them take care of the other matter."

"Yes, Sir."

Cronin rushed out of the office. Latten picked up the phone and made a call.

*          *          *

"Looks like we're going to make it," Fuchs said.

"Yeah. We'll know when we get clear of this plane if we made it or not."

"What the hell is going on, Jess?"

"We're caught in the middle of some heavy shit. No wonder the Commissioner told us to watch out, he knew."

"Knew what?"

"What we we're up against."

"Then why the hell didn't he tell us?" Fuchs said.

"Your guess is as good as mine."

The landing was hard, so hard the damn plane rocked. The Pilot taxied the plane to the end of the runway and parked near the emergency vehicles. The doors of the plane opened and the Marshals escorted their prisoners to a waiting van. Phillippe did exactly as he was told. He pulled the cap down a little to obstruct his face and walked towards the vehicles parked on the runway.

Two men dressed as Military Police stopped Phillippe and put him in their car. Jess approached the vehicle and was instructed to keep his distance. Jess reached for his identification and the soldier drew his gun and told Jess to get down on the ground. The Lead Marshall held his shield high and approached the soldiers. The taller of the two men fired at the Marshall and the Marshall dropped to the ground. Jess and Fuchs dropped to the ground and fired at the larger of the two men. The first shots lodged in the soldier's bulletproof vest, but Jess' last shot hit the soldier between the eyes and he went down. The driver of the MP's car sped off and raced across the field. He drove across an active runway and the car was struck by the landing gear of a 747. The plane landed uninterrupted, unaware of striking the vehicle and leaving a rolling flaming mass of metal in its wake.

The emergency vehicles charged in the direction of the flaming vehicle. The first one on the scene spayed the car with foam, but it was too late to save the men inside. During the confusion a neatly dressed technician boarded the plane, found the explosive device, removed it, and blended into the crowd at the scene. Jess and Fuchs were checked at the scene by the EMS crew and released, after which, they went to the Port

Authority Police Station to complete the paper work and called the Commissioner in New York.

Cronin arrived twenty-five minutes after the incident. He flashed his identification and questioned the cops at the scene. Satisfied that at least part of the problem had been solved he went to the Port Authority Police Station, flashed his identification again and stood in the rear of the room observing Jess and Fuchs. Later Cronin would get a copy of the phone call Jess made to the Commissioner. The lack of activity was enough for Cronin to conclude that Phillippe hadn't given them enough information to help them; otherwise they would be on their way to Washington.

Cronin told the Officer at the desk that he was not to tell anyone that he had been there; it was a matter of National Security. The Desk Officer told him that he would cooperate, but as soon as Cronin left he passed the news on to his superior who shared the information with Jess and Fuchs.

"We must be getting close if those boys are coming out into the open," Fuchs said.

"You'd better believe it. But to hell with that crowd, they would kill their own mothers," The Lieutenant said.

"Hey, thanks a lot for your help, and for the information. Say, is there anyway we can get a lift back to New York," Jess said.

"You bet! Say you New York guys aren't the only guys with special equipment. I'll have our copter take you wherever you want to go."

"Thanks, Lieutenant," Jess said.

"You're welcome," the Lieutenant said.

"By the way, did you get that agent's name?"

"No. All I saw was the magic initials."

"Well, thanks again."

Fuchs extended his hand to the Lieutenant. A macho looking kid entered the room and asked if there was anyone in the room looking for a lift? Jess looked at Fuchs and shook his head in disbelief.

"Don't worry, he's as good as he is cocky," the Lieutenant said.

Jess shook hands with the Lieutenant and the Desk Officer, picked up his briefcase and followed the swaggering pilot out to the helicopter.

*          *          *

"Baby, I've got to go to New York to take care of some business. I want you to stay here, okay?"

"Okay with me, but Juan you be careful, right?" Lisa said.

"It's all right. But from now on don't ask me anything about the business. Do what I ask and maybe you can get out of this shit. I'm stuck, but I think they will let you go."

"Hey, Baby, it don't mean nothing if we're not together, okay?"

"That's cool. I like that and I promise we're going to get out of this crap and enjoy some of this money." Juan kissed Lisa and picked up his clothing bag. He threw the strap across his shoulder and sighed. Lisa stood, threw her arms around him and kissed him again. When she released Juan he turned and walked out the door. He didn't want to look back, because this time they would be separated for a long time. Juan drove to the airport, cleared customs and waited for his lift out to his private plane. The airport van stopped near the door and the driver got out to open the door.

"Mr. Acevedo?"

"Yes."

"This way, sir. The Gulf stream five, right?"

"Right," Juan said.

The Flight Attendant saw the van approaching and hurried to the door to greet her boss. The Driver carried Juan's bag. He followed Juan up the steps and stopped when the Attendant took the bag from him and gave him a tip.

"Thank you."

The sleek looking Flight Attendants smiled and move inside the craft. The Pilot closed the door and secured the latch. He walked past Juan and tipped his cap.

"Good to see you, Mr. Acevedo."

"Thank you, Captain. How's the weather for our trip?"

"Clear all the way to New York. You have a choice of Newark or Tetaboro."

"It will be mid-day when we arrive, so let's take Newark."

"Yes, sir."

The Pilot tipped his cap again and returned to the cockpit. Moments later the sound of the engines whining filled the cabin. A chime sounded, followed by the plane moving forward to the line of aircraft waiting to take off.

*　　　　　　*　　　　　　*

Bee announced Jess and Fuchs after which the two detectives went into the Commissioner's office. The Commissioner stood at the window looking into the distance. He didn't move until Fuchs cleared his throat. The Commissioner took a deep breath and turned to face Jess and Fuchs.

"Have a seat, gentlemen."

The two detectives looked at each other and took seats in front of the Commissioner's desk.

"I'm glad you made it, how did you know?" the Commissioner asked.

"Phillippe told us," Jess said.

"Told you what?" the commissioner asked.

"He didn't tell us anything, it was what he said. He said that he was told that they were protected and that nobody could touch them. That meant only one thing to me," Jess said.

"What?" The Commissioner said.

"It meant that we were as good as dead. The lift on the marshal's plane confirmed it for me. Who the hell would care about a plane full of Federal prisoners crashing?"

"Good work. All right, to hell with security. There were a couple of people from some kind of high priority unit here in my office. After they left I couldn't find out anything about them. They were the same people who were at the hospital with your Perp."

Jess and Fuchs looked at each other.

"Well, they wanted to know where you and your partner were, and when I told them, they said that was good, at least you would be safe there. They left and I haven't heard anymore from them, except I wasn't supposed to tell you about them," the Commissioner said.

"If this is going where I think it's going, none of us are safe," Jess said.

"Exactly," the Commissioner said.

*          *          *

Fangio replaced the phone, sighed, picked up the receiver and called Duke at the special number Duke gave him. He replaced the phone a second time and used the intercom to order a car to Avitat to pick up Juan. Duke smiled and started to put the cellular phone into his pocket when it rang again, this time it was Monica giving Duke the location of their meeting.

"You gotta admit it, he's bold. Guess where they are meeting?" Duke said. Vic shrugged his shoulders.

"El Porte Restaurant, midtown Manhattan." Duke said.

"Or it is a quick way to get out of town," Vic said.

"Yeah. We don't have much time. Do you know this restaurant? " Duke said.

"Yeah. It's a small place, seats thirty people. The UN crowd hangs out there."

"Damn! "

"What's the problem?"

"Every fucking country in the UN probably has a wire in the place," Duke said.

"No way, they'd blow the fuses," Vic said.

Duke laughed and shook his head; it was the first time Vic had showed any signs of recovering.

"Have any ideas?" Duke asked

"They have a small bar in the place, why don't we stop by and have a drink?" Vic said.

"No good, Monica would give us away. With these guys one strange glance from her could blow the whole deal"

"Right. We can't go in and we can't sit on top of the place. Why don't we use Monica?" Vic said.

"Right, we'd better hurry."

Duke opened his desk draw and removed a tiny transmitting unit. He gave Vic the listening devices and cupped the small transmitter-mike in its small case. After checking the device he called Monica and asked her to meet them at the bookstore near her house. They would wire Monica and park around the corner until the meeting was over.

★          ★          ★

"Good afternoon, Mr. Acevedo, good to see you again."

"Lupe, good to see you. There will be two of us, you know what I like, and my guess will like it too."

"Very good, Sir," Lupe said.

Monica arrived and went directly to Juan's table. He stood and she gave him a show business kiss.

"Monica, how are you?"

"I don't know, suppose you tell me."

"What do you mean?"

"That was some job you did on Manero. He's still in a coma, and someone tried to kill me. Are we getting ambitious?"

"It's not necessary, I have everything I need. That is, that which is mine," Monica said.

Monica handed Juan a computer disk and took her seat.

"Then, this should make everything right. I tried to give this information to Manero, but he became ill before I could give it to him."

"Come on…let's be adults here. Didn't you try to whack Manero?"

"No, why should I?"

"Because of the hospital thing, you know, him putting you away like that?"

"That's no reason to kill him. I was going to take twenty percent of the money. That would have been enough revenge for me."

"Okay, I'll buy that. If the money is here, we can pick it up where we left off, and all is forgiven."

"Good," Monica said.

"Yes, let's enjoy our lunch," Juan said.

*       *       *

Vic gave Duke the high sign, and sat back in his seat. The tape was running and Monica's conversation with Juan had turned to small talk. Near the end of the conversation Juan told Monica that he had someone that wanted to meet her. The food arrived and Juan changed the conversation.

"Damn, just when he was about to open up," Duke said.

"Relax, Duke. We have this bastard," Vic said.

*       *       *

"Welcome back," Latten said.

"Sir."

"Well how did it go?"

"It cost us two men but we got our mark. And it appears that he hadn't given them anything of substance. I have a copy of his phone call to his boss."

"Let's hear it." Cronin put the small recorder on the desk and pressed play.

"Jess here."

"Where are you?"

"Philadelphia," Jess said.

"Philadelphia?"

"Yeah. The plane we were traveling on had engine problems, damn thing almost crashed."

"Are you guys all right?"

"We lost the prisoner?"

"What! How?"

"There's more to this thing than you told us, Commissioner. Two guys dress like MPs grabbed Phillippe and tried to kill us."

"I don't believe this," the Commissioner said.

"Well, he told us one thing. He said that we didn't know what we were up against. He was about to open up when the plane started acting up. I didn't know what to expect, so I had him dress in coverall and still they got him. Commissioner, they knew we were coming."

"How do you figure that?"

"We were supposed to land in New York. We made an emergency landing in Philly and they were there waiting for us."

"Okay, let's drops this now and you two get back here as fast as you can," the Commissioner said.

"Yes, Sir."

Two clicks and the tape ended.

"What do you make of that?" Latten asked

"They don't know anything," Cronin said.

Latten nodded his head.

"Just the same we'd better keep and eye on them. At least until we have completed our last project."

"Who do you want to handle it?"

"You," Latten said.

"Yes, Sir," Cronin said.

"I still want you to meet Monica, maybe we can kill two birds with one stone, so to speak." Director Latten said. Cronin nodded his head.

*      *      *

"How's your veal?" Juan asked.

"Its very special. I've never had such delicious veal."

"Its cooked in the true Spanish tradition, the wine is also Spanish," Juan said

"I can't believe that you are the same guy I used to meet on Crotona Avenue," Monica said.

"Money makes the difference. If we had money my father would have never left my mother. If we had money when I was growing up I would have gone to a good school..." Monica interrupted.

"But you did go to school..." Juan waved her off.

"After making a fortune in drugs," Juan said.

"Hey, at least you made it."

"That's the trouble with you rich people...."

"Hey don't knock us, who has a private jet parked at Newark?"

"How did you know about that?" Juan said.

"That's the only way to travel," Monica said, "Besides I have connections too."

"Like who?"

"Let's just say he works where my family keeps a plane, and you're parked next to it," Monica said.

"Go figure," Juan said.

"You said someone wanted to meet me."

"I did, but I'm going to wait until we get the money. This way the meeting will be pleasant."

"Good," Monica said.

"Can I drop you off anywhere?"

"How about Bloomingdale's?"

"That works," Juan said and signaled for the check. Lupe brought the check personally. Juan looked at it and dropped two one hundred dollar bills on the table.

"Thank you, Mr. Acevedo! Always a pleasure to serve you!" Lupe said, and held Monica's chair.

Vic looked at Duke and Duke started the car.

"We'd better get going," Vic said.

"What's the hurry, we know where they're going."

"Finally," Vic said.

"Finally what?"

"Finally we've hit on something you don't know anything about. Never take things for granite. Suppose Juan spotted the wire, suppose he plans to kill her and dump her body later?"

"How the hell is he going to do that in broad daylight?" Duke asked.

"In a dark limousine."

Duke gunned the car forward. They reached the corner just as the limousine turn west on Thirty-seventh Street. Duke jumped the light and made it to the corner just in time to see the limo turn right and head uptown on Third Avenue. He tweaked the siren two times and squeezed through the traffic in the block and made it to the corner. He jumped the light at the corner, cut off a panel truck, zig-zagged through the uptown traffic until he caught up with Fangio's limousine. They dropped back two cars and clued in on the limo's license plate, "FANGIO 53."

"Looks like they're going where she asked them to take her," Duke said.

"We'll know when she gets out of the car," Vic said.

"She'll get out," Duke said.

"We'll see," Vic said.

The limo stopped at the corner of Third Avenue and Sixtieth Street. The chauffeur got out of the limo and opened the door for Monica. Monica got out of the car, turned, and said something to Juan. A hand extended out of the car, Monica shook the hand, turned and went into the store.

"I told you she was going to get out," Duke said.

"This time," Vic said.

He waited for the limo to drive off before making his move. Vic got out of the car and asked Duke to stick with the limo. He went into the store and headed for the cheese bar. Monica was busy tasting a sample of cheese when Vic arrived.

"That looks good," Vic said.

The girl behind the counter offered Vic a sample.

"Thank you," Vic said.

"Vermont's best," Monica said.

"I prefer New York's cheeses," Vic said.

"How can you tell the difference?" Monica asked.

"I can't," Vic said.

"May I have a half pound, please?"

"Yes, Miss." The young girl adjusted the slicer, put the cheese on the block and measured a small piece.

"Say...would you like to have a drink?" Vic said.

"Why not?" Monica said.

The young girl weighed the cheese and said, "Its a little over."

"Fine, I'll take it," Monica said.

Vic continued his conversation with Monica until the cheese was wrapped.

"Can I help you, sir?"

"No thanks, I have what I need."

The young girl blushed, Monica took Vic' arm and left the counter with him.

"We'll take a taxi back to your place," Vic said and opened the taxi door.

"Where you going, Mack?" The taxi driver asked.

Monica ignored the driver and entered the taxi.

"Well, this is my last call. My garage is in Brooklyn, like, I hope you're not going uptown," the driver said.

"Consider this your lucky day," Vic said.

Monica laughed.

"Hey I don't want no trouble," the driver said.

"Move it!" Vic said.

"I guess he don't like black guys," Monica said.

"You think that's it? I mean, I would hate to think that was it," Vic said.

"Where are we going?" the driver asked.

"Just drive..." Vic whispered.

"Honey, did you have to shoot that guy?"

"He shouldn't have pissed me off."

"I know, but couldn't you just hit him or something?"

"Some of these guys you can't reason with, especially the ones that don't like black guys," Vic said.

Monica and Vic watched the driver's eyes in his rear view mirror. He did everything he could to avoid their eyes, but they wouldn't let him off the hook.

"Say, driver!" Vic said.

"Yes, sir..."

"You see, honey. I told you he was polite. The guy just wants to get home," Monica said.

"Well, if you think he's all right..." Vic said.

"Yeah. Hey, Michael, that's your name on that picture, right?"

"Yes, Miss."

"Michael, drop us off at Fifth Avenue and Eighth Street."

"Yes, Miss."

"Wait a minute. He was listening to us."

"Michael. Michael!"

Monica lowered her head; she couldn't look at the driver. She wanted to laugh, but that would have given them away.

"He wasn't listening to us, honey," Monica said.

The taxi picked up speed, cut a truck off, and pulled over to the curb at Eighth Street.

"Say, Michael. You forgot to drop your flag."

"Forget about it, it's on me," the Driver said.

Vic dropped a ten spot on the seat. The driver scuffled for some change, when he looked up Monica and Vic were nowhere to be found. The driver took a deep breath, sped away from the curb, and headed downtown.

# Chapter XI

*C*ronin stopped at the desk and presented his identification. The Correction Officer asked Cronin to check his weapon, after which, he took the pistol and locked it in a cabinet. He gave Cronin a visitor's badge and pointed toward the prison ward. Cronin presented his identification again and was admitted. At Fangio's cell the Officer on duty opened the cell and admitted Cronin. Cronin thanked the Officer and asked him to leave him alone with Fangio. The Officer locked the door and moved away from the cell.

"I'm a friend. I can get you out of here, but there is something you must do for us," Cronin said.

"How the hell are you going to get me out of here?"

"That's my business," Cronin said.

"Who needs you, my lawyer said he can get me off, I didn't know the guy was a cop."

"You know they're not going to let you off the hook, not those two, they're a nuisance. We want you to help us get rid of them."

"Fuck you, I ain't gonna kill no cops! Fuck you!"

"Shhh. You won't have to kill them. All you have to do is conduct business as usual and they'll come after you. That's when we'll take over," Cronin said.

"We and just who the hell are we, and how did you get in here? Fuck you, this is some kind of trick."

"I'm a friend of Juan," Cronin said and touched his lips with one finger." He waited for the idea to set in before he spoke again. Fangio's suddenly appeared to be listening.

"We're on the same team. Those two plan to use you and if you don't continue helping them they're going to take your business from you. At least with us you'll keep all your money, and you can have someone else run the business for you. Juan told me you didn't want to lose you business, right?"

"Nobody is going to take my business, shit!" Fangio said.

Cronin smiled.

"Here's the plan. I take you out of here and they come after you. All we want you to do is let us know what they want you to do and we'll take care of the rest," Cronin said.

"When can I get out."

"Now, pack your things. Guard!"

The Corrections Officer returned to the cell.

"Officer, this prisoner is leaving with me," Cronin said.

"I have strict instructions not to let him leave with anyone but the arresting officers."

"Get your supervisor over here."

"Yes, Sir."

"The Officer left the cell and went to the front desk. At the desk he called Vic before he asked his supervisor to go to the cell with him.

*       *       *

"We've got to get the hell out of here, now!"

"What's going on?" Duke asked.

"The Company just sprung Fangio."

"Bull shit!"

"No, that was the guy from the prison ward, he's gone. Now this thing is beginning to make sense," Vic said.

"What?" Duke said.

"The thing at the airport…we thought it was the bad guys, Duke we're in trouble," Vic said.

The ride to the hospital took less than twenty minutes. The visit there was short. The Supervisor of the shift had called the prison's commissioner before releasing the prisoner. He said that he was surprised when the Commissioner approved the release. Vic thanked the Supervisor and asked if he could borrow the Corrections Officer for a few minutes. Vic had an idea. He would take Officer Bland to the Security Office and see if he could identify the Agent that sprung Fangio.

The wall of the Video Surveillance room looked like a newsroom. Vic flashed his identification and asked for a review of the various entrances during the time of Fangio's liberator arrived. Their adversary was good. They didn't get anything from the tapes. They were leaving when on of the Special Officers suggested that they review the outside cameras. It worked like a charm, the Agent stood out like a sore thumb. The one thing the Company guys were famous for was their attire; their man favored Paul Stuart.

"I've seen that guy somewhere before," Vic said.

Duke watched the man get into the limousine, there was no question about him being the right man, Washington is full of his type.

"I don't know where you've seen him before, but this guy is top shelf all the way. We're getting close, Vic."

"Yeah. Thanks, Officer you were a big help. Now forget you ever saw us, you don't want to play around with these guys."

"Yes, Sir," The Special Officer said.

Vic and Duke returned to their car. A helicopter roared overhead, heading for the heliport near the hospital.

"You said you've seen that suit before, where?"

"That's it! The copter, I mean, that's where I saw him before. He was in the police station in Philly. I thought he was a boss, you know, the way he's dressed," Vic said.

"Are you sure?"

"How could I miss? It was his camel hair coat that made me notice him. That's the guy all right," Vic said.

"We'd better report this to Dad," Duke said.

"What are we going to do about Fangio?" Vic said.

"I think our friend just lost his business."

*     *     *

"I didn't believe you…man it's nice to be back home again."

"We take care of our own. Get yourself together, then I want you to call those two pricks and ask for a meeting."

"They won't go for that," Fangio said.

"They will if you tell them you can give them Juan for a price," Cronin said.

"That might work," Fangio said.

"Good let's get back to business at hand. I want one of your cars to take me to see Miss Woolford."

"Right."

*     *     *

Monica hung up and cursed. She picked up the phone again and called Jess. Jess asked her to meet him at Tony Roma's on Sixth Avenue. He hung up and asked for a sector car to shadow her to the restaurant, and grabbed his jacket.

"Fuchs we have a hot one!"

"Right," Fuchs said.

The Lieutenant gave Fuchs a questioning gesture and Fuchs shrugged his shoulder.

"Detective! Where the hell are you going, did you finish those reports?"

"Got'em right here. Gotta go, Sir, there's a young lady we know in trouble."

"You'll never learn," The Lieutenant said.

Jess threw the reports on the Lieutenant's desk and rushed out of the squad room, Fuchs right behind him.

"Screw you!" The Lieutenant shouted.

Jess took the wheel and started the car. Fuchs closed the door a moment before Jess backed the car out of the space burning rubber. The ride downtown to the restaurant took less than ten minutes. Jess parked on the bus stop and hurried into the restaurant. Monica was sitting in the back room in a corner.

"The lady is good," Jess said.

"Yeah, I would hate to think of anyone trying to rush her. I bet she has a weapon pointing at us," Fuchs said.

"No bet," Jess said.

Monica took a deep breath and closed her purse, her purse slipped off her lap onto the seat, the weight of the 9mm pistol gave her purse life as it pulled the purse across her lap.

"I'm glad you could make it. I just received a call from a man named Hank. He said it was urgent that we meet as soon as possible. They plan to kill me, " Monica said.

"How do you know that?" Jess asked.

"I gave them everything I had for them, what else could it be?"

"Maybe they want to use you again," Fuchs said.

"How?"

"You know who your father was dealing with. They probably want you to be the middleman, pardon me, middle person,"

"This is not time for joking, they're going to kill me," Monica said.

"I don't think so, they need you."

"But how can I help them?"

"Of course…your father kept records. He probably has the whole set up in his computer," Jess said.

Monica studied the idea for a moment.

"Yes, yes. That's it. He kept everything, that's what got him killed," Monica said.

"What do you mean?" Fuchs asked.

"Drop it," Jess said.

Monica froze and looked at Jess strangely.

"Is there something wrong?" Jess asked.

"No." Monica said, struggling with Jess' revelation.

*       *       *

The plans for the meeting with Hank Cronin proceeded, Monica nodding her head here and there, but her focus was elsewhere. The Courier hadn't lied and he had died for nothing. The meeting was set for a restaurant on City Island. Jess had picked the place because there was only one way in and one way out. A harbor patrol boat would be parked in the water near the meeting place, and extra coverage would be stationed near the bridge. It was set; their meeting was over, Fuchs and Jess escorted Monica back to her apartment.

At the apartment Monica fixed a stiff drink and put some soothing music on. It was hard to believe that her mother had killed her father, harder to believe that Vic Morgan and Jess Norman had squashed the killing. The Courier had seen the shooting and kept the secret until he met Monica. It wasn't enough to accept Monica's generous offer of money he wanted more. Monica had agreed and met him in a sleazy motel. The filthy little man stood there in front of her directing her to get on her knees and crawl to him. He hadn't bothered to notice the bulge in Monica's gown. He closed his eyes when she touched him. The cold touch of the silencer puzzled him, after which he shuddered. A wicked hiss from the pistol was followed by horrific pain. Pain so severe that he felt noting for a moment, then, he opened his mouth to scream and swallowed the barrel of the gun. Two more hisses and his body lay on the bed, his eyes staring at the ceiling.

Monica dressed, collected the bottle of Scotch and the glasses and dropped them into her overnight bag. She removed the Courier's keys from the table. Turned out the lights opened the door and looked around before getting into the little man's rented car and driving off…. The sound of a soulful trumpet interrupted Monica's thoughts.

"Mother, who would believe it…" she whispered.

# Chapter *XII*

"Y ou think you guys would pick a better restaurant," he said.

"Give us a raise and we'll do better," Duke said.

"How are you, Vic, Like working this side of the street?"

"It's different, Sir."

"Yes. What do you have for me?"

"It appears that we've bumped into another Company Operation," Duke said.

"I see."

"The prisoner was liberated."

"Do the two cops have any idea about who?"

"Knowing Jess, he's bound to put it together," Vic said.

"Then we'd better make sure they are protected," Dad said.

"We'll make it a priority," Duke said

"In the meantime I will start working the problem from my end. I think what we have here is an over active imagination," Dad said.

"What do you want us to do?" Duke asked.

"One of you take care of Miss Woolford, and the other the two cops."

"Yes, Sir."

Vic watched Dad walk calmly out of the diner and hail a taxi. Vic looked at Duke and shook his head.

"Who would believe this guy is who he is? Vic said.

"That's the point, isn't it?" Duke said.

"You guys are too much for me."

"Look you cops are just as bad as we are," Duke said.

"If we had the kind of budget you guys have."

"What you guys, you're one of us now," Duke said.

"Yeah. Well it's baby sitting time," Vic said.

"Vic, these guys don't miss…no resurrection this time, be careful."

"Gotcha," Vic said.

*        *        *

The weather was beautiful, on the cool side, just right for the quaint little piece of land just off the mainland Bronx. The little village looked nothing like the massive land mass just over the little bridge that separated it from the rest of the city. The restaurant had valet parking, one way in, and one way out. Monica chose one of Fangio's Town Cars for the trip, Jess had suggested using the car as an act of faith, and it worked.

Monica didn't know whom to expect at the meeting, but as soon as he entered, she recognized the person she was to meet. She had seen him on television, not as a principal, but the quiet man standing in the background while his boss answered question at news conferences. The rest was easy, Hank Cronin, hatchet man for James Latten, Director of the "DTF," Drug Task Force.

"Miss Woolford, I'm Hank Cronin."

"Mr. Cronin…" Monica said.

"I hear the lobster is great here?"

"It is," Monica said.

"Good."

The Waiter arrived and announced the specials of the day. Hank waited patiently until the Waiter was finished and ordered two large lobsters and a bottle or Chardonnay.

"Shall we deal with the business at hand, or have dinner first?"

"Business first, my Father always said."

"Yes, well…we know that you helped your father, from time to time."
Monica nodded her head.

"It is our feeling that you might have knowledge of his work and may want to continue helping us."

"I don't know too much. As you know my function was mostly as a courier," Monica said.

"Hmmm. Do you have access to your father's records?"

"I hadn't thought of that. That's a possibility," Monica said.

"Good. Why don't you check and get back to me?"

"Where?"

"Oh…" Hank said.

He fumbled in his jacket pocket for a pen, and then wrote his cellular phone number on a match book.

"Call me here when you get the information we need, please."

"Fine," Monica said.

"Perfect timing, our wine is here."

The Waiter poured the wine: waited for Cronin's approval, filled the glasses, after which he moved on to the next dinner guest.

"There's one thing about this I don't understand," Monica said.

"That is?"

"You're one of the good guys, why?"

"I won't give you the business about it being the security of the nation being at stake, but it is."

"Sure…"

"Don't be a wise ass. If we don't have some control of this business they will take over, just as they have in their country. You wouldn't want that to happen, would you?"

Monica pretends to mull over the idea.

"I…. guess…not, but?"

"Monica there is so much money involved in this business. Imagine these people and the control they could muster, if we weren't involved. As it is we're having trouble keeping things under control."

"So your part in this is legitimate?"

"Not for the record, but yes."

"And the President?"

"Presidents come and go, we have the duty of keeping the nation safe," Cronin said.

"I see."

Cronin smiled he was pleased.

"Father tried to tell me about the operation, but I didn't want to believe him. There were so many things we had to do that were wrong," Monica said.

"We are living in a very complex world today, Monica. Regrettably there are many unpleasant things that occur during the process."

"What about Juan?"

"You delivered the money, that's good enough for me. And what's good enough for me is good enough for the rest of them. From now on you will work closer with me."

Monica took a deep breath and sighed.

"That's it, relax, and welcome home," Cronin said.

The waiter returned, refilled their glasses, and told them that their dinner would be out shortly.

*      *      *

"Well things appear to be going smooth," Jess said.

"So far," Fuchs said.

Vic and Duke watched from their spot in the boat yard across the street. Duke handed Vic a scraping tool and kneeled down to work on the hull of the small boat above him. They played the cat and mouse game until Monica left the restaurant. Jess and Fuchs acknowledged the call from the Officer in the restaurant, and moved out a little before Monica and Cronin left the restaurant. Vic and Duke remained behind. Vic would stick with Monica. Duke alerted their backup that Monica was on the move. That was the backup teams clue to watch for Jess and Fuchs.

Jess parked near the old Department of Sanitation Dumpsite and waited for Cronin's car. Monica's car passed first, followed by Cronin's car. Jess and Fuchs fell in behind Cronin's car at a respectable distance and followed him onto the New England Thruway and exited onto the Bruckner Expressway Cronin's car in sight. Suddenly a large truck cut them off. Fuchs slammed on the brakes and swerved to the left to avoid the large vehicle. An oncoming car clipped his left front fender and spun their car around. It was over in seconds, but the motion inside the car was like a slow motion movie.

"What the hell happened?" Fuchs asked.

"I don't know. Are you all right?" Jess said.

"I guess so. Let's get the hell out of this car!"

Traffic on the expressway had stopped behind them. The exception was the one lane open on their left where rubber necking drivers moved slowly past the wreck scene. In the distance the sound of sirens screamed in the background. The front end of their car was totaled, the left front wheel bent under the car. The car that hit them rested on the concrete barrier that separated the expressway, the truck that cut them off was nowhere in sight.

"Fuchs, call for an ambulance, I'll try and help the people in the other car. Cronin looked back in the direction of the accident and smiled. The backup team was two cars ahead of Cronin's car when the truck cut Jess and Fuchs off. The second team car followed them under the expressway on Bruckner Boulevard. Cronin's car continued as, anticipated pass the backup team, onto the Triborough Bridge, their destination Manhattan. The second team car rushed to the on-ramp to the Triborough Bridge. They made it just in time to spot Cronin's car. Their partners stalled at the tollbooth in front of Cronin's car and had to be towed to the side. The action stopped all traffic and allowed the backup team to fall in behind Cronin's car, in the lane next to Cronin.

The Bridge Officers directed the traffic through the tie-up, alternating the lanes. Now the backup team was right behind Cronin's car. Once the two cars had cleared the tie-up the Officer from the second team thanked the Bridge Officers and hurried to catch the other cars. Cronin's car left the East River Drive at 53rd Street and drove across town. The evening traffic was slow and when they reached the theater district traffic slowed to a crawl. Cronin waited for the traffic light to cycle and in the middle of the process he told his driver to drive slow enough to get caught in the middle of the intersection. The light turned reds just as they entered the cross walk, leaving no room for anyone to follow them. Pedestrians gave them dirty looks as they squeezed between their car and the car ahead of them. The two surveillance cars were stuck in the middle of the other block behind them. Cronin got out of the car and walked casually across the street and entered the hotel. He rushed through the lobby and entered the subway entrance in the hotel and disappeared.

"We've lost him," the Driver in the lead car said.

"Stick with the car, let's see where they end up," Duke said.

Duke used his cellular phone to check with Vic. Monica had returned home and Vic was with her. Duke filled Vic in and continued their surveillance of Cronin's car. Cronin's car turned left and took the West Way down town. They turned left and parked near the "Intrepid Museum." One of the men got out and walked towards the entrance. Suddenly the doors of a large truck parked near the entrance opened and three men jumped out, and fired at the lead vehicle. The car exploded in flames. Duke watched one of the team jumped out of the front of the car and roll to the side of the car. Duke and his driver reached over the seat, simultaneously and removed the heavy weapons from the back of the car, moved away from their car and opened fire. Two of the three men from the truck went down. The third man rushed back to the truck, threw his weapon into the truck and leaped in. The men in Cronin's car used the confusion to escape.

Duke and his Driver rushed to the aid of their team. The Driver was dead; his partner had escaped with a few bruises.

"What the hell is going on here, they're supposed to be the good guys!" Duke said.

"If they're the good guys, I don't want to meet the bad guys."

"Sorry about your Partner," Duke said.

"Yeah…I'll stay here with him, get those bastards!"

Duke stood and tapped the Agent on the shoulder. Duke called in Cronin's plates, he knew there would be no record of the vehicle. He cursed when the return message confirmed his beliefs. Duke drove downtown, then it hit him, he knew where to find Cronin's car. He spotted it before he reached the East Side Heliport, parked outside the fence in plain view. Duke called headquarters and asked them to pick up the car, the car would be clean, but his people would check it anyway. He waited until the unmarked tow truck arrived and towed Cronin's car away, then he headed across town.

*      *      *

Duke waited for the Doorman to announce him, he had the same dumb expression on his face he had the first time he and Vic visited the apartment house. They say the servants take on the personalities of their employers; this Doorman had taken the quirk another step.

"This way, Sir…"

Duke looked at the man and pictured backing a eighteen-wheeler under his nose, there damn sure was enough room to do it. The elevator man on the other hand stood all of four-feet-eleven inches. What he lacked in height, he made up for in bravado. He had made Duke and Vic the first time they went to Monica's apartment.

"So, did you get the perps yet?"

"No, Louie, but we're close," Duke, said.

"You'd better get them before I get my hands on them, used to be a commando during the war, you know."

"Yeah, you told me, Louie."

"Used my size to get under the wires and find mines." Duke looked down at the little man and suppressed a smile. Louie was harmless, living in a world of his own creation. Monica said that he had been running the elevator every since she could remember.

"Here we are, remember be careful out there," Louie said.

"Thanks, Louie."

"You bet, and remember, I got your back."

Duke turned and gave Louie a salute. The little man's vest buttons almost popped off. Vic stood behind a curtain until he recognized Duke's voice. Monica opened the door and stepped aside in a manner of receiving royalty. Duke smiled, this gave Vic a start, he had never seen Duke smile.

"Have you heard?" Duke asked.Vic shrugged his shoulders. "Turn on the news station, you should have heard the racket from here." Monica turned on the radio.

"Three dead at the scene of one an outrageous incidents near the Intrepid Museum. In broad daylight tourist were forced to scramble to safety as a shoot-out took place near the Circle Line's dock. Three men in a truck apparently attacked two men in a car, a second car, in which two policemen were riding came to the aid of the men in the car, one of which was killed. The information surrounding this incident is still under investigation and all information is being withheld until the investigation is complete."

Duke motioned with his head towards the radio and Monica turned it off.

"Your man plays rough," Duke said. Monica nodded in agreement.

"Well, now that we know who he is, how do we nail him?"

"I can deliver him, but I want something in return," Monica said.

"Yes?" Duke said.

"When this is over I want to walk…"

Vic grimaced; Duke nodded his head slowly in agreement. He waved Vic off before he could protest.

"All right. But you've got to deliver him."

"Done."

"Just like that, huh?"

"You do what you do, and I do what I do."

"All right, Monica. But don't think that we're going to be sleeping."

"Do whatever you have to do, but if you crowd me it's all over."

Vic nudged Duke and tilted his head towards the door. Monica looked at Duke and smiled, a smile that defied Duke's stare.

"Come on, Duke.

Vic took Duke by the arm and pulled him gently towards the door. Duke took two steps towards the door and turned around, and looked at Monica, this time Monica blinked.

# CHAPTER *XIII*

"Well, well, well, you finally made it back. I heard you had a little trouble."

"They're good. I don't know how, but they were with us all the way. We took care of them, but the question is how did they know we were going to be there?"

"That's no problem, they're following Monica."

"How do we handle that?"

"No problem, I'll make a few phone calls and take care of it. How did it go with Monica?" Latten said.

"She's on board. She is going to find her father's records, update them, and get back to me."

"What is her position in this matter?"

"Now that she understands the complexities of this matter, she is willing to work with us."

"Good! How will we know she's being truthful with us?"

"She is going to call me when she finds the information. When she calls I will give her a test."

"Cronin, you're going a long way in this business."

"Thank you, sir."

★       ★       ★

Monica twisted the knob on her father's desk draw counter clockwise. The sound of a small motor hummed and the floor under the desk moved forward. A light came on when the door was half open revealing a panel of switches. A red light flashed intermittently and Monica scrambled to find the cut off switch. She kneeled and fumbled around the cavity beneath her until she felt a button and pushed it, the flashing red light stopped. She stood for a moment and wiped her brow. Monica walked over to the entrance, locked the door, and closed the curtains. A key switch at the upper left hand corner of the hidden cavity controlled the panel. Monica knew her father well; she ran her fingers across the bottom of the desk and found the key to turn on the panel. The panel opened and a small television screen blinked on. The touch-prompted CRT did the rest. Switch one, lowered the curtains in the cabin, obscuring daylight from the outside. Switch two, opened a wall panel and a huge safe moved forward.

The neat freak had been true to form. Monica twisted the handle on the large door and opened it, inside, a stack of computer disk, label neatly. Monica turned on the computer and used new disks to copy the disks she found in the safe and stuck the copies in her purse. She made copies of three financial disks, label them and put them in a separate envelope. Just as she was about to turn away she noticed a crack in the bottom of the draw she took the disks from. She slid the false panel back and gasped at the bundles of money stacked neatly in the false draw. Monica closed the panel, closed the safe and closed the wall safe from the control panel. She wanted to dance, that money was going to be her ticket to freedom.

*   *   *

The setting was pleasant, a new experience for Juan. Lisa had pleaded with him to take her to a spa. She wanted to take advantage of their money, but Juan couldn't see it, thought it was beyond their social skills. He smiled and reminisced about Lisa's joy when he told her they were going to Italy to enjoy the "baths." So far it had been everything Lisa dreamed of, silent servants delivering great food, the massages, and the water, warm and sensuous. Juan found the atmosphere pleasant too, Lisa had what she wanted and Juan was free to attend his meetings. And what a meeting it was, he wasn't prepared for the surprise Latten had for him.

"Manero! I thought…I,"

"Good to see you too, Juan."

Juan tried to submerge the picture of Manero in a wheel chair; he had lost weight, and his dark tropical tan.

"Why didn't you let me know you were going to be here?"

"I want everyone to think I'm still in a coma. You've done well…I'm pleased."

"Thank you."

"We have a lot to do. Everything must focus on the business, the business first. I would like to settle things with Monica, but the business comes first. First we recover the money, then we find someone to take her place; and that's not going to be easy, then I will settle with her."

Juan nodded his head in agreement.

"I am told that she will be delivering the money to Washington? Fine, let her think that we don't know about what she's doing with Latten. When the time comes she'll know," Manero said.

"Does he agree with you, I mean, he scares me," Juan said.

"You scared, bull shit!"

"What frightens me is his legitimacy. He can do anything he wants to and get away with it," Juan said.

Manero raised his hand, stopping for a moment to catch his breath. Juan moved closer and offered to help him, but Manero waved him away.

"Now you see why I want to kill that bitch personally. I will be like this the rest of my life; sitting in this damn chair tied to an oxygen tank."

Manero held the oxygen tube between his fingers, pointing it towards Juan.

"You will take over as I had planned. I'll advise you and help you with that prick in Washington."

Juan nodded his head.

"I'll let Latten know we've met. I've already told him what we are going to do. You keep the business going, I'll handle the director."

Manero motioned Juan forward. He beckoned Juan towards him, reached up slowly and embraced him. Luis entered the room as if he had been called.

"Luis will do his regular thing. He has no problem with you taking over," Manero said.

Juan nodded his head.

Manero pressed a button on his chair and his nurse entered the room.

"The people here are good to me, besides the waters are good for me."

Manero smiled, the Nurse wrapped a shawl around Manero's shoulders and pushed him towards the door. Manero raised his hand and she stopped.

"Call me if you need me," Manero said.

He raised his hand again and the Nurse pushed him out of the room.

"Luis, what's pressing?" Juan asked.

"I have to go back to the states, the big shipment will be coming in next week," Luis said.

"Good. I'll set up a meeting of the Combine. How did she do it?" Juan asked.

"She's good. If my brother's men hadn't got there when they did he would be dead. He almost died anyway. There was an Indian doctor in the emergency room, good thing; he saved my brother's life. We gave him ten-grand. He almost shit in his pants!" Luis said and laughed.

Juan frowned and gestured with his hands.

"Well, this Doctor recognized what was wrong with my brother. He said that he was bitten by a snake, a cobra."

"A cobra!"

"Yeah. Seems they had a lot of that where the doctor came from. The strange thing was there was no sign of a bite. But the Doctor was right, it was cobra venom."

Juan shook his head.

"They found it in his blood stream. They said the poison must have been put in his drink."

"How the hell did she do that?"

"I told you she was dangerous," Luis said.

"Yeah…."

*          *          *

The switch would be simple, a transfer of funds from one company to another. Monica put the computer disk in her purse and locked the copies in the wall safe. She looked at her purse on the coffee table and almost laughed at the thought of it containing twenty million dollars. She checked her watch, picked up her bag and left the apartment. The Doorman held the door for her, then hurried out to the street to hail a taxi. The taxi turned into the driveway and the Doorman rushed back to open the door for Monica. Monica waited until the Doorman returned. He opened the door for her and gave the taxi driver a dirty look.

"LaGuardia, please, the shuttle, " Monica said.

The driver dropped the flag and sped off.

*          *          *

"We should have waited at the shuttle for her," Vic said

"Then what, get on the plane with her?" Duke asked.

"You're right."

Vic moved a little closer to Monica's taxi.

"Don't get too close."

"She does know that we are following her, right?"

"Not really."

"I thought..." Duke interrupted. "I told her I trusted her and that we wouldn't follow her."

"Why did you do that?"

"She was concerned about us being spotted on her tail. As she said, that would blow the whole thing."

"What do we do now?"

"We see her onto the plane, watch it take off, and let Dad handle it from there," Duke said.

"I'll buy that," Vic said.

The taxi stopped in front of the departure building and Monica got out. Vic drove pass the taxi and stopped. Duke got out and Vic drove away, he would pick up Duke later at American Airlines at the other side of the airport. Duke made his way to the commuter counter to the left of security; Monica was to his right at the Security checkpoint. That was when he spotted the man tailing her and he knew it wasn't one of their men. Monica was right they were watching her. Monica entered the terminal, presented her ticket, and moved along the corridor towards her gate. Duke flashed his badge and asked for a place where he could watch Monica's plane take off. Moments later he watched a tractor push Monica's plane away from the finger ramp, unhitch the towing bar and move away from the plane. Duke watched the plane taxi out to the runway, and waited patiently until the plane took off.

*   *   *

Monica spotted a young man holding a sign with her name on it. She walked over to the young man and introduced herself.

"I have a car for you, the Director is expecting you," the young man said.

There was nothing fancy about the car; it had the same look as most law enforcement vehicles, black with black sidewalls, and the inevitable antenna protruding from one of the rear fenders. The young man opened the read door and waited for Monica to get in. He closed the door and joined his silent partner. Monica looked at the carbon copy haircuts and the Brooks Brothers suits and smiled. These were heavy hitters, not your run of the mill agents. She knew better than to ask them any questions, so she directed her attention elsewhere. They took old route one south and headed for the Virginia countryside. Thirty minutes later they turned off the road and left the real world.

She knew what to expect, a quite dignified home a quarter of a mile from the main road: a stable, horses, waterfowl, and television cameras hidden in the trees. The car stopped in front of the house and James Latten motioned her in from the veranda.

"Miss Woolford, so nice to see you," Latten said.

"Thank you, it's nice to finally meet you."

"Well…I didn't expect you to be so young."

"Thank you. It must be the effects of the hospital."

"Er, yes…unfortunate about that, but you know how those people are."

Monica didn't answer. Latten pointed to a comfortable chair and asked Monica to have a seat. Monica removed the disks from her purse and gave them to Latten before sitting.

"Right to the point, that's commendable, but you are among friends now.

"Can I be sure?"

"That's a promise, and I'll make sure our other friends understand that."

Monica looked at Latten strangely.

"Oh, its okay to talk here, we are in a safe zone. You understand that this is official, and that we are running it quietly?"

Latten watched Monica's expression, he was pleased, she was as cool as a cucumber.

"I have been told as much by your subordinate."

"Good. We are about to embark on a huge acquisition, the details I can't give you, but you will be needed to help us move the funds after the deal is consummated."

"What would you like for me to do?"

"I have made arrangements for you to function in your father's capacity. You will receive five percent of the net, just as your father did. Complete this operation successfully and we will be able to retire. You'll be happy to know that this move will result in a better control on the drug market is this country."

"I don't understand," Monica said.

"That's all you need to know. Just be ready when I call upon you. In the mean time let's go inside and confirm the transaction of funds."

Latten stood and pointed towards the entrance to the house.

*    *    *

"Eighty-four."

"Go ahead, eighty-four."

"Destination hot, we are abandoning."

"Confirmed, seek safe area."

"Eighty-four, out."

"I'll move south to the nearest intersection and wait there. You move north and cover that area. One of us should spot Monica when she leaves his place," the Agent said.

"Right. Is there a back way out?"

"I'm sure there is, but they will have to get on the main road no matter what."

"Gotcha."

*    *    *

"No one could say that Latten wasn't thorough. The basement was covered with special equipment and specialist. He handed one of them the desk and waited. The screen danced and loads of figures appeared. The Specialist waited until the last block of numbers appeared on the screen and pushed the return button. The computer flickered and dialed a phone number, more numbers and a request for a password. Monica moved forward and entered the password. The computer beeped again, this time confirming the transfer process.

"Excellent!" Latten said. " Now let's have lunch."

Monica followed Latten upstairs.

"I wasn't sure that I could count on you, but now that has been resolved."

"Thank you," Monica said.

"We'll have lunch here at the house, you understand that we can't be seen together?"

"Yes."

"By the way, how did you come by you magic portion?"

"Oh, its something I picked up while traveling in India."

"You aren't using today, are you?"

"Of course not, I save it for pigs."

"You're absolutely right, but we can't live with them, and we can't live without them."

"Where does that leave me?"

"Good question. Manero has agreed to abstain until the business is complete, after which I'm not sure what his intentions are."

"Can you control him?"

"Up to a point, but we do need him, for a while anyway. Juan is learning fast, but there are things he's not equipped to handle. I tell you what. I'll give Manero some specific instructions, and a bad promise. You can guess what that will be."

"You'll deliver me personally."

"Good girl! You are special," Latten said. " Eat up, the seafood here is delicious."

Latten broke open his blue shell crab and used his fingers to retrieve the meat inside. Monica followed suit.

"They are delicious," she said.

"The only place in the world where you can find them. They are special, just like us. Anything else is a waste of time.

Monica nodded her head, took a deep breath, and moved her chair closer to the table.

"Good..." Latten said.

# Chapter *XIV*

"*V*ic, its for you."

"Who is it?"

"Monica…"

Vic looked at Duke and raised his arm in celebration. He dropped one arm and used the other arm to accent a "yes!"

"Welcome back, Monica."

"It's good to be back. Thank you for trusting me."

"You're welcome. How did things go?"

"I gave them what they wanted…it appears that you were correct, they want me to work for them."

"We'll reel Latten in, and you're home free."

"I wouldn't be too hasty."

"And why not?" Vic asked.

"I'll tell you over a plate of ribs, no onions, okay?"

"Thirty minutes," Vic said.

"Right."

\*             \*             \*

The Commissioner gestured towards the two chairs in front of his desk, Jess and Fuchs walked around the chairs and sat down.

"You're back on the case," The Commissioner said.

The two detectives looked at each other.

"You're still behind the eight ball, but you are on the case. We're going to let the shipment go through."

The Commissioner raised his hand to silence Jess.

"We are going to track it and see where it takes us. The worse we can do is pick up some major dealers. That's not what we want, but, if we have to settle for that, we will."

"What about Juan Acevedo?"

"He has moved up in the organization, you won't be able to touch him."

"In a pig's ass, I won't."

"The Feds want us to lay off him, it seems he has clout. The clout behind him is what we are after. If we leave him alone, he'll take us to the big kahoona!"

"What do you want us to do?"

"We've made some arrangements for you and Fuchs to work with a special task force covering this mission. Thanks to you two we're closer to nailing these bastards. These bastards are so bold they think they're gonna drive two of the Navy's truck full of dope into this country and deliver it to their suppliers." The Commissioner pushed a button on the intercom and Bee entered the office carrying their new identification.

"Give them the tickets, Bee. You're going to Newport News Virginia. You'll meet the rest of the team there."

"Yes, Sir," Jess and Fuchs replied.

"Be careful, one slip and you're history."

"Thank you, sir," Fuchs said.

"Sir, " Jess said.

# Chapter XV

*T*he tugboats nudged the LST into the repair area bow forward and the dry-dock crew tied her in position, after which the bow opened and the crew drove the vehicles off. One of the trucks wouldn't start and it was decided to leave it and the two trucks it was blocking on board while custom checked the rest of the vehicles. The mechanics couldn't get the truck started and it was decided to leave them. The Custom's inspection took most of the day, and it was decided to leave the two trucks on the ship for the night crew to inspect. The drivers were ordered to stay with the trucks and bring them to the motor pool after the Custom inspection. They snapped to attention and gave a smart salute to the Lieutenant and returned to their trucks. Malone looked at Childers and smiled, they had crippled the ship according to plans, and things were on schedule.

*    *    *

"Welcome, gentlemen. We have to get a move on; they plan to move the stuff tonight. One of our people planted a tracking device on the two trucks, so all we have to do is wait for them to move the trucks."

"How are they going to do that? The still have to pass Customs."

"One of our people will be doing the inspection." Captain said."

"Yeah, but there's still the problem of the dog," Jess said.

"We've taken care of that too."

"Don't tell me," Fuchs said."

"What?" Jess asked

"They brought in a ringer," Fuchs said.

Everybody laughed

*       *       *

"Where's Charlie?"

"Down with the Flu, you got the call about me replacing him, right?"

"Yeah, sign in here. It's usually quiet around here, but we got these two trucks stuck on that LST over there."

"What's wrong?"

"Oh, they towed her in here with her propellers busted."

"I mean with the trucks."

"One of them wouldn't start, and it blocked the other one. They should be through in a few minutes, then we can sack out."

"Right."

"That Charlie's dog?"

"No Charlie has his dog, and I have mine."

"Oh that's right. I don't know why they have you guys checking anyway. Our boys are too smart to bring anything through here."

"Regulations."

"Yeah, fucking regulations. Why don't you go up there and check the trucks? That way we can sack our early…"

"Okay."

"By the way, what's your name corporal?"

"Hanson."

"Okay, Hanson."

Hanson patted the muscular little Beagle hound and tugged at its leash."

"Let's go boy." Hanson tugged the leash and the dog trotted along beside him. One of the drivers spotted Hanson and gave the look-alive-signal. The soldier under the hood of the first truck gave the signal to start the truck. The truck whined for a moment then roared once, back-fired, and settled down to a smooth hum.

"That's got it."

The Soldier closed the hood and wiped his hands. Hanson said hello to the four men and made his way to the truck. He walked around the first truck, opened the door to the cab and the dog hopped in. The dog jumped out almost as fast as it jumped in. Hanson did a thorough check of the two trucks, after which he gave the soldiers permission to drive the vehicles off the ship.

"How about a lift back to the gate?"

"You got it, Corporal."

Hanson picked up his dog and held it close to his body with one hand, and held onto the moving truck with the other hand. The truck stopped at the gate and Sentry checked each driver's orders, recorded the incident and returned the papers to the drivers. The two trucks drove through the gate and made a left turn. Jess looked at the tracking device and waved his hand.

"All units, they're on the move."

"Air thirteen, 10-4."

"Car three, 10-4."

"Car two, 10-4."

"Show time! Ten to one they head for Norfolk," Fuchs said.

"What makes you think that?" Jess asked.

"Its the quickest way north."

"No bet."

"Car two, take the lead. I want you to pass them and wait for them to enter Norfolk."

"Yes, sir!"

The Commander replaced the microphone and settled back in his seat. Jess sat directly behind him eyes focused on the tracking screen. Traffic was light and the trucks made good time getting into the city.

Fuchs was right they drove directly to Norfolk. They took a back street in Norfolk and drove towards the water.

"There's something screwy here, the base is in the other direction."

The streets were empty on the waterfront; the only traffic moving was the trucks. The Commander told his driver to pull over and stop.

"We're the only ones down here."

He reached for the microphone and called Air Thirteen.

"Air thirteen."

"Air thirteen, over"

"We're dropping back, its all yours."

"Ten, four."

"Car, two."

"Car two, go ahead."

"We're down by the warehouses, hold you position."

"Ten, four."

"Command, over."

"I've lost them in traffic, there's a lot of action below. Standby, I see them! They're heading back towards the highway."

"Ten-four, Air thirteen."

"They pulled a switch," Jess said.

"What do you mean?"

"I have them standing still."

"They couldn't have unloaded the stuff that fast."

"What do you mean?" The Commander asked.

"The tracking devices are planted on the loads."

"That makes the answer easy," Fuchs said.

"What, what!"

"They duped the trucks."

"What the hell are you talking about?" The Commander asked, Jess interrupted

"What's the easiest vehicle in the world to duplicate?"

"Of course! All they had to do was paint the same numbers on two other trucks and they're home free! Okay. Let's pinpoint the their location." The Commander said.

"Car two they're heading your way. It's a decoy, but we want you and Air Thirteen to track them."

"Car two, 10-4."

"Air thirteen, 10-4."

The Commander nodded to the Driver and he moved the car out slowly.

"Which way, Jess?"

"Two blocks east and one south."

They drove two blocks and turned right. The beeper sounded loudest in front of a wholesale seafood company. Jess noted the address as they drove past the location.

"Well, the good news is they use white trucks," Jess said.

"Dealers seem to have a passion for white vehicles," Fuchs said and they all laughed.

"Okay, we'll drive to the edge of the range of our tracking device and wait. When they move, we'll trail them.

"Air thirteen to command."

"Go ahead, Air thirteen."

"They drove into the base."

"Ten-four. Refuel and call us when you are ready, I think we're going on a long trip."

"Air thirteen, 10-4."

✳          ✳          ✳

"Get the loads into the other trucks, I want them out of here now!"

Luis motioned to one of the workers and the man nodded in agreement. The trucks were lined up rear end to the narrow doors of the refrigerator trucks, and a wooden ramp connected the trucks. Two men

loaded the dope onto hand trucks and pushed them into the refriger-
ated trucks where two men unloaded the hand trucks and stacked the
boxes of dope in neat stacks between the labeled fish orders for delivery.
Juan observed the operation from the office high above the loading
docks.

"This is neat. I don't know why we have to shut down. I could figure
out something that would get our stuff into the base without taking a
ship out of action," Juan said.

"Forget about it. This operation is used to move arms. We've used the
truck switch for almost a year, but that was for guns. The best thing you
can do is forget about this place."

"I guess you're right."

"One truck is for New York, and one for points west, that's a bitch."

"Hell, at one time I felt like I could consume a truck load, now I leave
it to the suckers," Juan said.

Juan opened his briefcase and emptied the money on the desk. The
money was neatly wrapped in plastic packs, two thousand dollars to a
pack.

Carmine counted he packs. "Fifty on the head, maybe you're
right…we could consider another shipment," he said and motioned for
his backup man to take the money.

"We shall see," Juan said.

Juan shook Carmine's hand. He closed he briefcase and headed for
the door, bodyguard behind him.

"It has been a pleasure doing business with you."

"Same here, Juan."

The door to the loading dock opened and Juan's car drove out of the
bay and headed for the airport.

"Get a load of this, its him, my friend Juan Acevedo! Got to admit he
looks good, like another person…" Jess said.

"Car three, cars heading your way, black Cadillac Brougham, two
passengers. Don't loose them, the Commander said.

"Get down!"

Two cars entered the block. The four men in Jess' car dove into the seats. Each of the approaching cars had four men in them, eight shooters. The Commander raised his head slowly and looked down the street.

"They're in front of the wholesale house. Fellows, I think the escorts have arrived," The Commander said.

The rest of the team sat up.

"I'm sure they're going to New York. What do you say we get you another car?"

"Works for me," Jess said.

"Good. We will work with you until they cross the state line. From there you and your partner can tail them. I'll keep the copter over the trucks all the way, that way we should have them covered from every angle."

"Thank, Commander. The Commander used the phone to request a vehicle or Jess and Fuchs.

"They will meet us on the other side of the bridge. The trucks are in sight, so we don't have to worry about them."

"I hope there's no way out of that tunnel that we don't know about."

"No, that's not a problem. Once they get on the bridge, we'll pass them and take you to your car. The good news is they don't have too many ways to travel until they cross the Delaware Bridge."

"That is good news," Jess said.

Air thirteen watched the four vehicles enter the tunnel, then moved on to the other side of the bridge to refuel and wait for the convoy. Daylight made its way across the bay, and the mist lingered over the water. In the distance silhouetted fishing boats dominated the horizon line. Air thirteen warmed up its engines and took off.

"Air thirteen is airborne."

"10-4 air thirteen, we have them in sight."

Jess and Fuchs used the few minutes they had left to pick up some breakfast. The coffee was lousy, and the food passable. Most of the traffic was heading south, getting away from the oncoming winter. Fuchs took a sip of his coffee and spat it out of the window.

"No Starbucks here," Fuchs said.

"Give you any ideas?"

"Yeah, yeah, you're right...a coffee joint. I could open it in the mornings and go fishing in the afternoon, great idea," Fuchs said.

"Here they come," Jess said.

"I like their escorts."

"You've got to give them credit. Anyone bothering those trucks is in deep do-doo."

# Chapter XVI

*T*ony Roma's was the perfect place to meet, one way in and one way out. Monica sat at her usual table, in the corner, in the back room. From that table she could see the front door and duck into the ladies room, if she didn't want to be seen. From the ladies room it was simple, put on a wig and the dark glasses she carried in her purse, and walk out of the restaurant, undiscovered. Duke parked on the bus stop near the restaurant and stayed with the car, Vic went into the restaurant.

"Hi, Monica."

"Vic. Good to see you."

"At least you made it back in one piece."

"Better than I had hoped for. I am employed again."

"Oh…"

"You were right, they need me. There's a big shipment of drugs coming in. From what I was told it is quite a haul."

"Do you know when it's coming in?"

"I don't know. I couldn't ask any questions, but I can tell you this, it's big enough to get Latten excited about it."

"What do they want you to do?"

"Nothing about the shipment. It's after the deal is done that I come into play. My job is to launder the money."

"That's good information, we'll check it out. You delivered, so I'll speak with the office and see what we can do for you."

"That's it…you're not locking me up?"

"No need for that, you've been straight with us."

"Thanks, like I promised, I'll deliver Latten," Monica said.

"Good. One more thing…the job you allegedly did on Manero, he's not going to let you get away with that."

"I know, but our friend in Washington said that he'll keep him off me."

"Yeah, until the crap hits the fan."

Monica nodded her head in agreement.

"We'll do what we can, but on the other hand, you don't need too much help."

Monica laughed.

"Well, that's it. I'll keep in touch," Vic said.

Monica left the restaurant first, Vic chose to stay behind and have a drink.

*    *    *

The trucks drove straight through to Newark Airport to the industrial area where several companies prepare food for the airlines. Their escort vehicles parked in the parking lot where one man from each car got out and got into each truck. Jess and Fuchs drove past the area and found a good spot to observe the trucks. The trucks backed up to a loading dock and the ritual of unloading began. Jess used his binoculars to watch the trucks. Two men dressed in a white butcher's coat rolled hand trucks into the trucks and pushed them out loaded with the shipment. It took them almost an hour to unload the trucks. One of the men stacked one hand truck on top of the other, his partner close the door and locked it, after which both drivers returned to their trucks.

The trucks drove back to the parking lot, the two escorts, got out, and returned to their cars. The cars backed out of the spaces and drove to a nearby motel; the truck drivers joined them there, and settled in. Jess stayed with the shipment, Fuchs parked in the motel parking lot and went into the lobby. The lobby was empty, except for the clerk on duty. Fuchs waved at him and entered the bar on the other side of the lobby. Fuchs ordered a Dewar's and water, after which he used the pay phone near the jukebox. Frank Sinatra coolly whispered about loneliness to the string of Gordon Jenkins, interrupted by the phone ringing at the Commissioner's home.

"Yes?"

"Fuchs. We are in Newark. I am at the Satellite Motel, Jess is with the principal at the food venders area of the airport, we need backup."

"Considered it done. Anything special?"

"Telephone trucks, or utility vehicles would help."

"Good," the Commissioner said. Fuchs cradled the phone and returned to the bar. Four men entered the bar. Fuchs recognized two of the men, drivers from the trucks. He didn't recognize the other two men. They sat at the other end of the bar in a booth. Three songs later, two drinks down, a redheaded looker entered the bar and walked over to Fuchs. The guys in the booth eyes followed the woman like they were all on the same string, Fuchs smiled, that was until the woman sat next to him.

"I heard you like utility vehicles," she said.

"Yeah. Don't tell me you're a phone truck…"

"You got it," she said.

"What are you drinking?"

"A Johnny Walker, black." Fuchs signaled the bartender.

"A Johnny Walker, black."

"How do you want it?" the bartender asked.

"On the rocks."

"The Commissioner thought you might need some help."

"I always knew the Commissioner was a smart man. That's part of our crew in the booth. The other four are probably watching the stuff. "

"They look mean."

"They are."

"What's the plan?"

"Go outside and see if you can get a couple of Jersey Troopers to happen by. I'll give you the rest when you get back."

"Officer Franklin used her best movements on her way to the ladies room. One of the men in the booth pursed his lips and made a sucking sound as she walked past, Fuchs gave him a dirty look and the four men laughed.

"Hey, Honey! What you need is a real man."

Franklin smiled at the man. Two minutes she returned to her seat at the bar.

"That's perfect. Did you get the backup?"

"Yes, they're outside. What's your plan?"

"I'll start a fight. When it starts you get out of here."

"And how..."

"Dirty bitch!"

Fuchs faked a slap against Franklin's face. Two of the men in the booth jumped up and ran towards Fuchs. Franklin screamed and ran for the door. Fuchs stepped aside and tripped the first man. The second man stumble and fell into Fuchs' arms. Fuchs clipped him with a rabbit punch and the man fell on top of the first man. One of the men reached inside his jacket, but hesitated just as a burly State Trooper entered the bar.

"All right, what the hell is going on here?"

The two men from the booth untangled and stood.

"This prick was hitting a woman."

"What woman?"

"She was right here a moment ago."

"All right, the three of you let's see some identification," the Trooper said. His partner stood at the entrance covering him. The two men in the booth got up, one of them paid the check and attempted to leave the bar. The Trooper's partner motioned for them to take a seat. The

Trooper took the identification from the two men and held out his hand for Fuchs' identification.

"I don't have any identification, I left it in our room."

"All of you sit down, you two over here, and you over there. Bartender, what happened here?"

"It's like they said. He knocked the crap out of the woman he was with."

"You two want to press charges?"

The two men shook their heads, indicating, no. The Trooper jotted their names in his notebook and returned their identification.

"All right you can go, but this had better be over. I don't want to have to come back here again tonight. Got me?"

"Yes, sir," the two men said.

"All right, get the hell out of here. You! Come with me!"

Fuchs got up and walked ahead of the trooper.

"Just a minute. Does he have a tab?" the Trooper asked

"Give me a break," Fuchs said.

"Twelve bucks," the Bartender said.

Fuchs dug into his pocket and pulled out a twenty-dollar bill and handed it to the Bartender.

"Don't even think about it," Fuchs said.

The Bartender shrugged his shoulders, counted out the change and pushed it towards Fuchs. The Trooper took a buck from the change and shoved it to the Bartender.

"I like the way you handle my money," Fuchs said.

"Don't want the man to think you're a cheapskate, right? Okay, lets go."

Fuchs left the bar Trooper walking closely behind him. They walked across the parking lot to the Trooper's car. The Trooper opened the door and pushed gently downward on Fuchs' head to prevent him from bumping it on the roof of the car. Across the lot on the second floor Escobar watched the action from his room until the Trooper drove off.

"Well...what do you think?" the Trooper asked.

"You convinced me."

"I hope we convinced them. By the way, I saw one of them watching us from a room on the second floor."

"Tell you what, we'd better follow through on this one."

"What do you mean?"

"These guys are connected. Book me under some assumed name, or give me a DAT for a future date, just in case."

"Right. What about the woman?"

"Let me use your Cellular phone."

Fuchs called the Commissioner and filled him in.

# CHAPTER *XVII*

"*E*scobar you're fucking crazy! Let him kick her ass and anybody else he wants too!! You almost got pinched for some fucking macho shit!!" Luis said.

"I'm sorry."

"Sorry don't get it. Come over here!

Escobar walked slowly toward Luis.

"You know what I do with fuck ups!"

"Si."

"You're gonna live for the same reason I'm kicking your ass."

Luis backed handed Escobar and he fell across a table. The lamp fell from the table and broke the bulb.

"Pick it up," Luis said.

Escobar crawled across the room to the lamp, sat the table upright, and put the lamp on top of it.

"You're gonna live because we need you, all of you! Understand!!"

Seven men nodded their heads as one.

"All right…you have your assignments. We have an all clear. Go to your assigned locations, and if you spot anything suspicious, anything, give the alarm. That's it, get the hell out of here."

Luis used his Cellular phone to call Juan.

            \*                      \*                    \*

"Holy shit! This is car one, they're moving, both cars."

"What about the shipment?"

"Its still there."

"Good keep an eye on the place, we'll take care of the escorts."

"Car 227 to Central K."

"Go ahead, 227."

"Pass this on to Special units 333. Target Vehicles headed for Newark Airport car rentals."

"10-4, 227. KEA 8—62."

Franklin parked a safe distance from the rental agency and watched the eight men get on the rental company's bus. Her task was easy. She followed the bus to the departure terminal, stopped and used her cellular to call the Commissioner.

Commissioner Chapman slammed down the phone and called the special number he had for Duke and Vic, after which he called Jess and Fuchs. Jess handed over the surveillance to the State Troopers and drove over to the barracks to pick up Fuchs.

"Hi, jailbird."

"Yeah."

"What's the scoop?"

"The drugs are still at the vender, but the escorts have left."

"What do you think?"

"You got me. They're at seven different airlines, all domestic."

"That make sense to you?" Jess asked.

"Maybe, maybe not."

"Yeah?"

"Suppose they're going to the places where the drugs are going to be delivered."

"Fuchs, you surprise me sometimes."

"I surprise myself sometimes."

"I'll call the Commissioner and share your idea with him," Jess said.

"Good."

*       *       *

Trooper Willis followed the beep on his tracking device. Truck 115 pulled out of the loading area and drove towards the airport. He called in the truck number and slumped down in his seat, two more trucks were leaving the food company.

"Got two more trucks heading in the same direction," the Trooper said and returned the mike to its cradle.

"Get a load of this, the truck from the food company is entering the service area," Fuchs said.

"So that's how they're gonna do it."

"Pretty slick, if you ask me," Fuchs said.

"Yeah, the food trucks on the other end pick up the shipment with the empties."

Jess called the Commissioner.

*        *        *

Franklin tugged at her blazer; the red wig had been stuffed into her bag. She opened her Laptop and pretended to check data. The last member of the escort team sat directly in front of her near a large picture window watching planes land and take off. She made an entry of each suspect's destination and closed the computer. One of the men departed to Miami, one to Jacksonville, two to New Orleans, two to Chicago. The plane for Los Angles was announced and the suspect gathered his luggage and moved towards the gate. Franklin walked ahead of him and stopped at the magazine stand near the boarding checkpoint. The suspect spotted her and made a friendly gesture to her, but it was nothing like the sucking sounds he had made the night before at the bar. Franklin shook her head and let her long black hair dance around her shoulders. Her suitor didn't give any indication that he recognized her. He put his bag on the conveyor belt and watched it move through the machine. He turned and looked at Franklin once more and gestured "what a pity."

*        *        *

Duke entered the task force headquarters Vic remained in the car. He didn't go in for two reasons, one is Jess might realize who he was, and the other, he didn't want to stir up too many memories. After all the old building on Wards Island was where he and Honey had spent so much time together. It was all the same a pheasant strolling across the lawn in front of the building. And, it had the same affect it had on him the first time he saw a pheasant there, how in the hell could it be in the middle of New York City? He looked towards Queens and whispered, "Honey its all most over, and I will do what is expected of me." Vic felt a cold chill and looked behind him, but there was nothing there, yet he could feel the presence of a being. Whatever it was, suddenly the importance of getting even didn't seem so important. Then it came to him.

*"Vic your problem is focus, focus on the wrong things.*
*That's why you're always in a bind. Define your goal,*
*then determine how you're to accomplish it."*

That was what Honey had said to him the first day they worked together, and she was right. If he didn't watch himself he would be the victim of his revenge. He looked towards the building and wished he could hear what they were saying. Inside the building the Commissioner stood in front of the special team he had assembled. His main concern was if they had a leak the whole game would be over, and they would all probably be dead.

"Okay! Listen up!! This is important, Men."

The noise in the room died down.

"You will leave here tonight and be taken to your special assignments in a few minutes. Don't call anyone, don't talk to anyone, and don't listen to anyone who is not a part of our team. Move from your vehicles to the planes. Get on board and maintain your posture of silence. We close them down tomorrow at 0300 Eastern time, that will be 2300 for you guys on the coast. Upon arrival at your local destinations, remain in the special vehicles until zero hour. At that time we will shut these guys down."

"Are we authorized to us deadly force?"

"Is the Pope Catholic? Use everything you have, these are dangerous people. If they get away they will find you and your families."

Someone in the room laughed.

"You think that's funny, huh?" No one replied.

"Roll the tape," the Commissioner said.

The lights were turned out and a small square opened on the wall in the rear of the room. The pictures were of the Bronx murders. Four people sat around a table, all dead, including a baby in the arms of one of the women.

"This is the work of the people you will be dealing with. You are to take orders from no one but you company commanders. No one? There's a lot at stake here, so don't blow it."

The Commissioner closed his book and nodded to his assistant. The man turned off the VCR and turned the room light on again.

"West Coast! Form a line on the right. You will draw you weapons at the end of the hall and proceed to the departure vehicles. If there are any questions, now is the time to ask them…"

The group was silent, the Commander continued. "All right! Let's do it, move out!!"

*      *      *

"I don't like it. We should have laid low for a while," Juan said.

"He knows what he's doing."

"That's not the problem."

"What problem? We're in good hands."

"The problem is we invested so much in this venture."

"I don't get it, what do you mean?" Manero asked.

"We put a lot of apples in one basket. If the basket falls we loose everything."

"If that happens, and I don't think it will, it will be his responsibility."

"He's hooked up."

"Nobody, and I mean nobody is that hooked up."

"Good, that's what I wanted to know," Juan said.

"Okay. Luis will handle that part of the deal. He knows how to get out of difficult situations. Should a situation arise I will expect you to take care of it. Use any amount of money you need, but get it done," Manero said.

"Consider it done."

The two men hung up their phones simultaneously.

\*    \*    \*

Vic watched the trucks roll out. Duke shook the Commissioner's hand and headed towards the car.

"We're lucky, we get to bring down the New York connection."

"What about Jess?"

"He'll be there, but he won't see us. We're the cover. You and I will be on a building across the street with scopes covering the operation," Duke said.

Vic nodded his head and looked towards the last truck. He started the car and followed it.

"What are we going to do, sit on this thing?"

"No. You and I are going to case our positions, secure them, and go home and get some rest. Those guys in the trucks have all of the comforts of home. You should see the way that damn truck is set up."

"I will when this thing is over" Vic said.

The ride to the site took less than ten minutes. The Overton Food Company was the pride of the Bronx. The owner had pulled himself up by his bootstraps and made a fortune. He had dined with Presidents, local politicians adored him, and he was one of New York's greatest campaign donors. Charlie Overton opened his private bar and removed a bottle of twenty-year-old scotch. He loosened the golden cord and used a finger to open the velvet pouch the bottle rested in. He opened the executive fridge and spooned two spoons of crushed ice into an old-fashion-glass, poured the scotch over it, and let the golden-brown liquid blend into the melting ice. He chose Beethoven's ninth symphony from his CD player to complete the ritual. The forte opening of the symphony filled his office. Slowly the music climbed its chromatic scale, crescendo-ing into its complex beauty. Charlie reached for his drink and took a slow sip of his prize.

He rejoiced in the idea that this would be the last shipment his company would have to handle, soon he would be free from the strangle hold the Cartel had on him. He walked over to the window and looked down at the entrance to the loading area, the trucks would be arriving soon. The processing plant was in full swing preparing the meals for the flights later in the day. He didn't notice the strange looking eighteen-wheeler parked at the factory next door, just another truck freak, he thought.

Vic focused his scope on the edge of the loading dock. He used a hand signal to Duke to let him know he was in place; Duke returned the signaled indicating ok. The street was quiet, except for the infrequent visit by the hookers and their Johns. The whine of the diesels broke the silence. The two trucks turned the corner and drove up to the processing plant's gate, the lead truck blinked its lights and the huge gate opened. Vic and Duke focused on the two heavily armed men that appeared out of nowhere. The trucks moved slowly through the gate, suddenly all hell broke loose. The special team moved in, one of the team secured the guard house; a second member blocked the gate. There were two men on each truck, one at each door. Vic and Duke took out the two men in the open yard, and the team moved forward.

A barrage of gunfire from the top on the factory building brought two of the special team down. Vic lifted his rifle and scanned the top of the factory building. He spun around and ducked behind a sign a moment before a barrage of missiles bit holes in the metal roof near him. Duke turned towards the flashes and fired without aiming and the shooters body rolled off the building. Vic spotted the other gunman on the building across the yard, and squeezed off a round. The bullet found its mark and the target's head exploded. Five minutes is a long time in a battle, but in five minutes the special team had the area under control. Two buses enter the street and parked in front of the processing factory's gate. Later the employees filed out through a gauntlet of heavily armed troops towards the waiting buses. Charlie re-dialed Manero again his line was busy. The door of his office opened and two battle dressed team members entered.

"Hands up! Move over to the wall, and assume the position!"

"Don't you guys know who I am?"

"Yeah, a dead man if you don't get up against that wall."

Jess and Fuchs entered the room, guns drawn. Charlie Overton stood still; one of the men cuffed him and moved him towards the door.

"Leave him here," Jess said.

"Yes, Sir!"

Luis sneaked across the roof of the building and used a rope he had planted there to get down to the street. He walked out of the area carrying a lunch box, there were two pistols in the box. Two blocks later Luis used the car he had planted to take him to the airport.

*       *       *

"I'm glad you came here," Manero said.

"Figured the waters would help me," Juan said.

"You were right. Now we have to figure out what went wrong," Manero said.

"How could this happen without him knowing it?" Juan asked

"Good question. There's something else, there wasn't anything about the hit in the news."

"I hadn't thought about that, damn! I hadn't thought about that!" Juan said.

"I think you'd better meet with him."

"He said we were not supposed to meet again," Juan said.

"Fuck what he said!" Manero reached for his oxygen. "I'm calling this meeting, and he had better be there!" Manero said.

"Easy, easy. I'll take care of it," Juan said.

"Good. I want you to meet him on our turf. This way we will have control."

"Where?"

"At your new place. If he brings anything, or anybody with him you'll be able to detect them a mile away. If that is the case you know what to do."

"Si."

"Good. Go, enjoy the baths, have a drink or whatever you want. This is what we work for," Manero said.

Manero raised his hand and his Nurse entered the room. Juan entertained the idea of approaching Manero's nurse until he saw Manero's hand comfortably resting on her well-rounded rear end.

*      *      *

"We have detained the workers, what do you want to do with them?" Duke asked.

"Separate the good from the bad, Condition the good, confirm the results, and release them."

"Yes, Sir."

"That was excellent work. If everything goes according to plan out Mr. Latten is in for quite a surprise."

"Vic, Juan is yours, and believe it or not there's a rumor that Manero is hiding out in Tuscany."

"Never mind Juan, let me have Manero," Vic said.

"It has to be clean," Dad said.

"It will be," Vic said.

"First you will have to find him."

"Right!"

*　　　　*　　　　*

"Juan!"

"Baby!"

Lisa rushed into Juan's arms. The greeting was brief, followed by ripping off their clothes, wrestling on the floor, the couch, and finally into the shower. The tropical air rippled through the windows and the smell of fruit trees permeated the room.

"It's good to be home again."

"Are you staying?" Lisa asked.

"Who knows...I have to meet someone and take care of a little business. If things work out I should be able to stay for a while, or take you with me from now on."

"I love you, baby, but no thanks I'll stay right here."

"I like what you've done with the place."

"I took some courses at the university!"

"Wow! Dynamite, what kind of courses?"

"Interior Design."

"Interior design, I love it, my baby going to school."

"I'll take care of the business I have to conduct, then we'll celebrate."

"Good."

Lisa rolled into Juan's arms....

*　　　　*　　　　*

"I'll be away for a few days, things have gotten out of hand. While I'm away look into this fiasco, there's a leak somewhere," Latten said.

"Yes, Sir. Sir, don't you think you should take a couple of specials with you?"

"No, this calls for openness, an act of good faith."

"But…" Cronin said.

Latten waved his hand.

"You take care of this end, I'll do the rest."

Latten got out of the car and walked towards a dark gray Hawker. There were no markings on the plane and the plane had been modified to minimize its radar profile. The plane's door closed and the red halo around the entrance faded to black. The plane moved forward quietly, too quiet for an ordinary jet. Cronin watched until the plane blended into the darkness and returned to his car. In the shadows near the hangar a figure called headquarters and reported Latten's flight. His partner waited near the gate and followed Cronin's car.

*       *       *

"Our man is on the move. Ten to one he's on his way to meet Manero." Dad said.

"You're on. He's not meeting Manero, he's meeting our friend Juan," Vic said.

"You're probably right, our friend is headed for Columbia."

"One thing you gotta admit, he's got balls," Duke said.

The Commissioner walked over to the window and looked towards New Jersey. He turned and studied the people in his office a moment before speaking.

"What's our next move?"

"We have him and we have the dope. What we want is Manero, without him we'll just be switching dancing partners. To kill this snake we have to cut off its head," Dad said.

The room was silent.

"Hey! Wait a minute! Why don't we set a trap for them?" Vic said.

"And how do we do that?" the Commissioner asked.

"Money, money is the key. Suppose one of our guys offered a part of the shipment for sale…"

"Vic I like it. We are the only ones who know we made the bust, that is, except the Cartel. Why not?"

"That's fine, but how do we set the trap?"

"Monica, Monica Woolford."

Silence, everyone looked at each other.

"I like it," the Commissioner said.

"Ditto. After all she has connections on both sides of this problem," Dad said.

"Can we trust her?"

"She doesn't have to know it's coming from us. We find someone on the inside to set it up, one of Latten's people. The other thing is, if she gets it and doesn't inform us we'll know where she stands."

"Can we trust Latten's people?"

"We'll make them an offer they can't refuse," Vic said.

"Done."

*           *           *

"They always use Fords. You could meet one of these big shots in the middle of the Rain Forrest and they would be driving a fucking Ford. You stay up here, baby. I don't want this guy to know what you look like."

"Si, Juan."

Juan went downstairs and waited for Latten in the library. Moments later Juan's Bodyguard ushered Latten into the room.

"Mr. Latten, so glad you could come."

"Juan, where's Manero?"

"The task is mine, Mr. Latten. Senior Manero is quite upset. His feelings are that the events that took place couldn't have happened without your knowledge."

"That's ridiculous…more likely it was from some of your people."

"Our people didn't have any knowledge of the operation until the day they performed their duties, they were recruited and sequestered in our compounds."

"Well I'm sure you are not of the opinion that I had anything to do with this foul up."

"Is there any way you can confirm the security on your end."

"We had one problem, but we took care of it."

"What kind of problem?"

"One of our people offered to sell us out, but like I said, we took care of it?"

"How?"

Latten gave Juan a dirty look, but didn't answer.

"I see…but the question is did he tell anyone before he left us?"

Latten hesitated a moment.

"That's possible. I'll check it and get back to you in a couple of days."

"Very well."

Latten stood and extended his hand. Juan nodded his head and pointed towards the door.

"We will wait two days," Juan said.

"We?"

Juan smiled.

*     *     *

"Miss Woolford there's a gentleman here to see you. He said he's from Washington."

"Send him up, thank you."

Monica met the young man at the door. It wasn't hard to remember him; he had been one of her observers at Latten's place.

"Please come in."

"Thank you," he said.

"I'm Carl. We didn't get a chance to speak to each other at the farm."

"No. What can I do for you?"

"I am responsible for many things down at the farm, one of them is security. In the last few days we lost a valuable shipment. Fortunately, I know where it is and how to recover it."

"What does that have to do with me?"

"I pulled your dossier, you're the right person all right. I want to return the drugs, for a price of course."

Monica frowned.

"And just how the hell do you propose to do that."

"The agency that raided the cache is going to destroy it. Somewhere along the way I will confiscate one of the trucks, for a price."

"How can I help you? I don't know anything about moving dope. My thing is moving money."

"Let's cut the crap…call Juan and tell him you can help him, then leave the rest to us."

"Us?"

"My man on the inside."

"This stinks! Are you trying to set me up?"

In one swift movement Monica drew her pistol from under a pillow and aimed at Carl's head.

"Whoa! Whoa…. I have something in my bag. May I show it to you?"

Monica gestured a yes with the gun pointed at Carl's midsection. Carl opened the bag and handed Monica a package.

"This is part of the shipment. Do what you want to do with it, then get back to me with a customer."

Monica put the gun away and reached for the dope.

"All right. How do I get in touch with you?"

"You can't. I'll call you and set a meet."

"All right," Monica said. She stood and offered her hand to Carl; he shook it and followed Monica to the door.

"Two days," he said.

Monica smiled and closed the door.

# CHAPTER *XVIII*

---

"We fouled up, they put one over on us," Latten said.

"Who?"

"Those two dumb detectives working on the case. They got it all and led us to believe they had nothing."

"That's not possible," Cronin said.

"Not possible…these are the maintenance records on that marshal's plane they arrived on. The plane left less than an hour after it landed in Philly, and it didn't need repairs. They were on to us."

"Damn! Who would think that they would be that clever?"

"The problem now is to clean this mess up, they know about us. Find them and take care of them!"

"Yes, Sir." Cronin hurried out of the office. Latten called Juan.

*         *         *

"Vic, its for you."

"Yes," Vic said

"Monica, can we share a plate of ribs?"

"You bet, but I thought you too busy enjoying life."

"Life is a bitch, and then we die."

"Twenty minutes," Vic said and hung up the phone.

"Get your jacket we have to meet a friend."

Duke put his papers into a draw, stood, and reached for his jacket. The two detectives rushed out of the building. Vic drove down the ramp, stopped at the sidewalk, looked in both directions, then headed towards the West Way. They rode downtown and exited at 14th Street, took fourteenth to Seventh Avenue, and 8th Street to Avenue of the Americas. Vic found a meter and parked two doors from the restaurant. Monica spotted them and hurried over to the car before they got out.

"Let's get out of here!" she said.

Vic swung out of the parking space and headed uptown.

"What's up?" Duke asked.

"That's what the hell I want to know! You guys said that I was clear…some clear."

"What are you talking about?"

"Don't give me that shit!"

"Monica, what are you talking about?" Vic asked.

"One of Latten's flunkies approached me about moving some dope you guys recovered."

"Dope we recovered?"

"Yes, the Overton Food Company."

"All right, but we didn't have anything to do with him contacting you, you're clear."

Monica let out a long sigh.

"Damn…will I ever be free of this thing?"

"You're free now, unless you want to help us bag this bunch."

"If I don't?"

"You don't."

"Okay, what do you want me to do?"

"Exactly what did Latten's man want from you?"

"He's going to divert one of the trucks, and he wants me to make contact with the Cartel to sell it to them."

"Is he nuts?"

"Must be," Monica said

"How do you propose to set it up?"

"Juan Acevedo. I don't know where he is, but I have a way to contact him."

"Good. We are going to supply you with a new maid. We don't want anything to happen to you."

"I can take care of myself," Monica said.

"Not if anything goes wrong. Don't forget our friend Manero."

"All right. Drop me off at the house and I'll contact you when the deal is ready."

"Good. You be careful, this one is going to be dangerous."

"Why, Vic, I didn't know you cared…"

"Get out of this car…"

"Okay, but I love you too."

Duke and Vic remained at the corner until Monica entered her building. Vic called Detective Franklin and gave her Monica's address. She was to stay with her and not let her out of her sight. In public she would protect her and maintain a low profile.

*    *    *

Juan walked out onto the terrace. He took a deep breath and looked towards the hills. He pondered the idea of calling Manero, but he knew how much Manero hated Monica. If Monica was setting him up he would have to take care of her. Suddenly he relaxed, that was the way to handle it, handle it on his own. He would call Luis at the last moment, this way Manero would know his intentions were honorable. The idea of buying back their property was preposterous, and why was Monica so good to him, he took a deep breath and called her number to set up the deal, after which he called Luis and asked him to meet him in New York on Monday.

Dad met with the Commissioner In New York to set the final plans for the project. It was at this meeting that Vic made an important suggestion.

"What if Latten were to learn about the plan, and the fact that it was being done without letting him know?"

"I like it," Dad said " I think you are beginning to think more like us!"

"Vic, its your ball, how do you propose to set it up."

"Monica has been straight with us, why not let her take part in the plan?"

"Good, you handle it."

"Yes, sir."

*　　　　　　*　　　　　　*

"Miss Woolford, Federal Express is here with a package for you. They won't accept my signature."

"All right send them up with the package."

Moments later a uniformed person rang the bell. Franklin answered the door.

"Package for Miss Woolford."

"Thank you, I'll take it."

"Sorry, but it requires her signature."

"Just a moment." Franklin closed the door. " He looks legit. I'll open the door and cover you," Franklin said. Monica nodded an approval. Detective Franklin slipped her Glock under her apron and opened the door.

"This way please."

Monica didn't recognized Carl right away. She smiled and asked Franklin to leave them alone. Franklin did a small curtsy and left the room.

"Any progress?"

"The principals will arrive in town Monday. They weren't happy about purchasing their property, but they agreed to do so."

"Good. I want five Million Dollars in small bills, untraceable. I want it delivered in a small pickup truck. My people will cover the operation. Anything goes wrong and everybody dies."

"How do I contact you?"

"You don't. Tuesday evening at nine o'clock a taxi will park at the Hack Stand in front of the Hilton hotel. The number of the taxi will be JN35G. Your people will get into the taxi and they will receive their instructions there. No phone calls, and no one must follow us. If everything goes well you'll receive one hundred big ones."

"That's it?"

"Yes. Now sign for your roses."

"Thank you."

Carl stood and tipped his cap to Monica and left. Franklin crossed his path and opened the door for him.

*      *      *

Vic's restaurant was the perfect place for a friendly meeting, besides the food is excellent. Monica didn't hesitate when Juan invited her to lunch. Luis' presence at the meeting gave her a start, but she could have sworn she detected a certain amount of respect in his demeanor.

"Monica, so good to see you," Juan said.

Luis nodded his head.

"I've taken the liberty of ordering for us."

"Fine."

"If this works out I'm sure it will make a great difference with Manero."

"I like that," she said.

"Who will we be dealing with?"

"One of Latten's people."

"We should have known."

Luis frowned.

"Its not what you think. He has a friend working with the people that confiscated your delivery. It seems that they are some kind of special unit."

"Well, that makes a difference. What does he want?"

"Five million in small untraceable bills. He wants it delivered in a pickup truck."

"Is that all?"

"That's all."

"What's your part in this?"

"He saw me when I was being held at Latten's place and thought I would help him."

"What did he promise you?"

"Nothing directly. He said that if everything went well I would get a hundred big ones, whatever that means."

"Set up the meeting."

"He's done that."

"What? How could he?"

"He wants you to go to the hack stand at the Hilton hotel. His cab will be parked there, taxi number JN35G. He'll meet you there tomorrow night at nine o'clock. I don't know how to contact him, so that's it."

"Do you think it's a trap?"

"I don't know, but he gave me this package to convince me."

Monica eased the package under the table to Juan."

"Is this what I think it is?"

Monica nodded her head.

"Okay, we'll do it his way. And like he said, if it works out we'll have a little something for you as well."

"I'll settle for letting by gones to be by gones, if you get what I mean."

Luis smiled.

"Business is business. I'll speak my brother, let's enjoy our food."

⋆　　　　⋆　　　　⋆

Latten chose St. Patrick's Cathedral as a meeting place. He waited in the shadows at the entrance close to one of the poor boxes. Monica entered, knelt, made the sign of the cross, walked towards the front of the church, and chose a pew. Latten waited five minutes, walked outside, and looked around. His bodyguard gave him the all-clear sign. He returned to the church and joined Monica. He neither made the sign of the cross nor did he kneel.

"Monica."

"James. I'm a little disturbed. Are you testing me again?"

"I don't understand."

"One of your people contacted me and asked me to make a connection for him."

"For what purpose?"

"I don't like playing games, James. I move the money and that's all."

"What the hell are you talking about?"

"Please...have you forgotten where we are?"

James took Monica's arm and stood.

"We'll go somewhere we can have a real talk."

"Just a minute...please..."

"Carl said that he wants to sell part of the shipment that was confiscated from the Cartel."

"What!"

James looked around the room, and then sat down.

"That's why I thought you were trying to check my loyalty," Monica said.

"What did you do?"

"I made the connection, they are going to do the deal tomorrow night around nine o'clock."

"Where?"

"I don't know the location, he's keeping that under raps. I'm not in that part of the deal. Once I made the connection he said he would contact me after the deal is done."

"So what you have is nothing."

"I have what you want and I want something."

"Name it."

"I want out. Out of this whole damn thing, I want my life back."

Latten didn't answer immediately. Monica looked at him like a small child opening a gift.

"All right."

"I mean I want my files purged from the data base, history and all."

"Done."

"He isn't telling anyone where the exchange will take place. They are going to meet him at the Hilton Hotel hack stand tomorrow night at nine o'clock. He will be driving hack number JN35G."

"That makes sense, the fool is using one of our vehicles. You've done a good thing and I will do what you asked, but remember we are there if you ever need us."

"Thank you."

"Yes. I'll leave first, you take care, Monica."

Franklin watched Latten leave the church. A limousine appeared from nowhere, followed by two men from inside the church. They entered the limo and drove away. Monica left the church moments later and hailed a taxi in front of the church. The taxi headed downtown, followed by a black Ford. Franklin waved her hand and her car moved forward. The three-car caravan stopped in front of Monica's house. The black Ford left as soon as Monica entered her building.

∗      ∗      ∗

"Gentlemen have a seat. Well it looks like we are going to close this case after all. Tonight our principals are going to meet and liberate part of the shipment we confiscated. As usual it will be a combined operation. Those Washington people, whoever they are, will have part of it, and we will have the rest."

"What part will we have, Commissioner?" Jess asked.

"The good part, we'll take Juan and they'll take Latten."

"How about the plant?" Fuchs asked.

"Turns out that he was looking for a way out."

"Sir?"

"Not all of Latten's people are happy in their work. Our man jumped at the chance to expose him."

"How much does he know about us?"

"Nothing, he was recruited by the Washington group."

"Do we get to have a face to face with them?"

Commissioner studied Jess for a moment.

"The easy answer is no, but it goes deeper than that, we have to forget about them after this is over."

Fuchs shrugged his shoulders Jess frowned.

"Believe me, Jess, you don't want to know these people," the Commissioner said.

"Where's the meet?" Jess asked.

"Near the Hunts Point Market. We'll cover it and nail Juan when he makes the pick up."

"That's good, I have something special for him," Jess said.

"It had better be legal," the Commissioner said.

"What time do you want us there?" Fuchs asked

"They meet the mark at nine, we should be in place by eight-thirty."

Jess and Fuchs nodded their approval.

"That's it. Meet me at Southern Boulevard and Buckner tomorrow night at 1930 hours."

"Yes, Sir."

"All right get the hell out of here and take the wise cracks with you," the Commissioner said.

*　　　　*　　　　*

"Imagine that…Juan recovering part of the shipment and not letting us know," Latten said.

"We don't have too much time to get ready," Cronin said.

"He's using our equipment and he's probably using our drop."

"You're kidding!"

"No, he was muscle…he'll use one of our plans, and that's how we will nail them."

"What about Juan?" Cronin asked.

"What about him…let him think he's getting away with it, then we nail him."

"What are you going to do?"

"Accidents happen. We recover the dope and deliver it to Manero."

"And Carl?"

"We will make and example of him?"

"Yes," Cronin said.

*　　　　*　　　　*

Duke checked the rear view mirror, made a left hand turn and headed for City Island. Vic was sound asleep. They had been up all night keeping an eye on Carl. The streets were deserted and most of the businesses were closed. He crossed the bridge and drove to the end of the main street, made a U-turn and parked in front of the barrier to face traffic heading his way. A sector car rolled slowly towards them. Duke blinked their running lights mounted under the hood behind the grill. The sector car made a U-turn and left the area. Ten minutes later Carl's car came into view as it moved towards them. Duke nudged Vic.

"He's here."

Carl made a U-turn, parked next to Duke, rolled down the window on the passenger side of his car and leaned forward.

"Its all set, tomorrow at the market. We verify the product and exchange trucks," Carl said.

"Are they going to have the truck with them?"

"No, they don't know where the exchange is taking place. I tell them where to bring it when we are in route."

"Good. You be careful."

"I will," Carl said.

"If this works out we have a place for you with us."

"Hey! I love it! Things are going to work out fine," Carl said.

Duke motioned towards the bridge. Carl closed the window and drove away."

"I can't wait to get my hands on Juan Acevedo," Vic said.

"Don't press too hard, remember we want Manero, he's the bum that killed your wife."

Vic flinched.

"Sorry, Vic...I mean...it was said in the best of intentions.

Vic nodded his head.

*       *       *

Carl chose a perfect time for the rendezvous, an hour before the theater break. Most of the taxi drivers took a break around nine. He parked at the end of the line, walked across the street, and stood in the shadows. At nine exactly Juan's car stopped at the corner and Luis got out. He looked around for a moment, then walked over to the cab and tried the door. He opened the door and got in, after which he nodded to Juan to drive on. Juan drove across the wide avenue and parked. Carl crossed the street and got into his cab.

"I told you that no one must follow us."

"He's not going to follow us, we just wanted to make sure this wasn't some kind of trap. Who the hell are you?" Luis asked.

"That's not important."

"It is if you want to do business with us."

"This will be a one time thing. Look on the floor to your left there's something there to verify my intentions."

Luis pulled the box towards him. He recognized the package at once.

"All right, you are who you say you are. Do you mind?"

Luis reached for the door.

"Go ahead."

Luis got out of the taxi and signaled for Juan to join them. Cronin focused on the taxi and pressed the shutter release when Juan stooped to enter the cab. He used his phone and called Latten.

"Phase one complete."

Carl drove across town to Park Avenue, at Sixty-fifth Street he made a right and drove towards the East River Drive. At First Avenue he made another left and drove uptown. His phone rang and he answered it, said "Okay" and closed the phone. At Ninety-six Street he made another right turn and took ninety-six street to the drive and drove towards the bridge.

"So far, so good. At least you are smart enough not to have anyone follow us. Now it's time to verify your intentions."

Juan passed a briefcase to Luis.

"Give it to him."

"Open it, I'm not a magician," Carl said.

Carl stopped at the toll booth and paid the toll. Luis waited until they moved on before opening the case. Carl looked back.

"That looks good, but that's not what I asked for."

"There are thirty packs in this case. That is sixty thousand dollars. The rest is in the pick up truck in the tool compartment you insisted on. The driver is following us discretely and will deliver when we send him the signal," Juan said.

"Good. At the right time we will exchange trucks."

"After we check the contents."

"No problem. I rented a small stall large enough for the two trucks. My truck is there."

"Very well. One thing, how did you get your hands on our merchandise?"

"That's none of your business, but if it helps, it was an accident."

Luis laughed.

"I have a friend in the unit that confiscated your dope. Imagine this they were going to burn it!"

"You're kidding?"

"No. They are some kind of goody-two-shoes operation, you know, save the world. My friend, on the other hand, happens to realizes a good thing when he sees it."

"That clears a few things up. At first we thought you were trying to rip us off."

"No way. An opportunity comes your way once in a lifetime this was my opportunity. I'm getting the hell out."

Carl made a left and stopped in front of a dilapidated stall, blew the horn, and entered when the door opened.

"Call your people and tell then to bring the stuff here."

"First we examine the product," Luis said.

"Right!"

Luis climbed into the back of the truck and inspected the cargo. He moved to the tailgate and jumped down.

"It's all there, call them in."

Juan opened his phone and called the truck.

*       *       *

"Just as I told you it would be. He doesn't have the brains of a.... you'd think that he would find a place of his own," Latten said.

"What now?"

"We sit and wait."

"What if they get away?"

"Where are they going to go? This is too easy…wait a minute, wait…"

"What is it?"

"Take a look on the roof tops and tell me what you see."

"Damn, special Oops!"

"Why don't we just sit back and watch the show?"

"Yes, Sir," Cronin said.

The pickup truck was bright red. The heavy-duty tires and the high ride exuded strength. The truck's tailpipes played their power song, rumbling its way into the stall. The driver made a three-sixty turn and backed up to the platform. Two heavily armed men got out of the truck and gave the keys to Luis. Luis handed the keys to Carl.

"In the tool box," he said.

Carl wiped his hand and climbed into the back of the truck and opened the toolbox. Three huge plastic wrapped parcels were jammed into the toolbox so tight he couldn't get his hands between them. The parcels were plastic and transparent. Luis handed Carl a knife. Carl took the knife and opened one of the packages and removed a bundle of money.

"Yeah!" He shouted and tossed the keys to the truck to Luis.

Luis gave the keys to his man and told him to wait until they were out of the area before moving the trucks. Luis and Juan asked for the keys to the taxi.

"I can't give you the car," Carl said.

"Humor us. We'll leave it at the hotel," Luis said.

"How am I supposed to get out of here?"

"In your new truck," Juan said. " Is there a problem?"

"No problem.

*               *                *              *

"What's holding things up, why hasn't he given the signal?" Jess asked.

"He will," Fuchs said.

"I don't like it, I'm moving closer," Jess said.

"What the hell is Jess doing?" Duke said.

"That's my old partner, always making things happen."

"Damn! The door is opening," Duke said.

Jess stepped out of the shadows just as Juan and Luis exited the garage.

"Police! Hold it right there!!" Jess shouted. In the background sirens blared and bubble gum lights lit the night.

"We have to get closer," Vic said.

Luis lowered his window and fired point blank at Jess. Jess fell and Luis aimed for his head. Jess lay motionless, eyes on Luis' gun. He wanted to do something, but he couldn't move, he mumbled a prayer instead. Suddenly out of the darkness two shots and Luis' head exploded. Jess felt himself slipping. In the mist surrounding him a man leaned over him as said "you always jump the damn gun. When will you learn?" Jess couldn't see the man, but he could have sworn it was Vic's voice. A man stood over him saying something, but he couldn't hear him, then the warm comforting darkness engulfed him.

"Damn, we have to get out of here now!" Latten said.

"Sir?"

"Move it!"

Cronin backed the car out slowly and left the scene.

"Take me to the plane."

"Yes, Sir."

*       *       *

"We have them in the van."

"Good work, get them out of here."

"Yes, Sir."

"Well you got part of your wish. The perp you took out was Manero's brother."

Vic reloaded his weapon.

"Who is the guy we took into custody?"

"That's your old friend Juan Acevedo. Vic, Vic…."

"I just want to talk to him."

"He wants a lawyer," Duke said.

"I'll be his lawyer."

"You can't have direct contact with him, he might recognize you."

"I just want to ask him a few questions!"

"You know better than that, Vic."

Vic kicked an empty shell and watched it dance towards a burning vehicle.

"Come on. We have to get out of here before the regulars get here."

Vic shouldered his weapon and followed Duke to their car.

*          *          *

The temperature had reached ninety degrees by eight in the morning. Cronin nudged his horse and followed his benefactor's up the steep trail. From their vantage point El Paso looked like a miniature model. Trechert stopped, got off his horse and beckoned to Cronin.

"Pretty, ain't it? This means more to me than all of my money, hell I could sit here all day and enjoy this, if it wasn't for the bastards that are trying to ruin this country of ours."

Cronin nodded his head.

"The problem is the people we got running things ain't worth a armadillo's fart. Put'em all together and you couldn't make a turd."

Cronin winced, and turned to avoid Trechert's eyes.

"Looks like I have to do everything myself. Don't worry 'bout what they got on you. You can resign for the good of the service. Our people will take care of the rest."

"What about the operation?" Cronin asked.

"The thing is we have to control it. Let these people do what they want to do and they'll turn this land of ours into a taco shell." Trechert said.

"Manero is going to go crazy, they killed his brother."

"Let me worry about that. This is war and he has to realize in war there are casualties."

"Its, just that…"

"You did your job. When the time comes, go back to Washington and resign."

"Yes, Sir."

"You did a fine job and I won't forget that," Trechert said.

"Thank you, Sir."

"Saddle up. I have a little lunch set up around the bend."

"Yes, Sir."

Cronin followed Trechert and waited for some one to say "Action!"

Polite black servants moved silently in and out of the huge lunch tent. Cronin followed Trechert into the tent; he bent down to avoid the top of the entrance. The little man walked briskly ahead of him. A servant waited at the head of the table and moved Trechert's chair forward as he sat.

"This is what America has done for me."

Cronin moved his shoulders slowly and sat back in his chair, mouth wide open, the tent was air-conditioned.

"Didn't get my chance, but this is what I would have done for America. Problem is Washington is it's broken and they won't fix it!"

"Yes, Sir."

Cronin reached for his champagne and took a sip. Could it be, Heisike 52?

"I'm glad you recognize a good drink. I'll have my folks send you a case. Tasted the damn stuff and bought a box car full in 52."

"You are remarkable, Sir."

"You mean for a hick, right?"

"No, Sir, er…"

"I don't give a shit about what you think, as long as you do what I tell you to do."

"Yes, Sir."

Trechert looked at one of the servants and everyone left the tent.

"Do you think this Manero can get over what that woman did to him?"

"So far he's kept his word," Cronin said.

"Good. You see him and tell him we'll make good for the last shipment. Tell him our relationship is important to us. Tell him to stop the operation in his country until we can clean up this mess. Also tell him if he agrees I will guarantee his safety, and a return to his country."

"Yes, Sir."

"Relax and let's enjoy some of the fine Texas meat."

# Chapter XIX

"**I** have a message for you. Don't give them anything, you'll be out of here before nightfall."

The Correction Officer slipped Juan a note and left the block.

"It's time for the baths."

Juan read the note, then destroyed it. The sound of doors sliding open broke the rhythm of insanity. The stir-crazies songs fell silent as they joined the men filing out of their cells. A signal was given somewhere up front; the men turned and lined up behind each other. Juan followed the motions of the man in front of him. He had no idea of where they were going, but if the note was correct they were going to the baths. A man screamed behind Juan and all hell broke loose. Juan dived to the floor and crawled towards an open cell. A huge guard leaned down and pulled him to his feet. He put one finger to his lips and pointed towards the door.

"We're getting out of here. Just keep quiet and do what I tell you and everything will be all right," the Guard said.

A special team entered the melee and fired tear gas shells into the rioting prisoners. Juan was shoved through an open door and pushed along a long corridor. At the end of the corridor a door opened and Juan was rushed into a waiting car.

"Good to see you, Juan."

"How did you get here?"

"That's not important, what's important is that I am here," Manero said.

The car drove casually towards the main gate, waited until it was inspected, then drove out of the prison onto the highway. Juan looked back at the prison and pinched himself…it was real all right.

"We have a job to do. I want those cops, the ones that killed my brother."

"I don't know where to start, who are they?"

"Leave that to me, I know who they are. Put these clothes on. You don't want to get out of the car wearing those clothes."

"Thanks," Juan said.

"We're dealing with a tough group. That creep down in Washington finally got the information we need. You know something those pricks are worse than we are, they kill their own. I'm fed up with all of them, it's time for us to go back to the old ways," Manero said and pretended to spit on his enemies.

Juan sat quietly studying Manero. He waited until he finished before speaking

"The old ways?"

"Yes. We didn't get in bed with these pricks. We were the bad guys and they were the good guys. Oh, there was one or two we used, but they were just like us, kids we grew up with, turkeys who became cops."

Juan looked Manero in the eye and shifted in his seat.

"You should have told me about the move…there are things that I can do that you can't do yet, remember that. I guess Luis thought that you had told me what you were going to do?"

Juan nodded his head to confirm Manero's statement.

"Well, you had good intentions, but from now on every move comes through me."

"Right," Juan said.

"It's time to go," Manero said. His Nurse appeared as if by magic and assisted him out of the car.

The limo entered the gate leading Manero's private plane. Juan looked across the field, the commercial flights were lining up for take off. He hated Loggerhead; they would probably have to wait for an hour before taking off.

*         *         *

"Vic you're gonna love this one!"

"What?"

"Juan Acevedo escaped. There was a riot at the prison and he got away!"

"That's too convenient," Vic said.

"I should've let you burn him at the bust," Duke said and lowered his head to avoid Vic's eyes.

"You did the right thing. Now we are going to do it my way."

"Mind if I join you?"

"Dad isn't gonna like it."

"So what, where do we start?"

"New York."

"Why New York?"

"Because that's where this all started, and that's where we'll find the answers we need."

"I don't get it." Duke said.

"We've been chasing the wrong thing. This is about money, dope is the product, but this is and always has been about money."

"You're doing the talking."

"They killed my wife because they thought we had taken their money, and that's how we are going to nail them. We follow the money trail."

"And just how are we going to do that?"

Both men spoke at the same time "Monica!"

*         *         *

Juan watched the rolling hills of Texas pass beneath the plane. Occasionally he saw trails through the mountains that seem to lead to nowhere, a single dirt road snaking across the hills. The plane banked to the left and made a steep descent, too deep, for a commercial field. The plane leveled off at three hundred feet and surged towards Trechert's private airfield. The pilot sat the Hawker down as if he were landing on eggs and used the reverse thrusters to bring the jet to a stop just outside a huge hangar. Two Surburbans rolled up to the plane and stopped. Trechert got out of the first car and met Manero at the lift. A special van appeared and moved towards Manero's wheelchair.

"Welcome to Texas, Senior Manero!"

"Thank you, Sir."

"And you must be Senior Acevedo, I've heard a lot of good things about you."

"Thank you."

"I'll ride with Sr. Manero, you take the first car, and we'll meet you at the house."

Juan nodded and followed the driver to the first vehicle. This was no ordinary suburban. The damn thing was a tank bulletproof glass, extra thick doors, and special tires. They left the field and took an endless dirt road west. Juan looked back at the dust trail behind the vehicle.

"Mr. Trechert says that if anyone tries to come down this road he'll be able to see them two days before they get to the house," the Driver spoke as if he were reading Juan's mind.

Juan smiled, sat back in his seat and observed the wild game in the distance. Moments later they entered a paved road, after which the special van passed them.

"Manero, I want to thank you for keeping your word about the Woolford girl. She behaving herself, and she can help us."

"It is not easy, but the business must come first."

"Glad to hear you say that. I've transferred thirteen million dollars to your account. That will make up for what you lost in the shipment."

"Thank you Mr. Trechert. I appreciate that, but we have a big problem."

"The problem is not as large as you might think. What you consider a problem will end today at 5 p.m."

Manero studied Trechert's face for a clue to what he was talking about.

"Watch the evening news, that will explain it."

"Yes, Sir."

"Money don't grow on trees, so we are going to have to get busy to make up for the losses."

"That I like," Manero said.

*       *       *

Monica sailed into the South Street yacht basin and docked. The boat had been modified to satisfy Monica's taste. She had seen Malcolm Forbes boat and loved the color, but she had requested the color to be a touch brighter.

"Vic hadn't considered the impact of going to the boat, it wasn't until they reached the mooring that he felt the first tinge. It reminded him of Honey. He could feel the anger rising and then he remembered Honey's visit, the dream in which she warned him to think.

"Welcome aboard, gentlemen."

"Monica," Vic said.

"Miss Woolford," Duke said.

"I thought you guys were through with me. Did…no don't tell me, he got away."

"Right and wrong. Manero wasn't there, and Juan escaped."

"So, what else is new…you guys are never going to get them, they're too big."

"We're picking up Latten today," Vic said.

"Don't count on it. You still don't know who you are dealing with."

"And I suppose you do?" Vic said.

"I got a call this morning. I don't know who it was but I think I recognized the voice. If it's who I think it is, we're in big trouble," Monica said.

"Why didn't you call us?"

"I wanted to wait until I can find out what our mystery man wants."

Vic's beeper sounded.

"May I use your phone?"

Monica pointed across the room.

"Over there."

Vic dialed the number and waited for a response.

"You called, yes, yes, what! Right away. Any survivors? Damn!"

"What's up?" Duke asked.

"Latten and half of his staff were killed in a plane crash. It seems they were on the way to his place on Hilton Head and the damn plane crashed about five miles from the airport," Vic said.

"I told you. Now I know I'm right!"

"About what?" Vic asked.

"The man that called me was Walter Trechert."

"Holy shit! He's one of the riches men in Texas. He can't be part of this."

"Then why is he calling me?"

Monica got up from the sofa and walked across the room. She sat down at her computer and booted it up.

"If I'm right it will be here somewhere, and if I'm right you guys had better stay a mile away from me until I can give you something."

The screen in front of Monica turned six different colors, finally settling to a blue desktop with thirty small icons.

"It has to be here," she said

There were no names just numbers. It appeared to be an accounting file, but Vic noticed the addition was wrong and pointed it out to Monica.

"Let's do random number searches," Monica said.

The computer beeped each time she chose a number, indicating no information from her search. She chose the simplest entry —1234— and hit the search button. A special file opened revealing some new money figures and a phone number with a Texas area code."

"There we are. We don't have to check to find out who this number belongs to."

"Right," both men said.

"What did he say to you?"

"He said I'm a friend of Manero's. I know your phone situation and will contact you again soon. We need you. That was it."

"Okay. We'd better get the hell out of here and give you some room. You know the emergency number. Call us if you need us, we're going back to Washington," Duke said.

"I will."

*    *    *

The apartment had a great view of Central Park, and twenty-two rooms of splendor. One of the rooms was imported piece by piece from a castle in Spain. Walter Trechert loved weapons; naturally one room had to be dedicated to weapons, everything from a primitive bow to the latest in NATO arms. He enjoyed his time in the service, every moment of it. That was where he made his first million the rest was easy…He turned from the window, a chime in the background broke the magic spell and he looked towards a monitor behind his desk. Monica had just passed the desk and entered the elevator. He pressed a button and switched his view to the elevator. Everything appeared normal; there were certainly no electronic devices on her person.

"Mr. Trechert, Miss Woolford is here."

"Show her in, Eli!"

"Yes, Sir." Eli turned and left the room. Moments later he returned and presented Monica.

"Good to see you, Miss Woolford."

"Monica, please."

"Thank you. You're much prettier than I was told."

"Flattery will get you everything."

"Good. Won't you please have a seat, and can I get you anything to drink?"

"No thank you."

"Mind if I have one?"

Monica smiled.

Eli entered and poured a glass of champagne for Mr. Trechert.

"A friend of yours was here and he loved my champagne."

"Oh…" Monica said.

"Yes, Mr. Cronin. Too bad about his boss…terrible thing dying like that."

Monica kept her cool; she couldn't let Trechert intimidate her.

"Yes, but these things happen, and none of us are immune to tragedy."

Trechert smiled, he liked her.

"I think you and me are going to get along fine. Cronin is going to be our point man for now; if he works out we'll stick with him. Your job is vital. Can I depend on you?"

Monica nodded her head.

"Good! We're going to shut down for a month. In that month I want you to become familiar with our operation. Do you have any preference to where you would like to work?"

"I'd rather work in New York."

Trechert pondered the idea.

"That will work, if you are willing to spend a couple of weeks down home learning the operation."

"I'll have to go home to get my clothes."

"That won't be necessary. We can leave now. When you get to Texas, go down to Neiman Marcus and purchase anything you need. I'll call them and have a Shopping Assistant work with you."

"But I have clothes, more than I really need at home."

Trechert studied the idea for a moment.

"All right. Eli! I'll have Eli take you to your place and help you pack. He'll bring you to my plane and we'll be on our way."

"As you wish," Monica said.

Eli entered the room.

"Take Miss Woolford home and help her get a few things together, then I want you to bring her to the plane. She's going home with us."

"Yes, Sir."

Monica took a good look at Eli he was no ordinary servant. Everything about him spelled marine, spit and polish from head to toe. She wouldn't chance calling Vic and Duke.

*   *   *

"I don't like it," Vic said.

"What?" Dad asked.

"Monica out there alone."

"And just how do we arrange to cover her?"

"There must be a way…"

"No way." Dad said.

"There's always a way, right Dad?"

"There is, but whey risk it? She's with him, and he's at his place. Nothing is going to happen until she leaves."

"She will leave. Her problem will be contacting us."

"Is he that good?" Duke asked.

"We trained him," Dad said.

"Well…that takes care of that," Vic said

"Let's review what we have. She returned home and picked up some clothes, and then they flew to his place. My guess is that she's there mapping out a new strategy, or something," Vic said.

Dad and Duke nodded an approval.

"I like this guy," Dad said.

"We can't tap her place, and we can't contact her."

"Why don't we relax and wait, she'll come through," Duke said

"Why should she?" Vic asked.

"Because she wants Manero as bad as we do," Dad said.

"Hadn't thought of that," Duke said.

"All right, both of you. I want you to go downstairs and check the incoming reports. There might be something in them to give us a clue to what's going on down there in Texas," Dad said.

Vic and Duke nodded in agreement and left the room.

⋆       ⋆       ⋆

"I'll work with the bitch, but I don't ever want to see her," Manero said.

"Good enough. The place is large enough for the two of you not to cross each other's path. You keep to the West Wing and I'll make sure she stays away from your area. How's that?"

"I can live with that. You say she's important, she had better be," Manero said.

"I thought you had reconciled those feelings."

"Never! But I will keep my word, business is business, and the rest is bullshit."

"We are going to make a fortune if you can keep that attitude," Trechert said.

"That's what I'm about."

"Good. Map out the players in your area for me. I'll give her a copy and see how she handles the information."

Manero looked at his nurse. She pushed his wheelchair towards a desk in the corner of the room. Manero opened one of the draws and removed a floppy disk. He motioned again with his head and the Nurse pushed him towards Trechert.

"Its all here."

"Super! I have her get on it right away."

Manero nodded his head.

"I want you to relax now and let me take care of things. You'll be busy enough when we get the business going again," Trechert said.

"I hope so, in the meantime I'm going to enjoy some of this Texas sun."

Trechert smiled and watched Manero's Nurse push him out of the room, great ass, he thought.

*        *        *

Monica had followed Trechert's suggestion and chose one of his great stallions for a morning ride. When she returned from her ride Trechert was waiting for her in her room. He appeared to be excited, unusual for him.

"Do you have any idea of what I am holding in my hand? Just think of it! I'm holding the key to eighteen billion dollars."

"I'm impressed, you mean he actually gave you the information?"

"Yes, but he's very unhappy about you being here."

Monica shrugged her shoulders.

"Monica, this is a serious matter. I made a deal with him…he stays in the West wing and I want you to avoid that wing like the plague."

"Fine with me."

"Good. Crank up that machine and let's go to work."

Monica extended her hand to Trechert for the disk.

*        *        *

The days passed in a flash. Monica hadn't realized how much Juan had changed. She stood behind him, looking over his shoulders. Juan made the database dance; she had never seen anything like it.

"I'm impressed. I thought I was good, but…."

Juan stopped, turned around in the swivel chair and looked at Monica.

"Its like I said, give a person enough money, and if that person has sense enough to change, Walla!" Juan said.

"I know, but you were on drugs, I mean…"

"You mean I was an ignorant stinking junkie."

"Well…"

"You fucking blue-bloods kill me. You think that you are the only ones on earth with class. My people were building cities while your people were living in caves."

"Come on…what is this crap, your people?"

"Forget about it!"

"If you say so, Mr. Acevedo."

"I say that I am finished, now we can both get the hell out of here."

"Dynamite!"

"I wrote the password on the back of the disk, reverse what you see and that will do it."

"Thanks, and you didn't let me finish, I'm proud of you," Monica said.

Juan smiled and pushed a button on the intercom.

"We're finished in here," Juan said.

"Good. Come on up to the big house and we'll have a drink," Trechert said.

Manero finished his drink and asked his nurse to take him back to his quarter. He raised his hand and the Nurse hesitated.

"Trechert, you're in control now, don't fuck it up," Manero said. He looked at the Nurse once more and she pushed his wheelchair forward.

"I'll call you as soon as we are able to move again," Trechert said.

Manero left the room through one door and Monica and Juan entered through another.

"Come on in and set a spell," Trechert said. He looked at Eli and nodded his head.

"Monica, Juan…what you have done in the last few days some would say it wasn't possible, thanks."

It was the first time Monica has seen any sign of Trechert as a person. For the most part he appeared to be some kind of fucked up machine. Monica didn't refuse the drink this time. Trechert was right the champagne was something special.

"Let's drink a toast to us for being very special people," Trechert said.

*       *       *

Monica stepped off Trechert's plane and into a private limousine, Eli at her side. It was as Dad said, she was safe, Trechert wouldn't jeopardize his cover. They would have to wait for Monica to make a move Trechert always covered his bets.

"They're on the move," Dad said.

"That's interesting. Monica is back in New York, and we just received information that Manero is returning to his country."

"I don't believe it! You mean he's got the balls to go home?"

"He wouldn't do it if he didn't have protection," Duke said.

"Leave it alone," Dad said.

"I can't promise you that."

"Vic, we all have to answer to someone, leave it alone."

"He shot my wife!"

"He also killed a member of my family in the Bronx. Have you forgotten that? This come from the top, leave it alone," Dad said.

Vic stormed out of the room.

"Go after him."

"Yes, Sir," Duke said.

Duke rushed out of the room and caught Vic in the parking lot.

"What do you think you're doing?"

"I'm going after that bastard."

"Vic, I never told you this before, but we're just beginning to scratch the surface on this operation. Don't do anything to blow it now, we want them all."

Vic looked puzzled.

"You mean…"

Duke nodded his head.

"Damn!"

"The operation got out of hand, they got greedy. We've known about it for a while. What we didn't know is to what extent it had reached. We'll nail them, some of them, and some of them will come out of this stink smelling like perfume."

Vic kicked a small rock almost twenty feet away.

"What do you want from me?"

"Just take it easy and we'll get it done."

"All right."

"Good. We have to go to New York."

*       *       *

"I appreciate your help, Eli, but is it necessary for you to do everything for me?"

Eli didn't answer. He smiled and placed a coaster in front of Monica. Monica sipped her champagne, put the glass down and picked up the phone. Eli left the room. There was no mystery; Eli had a listening device somewhere in the house. The conversation was short; she invited her mother to join her in a shopping trip. Monica hated her escort. Eli went with her everywhere. The fact that he assumed the role in the attire of a servant didn't make her feel any better. Her mother thought it was a splendid idea, and offered to steal Eli away from her.

The one place that was safe was the dressing rooms. Safe they might be, but Monica wasn't going to take any chances. If she knew Trechert he had people everywhere. Sooner or later he would learn to trust her, but until that time, Eli the merchant of swift and silent death was there if she screwed up. She bought two expensive dresses, her mother argued with her about one of her choices, the dress wasn't for her, she said. Monica bought it anyway, Eli approved. The dined at their favorite restaurants, met old friends and went to the theater later that evening. It had been a pleasant evening, and she was right, Trechert had people everywhere.

Two days later the transactions were complete and Eli left, no ceremony, the damn man never spoke. One moment here was there and the next he was gone. Later that day the phone rang and Trechert thanked Monica for her help. This would be the true test. That rabbit looking creep would be really keeping tabs on her now. The idea of him saying that she could take a few weeks off, fuck him! She picked up the phone and called the emergency number. The tap on her phone wasn't even subtle; there was a distinguished click after the dial tone.

"This is Miss Woolford. Would you have someone pick up my cleaning?"

Monica hung up the phone and smiled. She removed the clothes she had worn at the ranch and pressed the intercom.

"This is Miss Woolford. Will someone come to the apartment I have some things for the cleaners?" Moments later the Elevator Operator knocked on the door. He took the clothes, a generous tip, and left.

At the cleaners one of the workers removed the message from the label in the dress and called Duke to let him know that Monica had made contact.

"Well, she's back. We'd better get over to the shop and see what she has for us," Duke said.

"Is that safe?" Vic asked.

"What do you mean?"

"Didn't you say that Trechert was trained at our facility?"

"Yeah, but that was a long time ago. When that prick worked for us we didn't even use women."

"How about the cleaners?" Vic asked.

"That's special, just for Monica."

"I like it," Vic said.

They rode uptown to the cleaners and used the rear entrance, a narrow alley that led to three different businesses. The back door to the cleaners required a special key to open it, just one of the little surprises for anyone trying to break in. The cleaner was a legitimate business that made a profit while functioning as a drop. It was perfect cover for the space in which vital information was discussed. Duke pushed a button and the door to the special area opened.

"On your desk, Sir," the young Agent said.

Vic followed duke and sat down in front of the desk. Duke looked at the disk and waved it a Vic.

"If this is what I think it is we're almost home."

Duke slipped the disk into the computer and waited for the file to open.

"Damn!"

"What's wrong?" Vic asked.

"There's nothing worse than too much inside information."

"How's that?"

"Churchill had the same problem once. The town of Canterbury was going to be bombed. He had the information, but if he used it, it would have tipped of the Germans that they had broken their codes."

"Nobody's going to bomb us," Vic said.

"I know, but we are limited to what we can use here, if we want the top man."

"The top man?"

"Trechert?" Vic said.

"Yes, Mr. Trechert, the one and only. The other thing is Monica. She's too important to us. Touch them now and we blow a vital source."

"So, what do we do?"

"Just as we've always done. We hit them on a percentage basis. We hit them hard enough to cause some internal problems, but we don't shut them down until we get him!"

Duke encrypted a message and planted it in Monica's dress, and then he pressed a button, after which a man came into the room and took the dress.

# Chapter XX

---

"*M*iss Woolford, there's a gentleman here to see you. He said that he's from Texas and that you know him."

"Send him up."

Monica poured herself a stiff drink. Moments later the doorbell rang. Monica waited almost thirty seconds before opening the door.

"Walter, how nice to see you."

"Thank you. I didn't mean to burst in on you, but I am very pleased with your work."

"What brought this on?"

"Well, I had my doubts about you, but I was wrong."

"And just how did you determine that?"

"We'd be foolish it we didn't take care of ourselves. I put you in a position to wipe us out. We would have been able to come back, but you could have hurt us."

"Why would I do that?"

"The point is that you didn't hurt us."

Monica extended her hand towards a chair. Trechert tilted his head in gesture of acceptance and sat down.

"Now that I know I can trust you I'll bring you into the whole operation."

"Oh!"

"This drug business is an all consuming thing. What we do is keep things in balance. If we don't these people will take over the whole world."

Monica nodded her head.

"The other part of this is we have to protect our interest. For instance, you were hassled by two special agents and one of them has an ax to grind. I want you to contact them..." Trechert reached into his pocket and produce a small piece of paper. "Call this number and ask for Agent Edmund Duke Junior, he's part of the team that questioned you."

Monica looked at Trechert and shrugged her shoulders.

"It's all right. We have to give something to get something. In the process you might make a friend. If so, he will be valuable to us as a source of information."

"That's dangerous."

"You can handle it. Besides it will solve one of your biggest problems."

"What problem?"

"Manero."

Monica took a deep breath.

"Give them this address and tell them they will find Manero there."

Monica took another swig of her drink and offered Trechert one.

"No thanks."

"All right," Monica said.

"Good. Don't worry we have them covered. You take care, everything will be fine."

Trechert stood, and offered his hand to Monica. Monica shook his hand and followed Trechert to the door. She closed the door and went straight to the bar and poured a double of Royal Salute, sipped it slowly, and picked up the phone. The familiar click was no longer there, her line was clear.

Dad was a little shaken when Monica asked for Duke on his private line. He wanted to ask her where she got the number from, but he didn't want her to hang up. He asked her to hold and transferred the call to Duke.

"Monica?"

"Yes."

"Where the hell did you get Dad's number from?"

"Guess?"

"Never mind. What's up?"

"When can we meet?"

"Right now! But what about your safety?"

"I was instructed to call you."

"Whew! Where do you want to meet?"

"My place."

"Thirty minutes," Duke said.

"Fine," Monica said and hung up the phone.

Duke broke the phone patch and called Dad.

"We're meeting Monica at her house."

"One thing you can say about our friend is that he has class. Imagine giving Monica my private number."

"Yes, Sir."

"Keep your eyes open," Dad said

"Yes, Sir."

Duke hung up the phone and motioned for Vic to follow him. On the way to Monica's apartment he filled Vic in on what had happened.

"Why do you think he's bringing us in?" Duke asked.

"To kill us, or to set someone else up."

"Good thinking."

Duke parked on West Eighth Street near the corner of Fifth Avenue and walked the short distance to Monica's house.

The doorman announced them and they took the elevator to Monica's apartment. Louie was in fine shape.

"You'll never guess who was here today?"

"No, who?" Vic asked.

"Walter Trechert! Right here in this elevator! I voted for him last time."

"Great, who did he visit?"

"Miss Woolford, but you won't tell her I told you, you know, privacy and all that. But you guys are special, right?"

"Right, Louie. Did he take care of you?"

"Yeah! I'm not supposed to, but I asked him for his autograph."

Louie let the elevator come to a stop a Monica's floor, but kept the door shut until he produced the autograph. He held it up to the two Agents.

"That's great, Louie," Duke said. Vic nodded his head and looked towards the door.

"Sorry!"

Louie flung the doors open. Monica was waiting in her doorway.

"Come in, gentlemen," she said.

Monica led them in and closed the door.

"This is scary," she said.

"What?"

"Trechert is giving up Manero. He figures if Vic kills him the pressure will be off."

"Son of a bitch! He wants his cake and eat it too," Duke said.

"This is one cake I won't mind delivering," Vic said.

"If we take out Manero, who's going to run the operation?"

"You won't believe this, but Juan Acevedo."

"Bull shit!"

"Senior Acevedo had turned his life around, college, the whole bit."

"He's a junkie!" Duke said.

"Not anymore," Monica said.

"Damn, if we don't take out Manero we blow the whole gig. Vic you must live right."

"It's about time I got a break."

Monica handed Duke the address.

"Looks like we're going to take a trip," Duke said.

"Yes!" Vic said, his right arm pumping like a sport's fan.

*          *          *

Manero, confident of his protection had chosen a place in town. He wasn't stupid; his apartment was on the top floor, the entire top floor. His life had been relegated to a view from his terrace. The view was excellent, especially at night. On warm evenings his nurse would push his chair out to the terrace, mix his favorite drink, then let him sit there and enjoy the view. Occasionally a few friends or associates would drop by and bring him a young lady reaching for the stars, and who thought her ticket would be a tryst with Manero. One of his friends had said, "think of it, he can't walk, but everything else works." What they didn't know was that he enjoyed the negotiations more than the sex. The idea of him being able to manipulate the young women to their desired goals, most of all, how little they settled for. A plane ticket to the States and a little money to get settled, or less…it was the trading that gave him the most pleasure.

It was a perfect night; stars filled the perfect blue the sky, not a cloud anywhere. It was the most beautiful night Manero had ever witnessed. He looked towards the harbor and watched the private yachts bobbing gently in the waters. He took a deep breath and held back a tear. She had done this to him and he had to tolerate her. Maybe a little visit, yeah, watch her bargain for her life as she bounced in his lap. That was it that was what he would ask Cronin for. If she agreed, he would forgive her.

Manero didn't here the special copter land on the roof above him. It all happened so fast, one moment the beautiful sky filling the night, the next, Vic Morgan was standing in front of him dress in a black suit of death. A second person dropped from the rim of the terrace above him and entered the apartment. He couldn't see it, but he heard the whimper when his nurse collapsed to the floor. He had pressed the panic button, but there was nothing to do now but await the outcome. Vic removed his mask and looked Manero in the eyes.

"Remember me?"

Manero gasp for air and shook his head, indicating no.

"Sure you do. San Juan, the night you killed my wife," Vic said.

The sound of silenced automatic weapons interrupted the moment.

"That's right. What you hear is your boys going down."

Duke returned to the terrace and motioned for Vic to hurry.

"I thought you were dead!"

Manero struggled to place the oxygen tubes in nose and took a deep breath.

"Vic, get it over with! We have to get out of here!"

"Anything you want…names, date…anything," Manero said.

Vic took a step forward and snatched the oxygen tank from the wheel chair and shut it off.

"I need that! I can't breathe without it…"

"Duke, you go ahead. I'll be here for a few moments."

Manero struggled to breathe, his hand reaching out, fingers pleading for the oxygen. Duke turned his gun on Manero and shot him between the eyes. Manero folded into a helpless mass. Vic just stood there, as if he didn't believe what had happened. Duke pushed him toward the rope dangling from the top of the ceiling.

"Let's go!"

Later on the plane heading home Vic spoke for the first time.

"Its like Honey warned me it would be, she's not coming back, no matter what…"

Vic lowered his head and cried. Duke patted him on the shoulder.

*    *    *

The next morning at headquarters Vic got the shock of his life. Walter Trechert was sitting in Dad's office as big as day. Duke didn't appear to be surprised. Vic and Duke joined Dad and Trechert at the conference table. Dad offered them a drink, Duke declined, Vic asked for a large scotch.

"Fellows, this is Walter Trechert."

Duke and Vic nodded their heads.

"Mr. Trechert is here to inform us that the situation is in hand, and that we can move on to bigger and better things. He also wants to thank you for the wonderful work you have done on this case."

Trechert was silent, but there was no question as to who was in charge. That was when it hit Vic to leave it alone. Dad's words finally made sense.

"As a reward for your good work we want you to take a little vacation. You choose the destination, money is no object."

"I'm told that you are partial to Spain, young man," Trechert said and looked directly at Vic. There it was, as plain as the nose on his face, time to get out of this crap.

"Yes, Sir. I was thinking of buying a little ranch there."

Dad was shocked; he hadn't expected Vic to react that way.

"You pick the spot and we'll take care of the rest. I guess with the money Ellis gave you you'll be fine. Maybe, pick one of the senoritas and make a life for yourself," Trechert said.

There it was again, Vic thought, get out and stay out.

"I can live with that," Vic said.

Trechert stood, smiled, and left the room.

"Sooo, everybody seems to be happy...gooood," Dad said.

Duke looked at Vic as if puzzled. Vic nodded and smiled.

"If Vic is happy, I'm happy," Duke said.

"Duke, you've earned a rest. Take a month off. When you return I'll have another assignment for you."

"Vic, I have some papers for you to sign. A kind of forget about the organization thing. The good news is that you can contact your friends and family now," Dad said.

Vic read the papers, signed them, and accepted a transfer form to an account in Switzerland, from which he was to draw funds as needed.

*   *   *

The Shuttle banked to the left and made its descent across the Bronx. The plane was descending and at its height you could count the seats in Yankee Stadium. In the next instance the plane landed roughly on the runway at LaGuardia. Vic hated that runway. He made his way to the taxi stand, waited his turn, and asked to be taken to Police Headquarters. He couldn't imagine what it was going to be like to revive his life, to contact his family and friends. Would they believe him, better would they accept, or forgive him? The midtown traffic gave him plenty time to think, and he almost abandoned the idea of going to see Bee, but that didn't last long. The taxi let him out at the rear of the building and he took the back stairs to the entrance. He showed his identification, and was admitted to the building.

"Can I help you, Sir?" Bee asked.

"Bee, don't you recognize me?"

Bee screamed, so loud, the Security Officer and the Commissioner rushed into her area.

"What is it? My God! Vic is that you?"

Vic smiled.

"What have they done to you? We thought you were dead!"

"I'm sorry. It was the only way we could catch them."

"Jess was right! He said that you had saved him in that shoot-out in the Bronx!" Bee said.

"But you know how that went, we thought he was drinking again," The Commissioner said.

"Yeah, yeah!" Bee said and hugged Vic.

"What are we doing standing out here?" The Commissioners said and used hand signals to send the security people to their stations. Bee punched Vic on the shoulder hard.

"You could have told us," she said.

"No, there were too many things at stake."

"What about the man that killed Honey."

"He's gone," Vic said.

"Vic, did you?"

"I tried, but I couldn't, but he's gone and I saw him go."

"Enough of this. Let's call Jess and get him down here. I feel sorry for you, Vic. You know how much hell Jess is going to raise."

"After what I've been through it will be a pleasure."

*      *      *

Dad watched a beautiful yacht under full sail cruise across the bay. The fish was excellent, the wine divine, the company sucked. He had watched Trechert attack his food like it was a villain. He didn't know why he had been asked to lunch, but he hoped it wasn't for what he thought it would be.

*So much for wishful thinking.*

"I guess you know we have a problem."

"No."

"Those two agents."

"What about them?"

"My ole pappy once said "they only way to keep a secret is to keep it to yourself." They know too much about me. Until now you were the only one that knew, and that's fine, but…"

"They're loyal."

"Loyalty ain't what concerns me."

"Yes, Sir." Dad said.

"Make sure it looks like an accidents. All we need is to have this thing backfire on us."

"Yes, Sir."

The rest of the meal was silent. Dad used everything he had to maintain his countenance. He wanted Mr. Trechert relaxed for what he had in store for him. Trechert signed the check and looked to Dad for him to give the tip. Dad laughed and gave the waiter a twenty.

"You don't give a damn about what you do with the taxpayer's money, do you?" Trechert asked.

"It was for a good cause."

The two men entered Trechert's limousine and rode back to Dad's headquarters. The new headquarters was located in a bookstore on New Hampshire Avenue. Dad got out of the car and shook Trechert's hand. The needle was hidden in his cuff link. Trechert didn't even feel the tiny penetrations.

"Call me when it's done," Trechert said.

"Yes, Sir."

Dad stood at the curb and watched the limo until it was out of sight.

*   *   *

The food was excellent. This time it really was a party, Bee had chosen the restaurant, The Downtown Athletic Club. In the middle of the dinner Vic stopped eating and stood. He couldn't believe his eyes. That face on the screen, Walter Trechert, but what was all the fuss about. He walked over the counter and asked the young lady behind the bar to turn up the sound.

"In a startling turn of events Walter Trechert, billionaire, and political candidate, collapsed today in Washington. He was returning to his plane after having lunch with friends. The cause of death has not been determined, but it is assumed that his death was due to a heart attack."

Vic went to a phone booth and called Washington. He held the phone as if it were a strange kind of instrument he couldn't believe what he had heard.

**"THE NUMBER YOU HAVE REACHED IS NO LONGER IN SERVICE."**

"Way to go, Dad," Vic whispered and returned to the table.

"Vic, what's wrong?" Bee asked.

"Nothing, everything is fine. Say how would you guys like to spend a few weeks in Spain with me?"

"You're kidding," Jess said.

"No, I want to visit all of those wonderful places Honey told me about. I think it will help.

"I think it would be better if you went alone," Bee said.

The party nodded in unison.

＊          ＊          ＊

Miles away in San Juan, Juan Acevedo asked if it is over?"

Dad said, "Who knows?"

**The End**

*Finished*
*4-20-15*
*BLRB*

# AFTERWORD

*Cliff Chandler does it again, this time with the sequel to The Paragons.
If you liked The Paragons you'll love Vengeance Is Mine. And as usual,
author Cliff Chandler continues his journey of twists and turns; just
when you think you've got it; you learn that you are wrong. The tragedy
at the beginning of this story has disturbed so many of his fans that
Cliff was forced to bring Honey back. It was a difficult task, but also a
fun task. Honey is as tough as she is beautiful. . It seems that she was
seriously injured, but not murdered as we were led to believe. Her
recovery is believable but we won't learn how it is possible until his next
book, so climb onboard and enjoy Vengeance Is Mine, and then wait
patiently for his next book. . Vengeance Is Mine, or is it?*

*Richard Cummings
Author of The Pied Piper*

Vic Morgan is back, this time with a vengeance! A great tragedy
enters Vic's life, one that will take him to strange places. And like *The
Paragons, Vengeance* is a page-turner. If you missed his first book *The
Paragons,* Author Cliff Chandler's new book *Vengeance Is Mine...*will
drive you to seek in *The Paragons* the events that has led to the
author's latest offering, and it doesn't stop there. Cliff is busy with the
third book of the series, in which, I'm told Honey returns. Sorry, I
can't tell you how she returns, you'll have to wait for the book, but you

will understand why she is returning after you read *Vengeance Is Mine*. Cliff Chandler has done it again, and done it in style.

Jackie Cooper
Movie / Book Critic
WPGA TV

It starts as the perfect honeymoon, but turns into a nightmare for Vic Morgan. Then the trapdoor opens and a whole new cast of demons crawl out, some of which are inside Vic's head, giving him the fight of his life. And as we found in the Paragons, Chandler's characters are seldom what they seem. This novel is explosive, and one not to be missed, because Vic Morgan
is back…with a vengeance.

Paul Carr

Author of the

Sam Mackenzie novels

Author, Cliff Chandler

# About Cliff Chandler

Author Cliff Chandler was born in New York City during the thirties, and spent part of his life in Macon, Georgia. His father was a sailor from Barbados and wanted to send him to the West Indies to be reared by his parents, that was the custom during the thirties. His mother thought otherwise and sent him to her parents in Georgia instead. Cliff returned to New York as a teenager, attended school at night, and worked in various occupations: Like most artist he has worked as a taxi driver, Hospital Aide, Paramedic, Professional Photographer – *Germain School of Photography,* Jazz Musician, and editorial writer for a local newspaper. During the sixties his career in Law Enforcement began. He was trained and served as a Special Officer in the New York City Police Department, but spent most of his time as a private detective. While he claims the work was dull, his novel, gives us a different view of what his life must have been like.

He says that he has been a writer all of his life, but his first taste of success was with his high school newspaper, *The Ballardite* in Macon, Georgia. He likes to tell everyone he has been everything but rich. We like to think that his life's experiences prove him wrong.

Ken may 27 '04